Copyright ©2025 by Lionel H. Santos

All rights reserved. No part of this book may be reproduced in any form or by any electronic or mechanical means, including information storage and retrieval systems, without permission in writing from the publisher, except by a reviewer who may quote brief passages in a review.

Electronic Book, ISBN: 978-1-0694938-0-4

Paperback Book, ISBN: 978-1-0694938-1-1

Hardcover Book, ISBN: 978-1-0694938-2-8

Audio Book, ISBN: 978-1-0694938-3-5

This book is dedicated to my children, whose own journeys into the world; raising a family on the coast, finding adventure in nature's heartland, and pursuing the echoes of Greek myth, have inspired the adventures within these pages.

And especially to my wife, Cheryl. Thank you for enduring the writer's solitude alongside me. Without your love, patience, and encouragement, this story would never have seen the light of day.

I love you all more than words can say.

Contents

Prologue	1
1. The Vault and the Scholar	6
2. Nightingale's Song	22
3. Moscow's Response	34
4. An Unlikely Partnership	42
5. The Istanbul Connection	53
6. The Unquiet Earth	69
7. Behind the Iron Curtain	88
8. Tatul's Shadow	103
9. The Hunted	108
10. The Cautious Curator	118
11. Running Blind	129
12. Plateau of the Ancients	142
13. Cornered on Sacred Ground	151
14. Into the Mountain's Heart	160

15. The Awakening Sphere	170
16. Descent into Chaos	178
17. Cretan Sanctuary	191
18. Map of Stars	203
19. Into the Labyrinth	215
20. Bridge of Sorrows	224
21. Taps in the Dark	231
22. Light of Annihilation	239
23. Confrontation	247
24. Overload	256
25. The Final Collapse	265
26. Blood and Stone	272
27. Rescue from the Edge	281
28. Calm After the Storm	289
Epilogue	298
Acknowledgements	302

Prologue

ECHOES FROM DELPHI

Northern Greece, August 1986.

The late afternoon sun hammered the dry, rocky hillside near Mount Parnassus with relentless fury, baking the air until it shimmered. The sharp, aromatic scent of crushed wild thyme and sun-baked dust mingled with the incessant, hypnotic buzz of cicadas, a sound that seemed to amplify the oppressive heat. Dr. Elias Vassilis, his face a sun-leathered roadmap of wrinkles mapping forty years spent under the Hellenic sun, dragged a dirt-stained hand across his sweating brow, squinting against the glare. Grit lodged itself under his fingernails.

For three long, frustratingly hot months, his unfunded team of inexperienced university interns had scraped and dug at this unassuming mound. Local shepherds avoided the spot, muttering old tales about unsettled spirits and bad luck. Elias was driven by his stubborn, academic hunch that defied logic but had served him well throughout his long career. Fragmented lines in an obscure text hinted of a forgotten shrine near the ancient pathways to Delphi. His colleagues in Athens thought him mad, chasing ghosts on a shoestring budget. But Elias felt something here, an echo resonating across millennia.

Today, finally, something shifted. Not just the loose scree underfoot, but the very atmosphere of the dig site. Yannis, the youngest intern, his voice cracking with exhaustion and disbelief, called out from the deeper trench. "Doctor! Doctor Vassilis! You...you need to see this!"

Elias scrambled to the trench edge, ignoring the protest of his aging knees, his heart suddenly pounding a frantic drum against his ribs. He peered down. There, nestled in the crumbling embrace of dark, time-worn stones that formed the undeniable foundation of a small, forgotten shrine, lay a flash of dulled metal. Not iron, not lead. It was bronze.

Carefully, painstakingly, brushing away the accumulated dirt of centuries with trembling hands, they unearthed it. A broken tablet, roughly palm-sized, its edges jagged where it had fractured long ago. It was etched with the elegant, unmistakable curves of ancient Greek script. The bronze was heavily patinated, greened with age, yet the lettering, though blurred by time and coated with grime, seemed almost to pulse with a strange, residual energy in the harsh sunlight. It felt... warm, almost alive, beneath Elias's probing fingertips.

Elias, a man who'd dedicated his life to the cool logic of archaeology and the faded echoes of the classical world, felt an electric jolt he hadn't known since unearthing the Minoan seal stone on Crete decades earlier. This wasn't just another pottery shard or a corroded coin; it hummed with something, an almost physical presence. A secret clung to it, a potent whisper from a dead age, refusing to stay buried.

Back at their rough, makeshift camp later that evening, under the sputtering light of a single kerosene lamp that cast long, dancing shadows, Elias meticulously cleaned the tablet fragment. Using soft brushes and distilled water, he worked with the reverence usually reserved for sacred relics. As more of the encrusted dirt fell away, revealing the characters beneath, the initial thrill of discovery slowly morphed into a knot of unease tightening in his gut. The Greek was old, really old. Archaic, pre-classical, hinting at a time when gods and monsters were perceived to walk the earth. And the message... it wasn't a dedication, not a prayer, not an inventory list. It was a prophecy.

He and Yannis, the only other member of the team with passable ancient Greek, pieced the fragmented lines together, their hushed voices stark against the chirping night chorus outside the tent. The text explicitly attributed the words to the Oracle of Delphi herself, Pythia, the mouthpiece of Apollo. But this wasn't one of the famously ambiguous political fortunes recorded by Herodotus. This was dark, foreboding, its cadence echoing the grim finality of tragedy. It spoke of a "shadow crawling from the East," an unseen blight, a power that would "unmake the stars" and "break the world upon its knee."

Elias, a man grounded in empirical evidence and rational explanations, instinctively scoffed at superstition. Prophecy? Nonsense born of fumes and desperate hopes. But the raw, poetic power of the words, the almost physical sense of dread emanating from the cold bronze in his hands, prickled the hairs on the back of his neck. He couldn't dismiss the palpable wrongness that clung to the artifact. He knew, with a certainty that chilled him despite the warm night, this discovery was bigger, and potentially far more dangerous, than anything he had ever stumbled upon. This fragment wasn't just history; it felt like a harbinger.

While Dr. Vassilis wrestled with the tablet's dark message under the lonely Greek stars, news of his unlikely discovery began its unstoppable journey. Driven by excitement yet tempered by a researcher's inherent caution, Vassilis sent a carefully worded telex to a renowned colleague in Athens. He hinted at a 'Delphic prophecy of unprecedented significance'. Just enough to spark intense curiosity, not enough, he prayed, to attract the wrong kind of attention. But even carefully chosen whispers had a way of echoing in the corridors of power.

***

That single communication, a tiny signal in a vast ocean of electronic noise, was silently snagged and amplified by the listening posts of global surveillance.

***

From the digital ether, keywords – 'Delphi,' 'Oracle,' 'archaic script,' 'artifact of power' – blazed like wildfire on analyst screens deep within fortified government buildings from Washington to Moscow. The Protocol, a deeply buried directive within these shadowy organizations, instantly kicked into high gear. For these players in the great game, whose currency was secrets and whose battlefield was the precarious peace of a world on a knife's edge, Vassilis's find wasn't just ancient history. It was live ammunition: a perilous new threat, a potent opportunity, a prize to be snatched from the dust. And none of them, least of all the old archaeologist himself, yet knew the true, terrifying weight of the words he had just dragged into the harsh glare of the 20th century.

Chapter One

The Vault and the Scholar

The call had come into Section M's ultra-secure comms center forty-eight hours after the Delphi Protocol first flashed red. The initial intercept from Greece was fragmented, academic, but the keywords were undeniable. Within six hours, a ghost flight was wheels up from Andrews, its manifest listing 'agricultural survey equipment.' Onboard, a lean, two-man 'recovery team' studied satellite imagery of a dusty hillside near Mount Parnassus.

Their brief was simple: locate the Vassilis dig, secure the target artifact – codenamed 'Oracle's Whisper' – and be airborne again before Athens even knew something was amiss. Discretion was paramount; diplomatic channels were too slow, too noisy. The operation was smooth, almost silent. Dr. Vassilis, though initially bewildered by the official-looking but unidentifiable Americans who descended on his camp in the dead of night, was eventually persuaded by the chillingly specific (and classified) satellite photos of Soviet military buildup they showed him. A buildup that, they hinted, his discovery might inexplicably be linked to. He hadn't understood the connection, but the grim certainty in their eyes had been enough.

Now, less than three days after its unearthing, the bronze fragment rested not in an Athens museum, but deep beneath the unassuming facade of the Mid-Atlantic Regional Government Records Depository.

From the outside, the building looked deliberately, aggressively mundane. It was just another anonymous brick box, squatting unremarkably amidst the sprawling, humid suburbs of Maryland. Decades of freeze-thaw cycles and sticky, pollen-laden summers had weathered its utilitarian facade to a dull, mottled brown, allowing it to blend seamlessly into the landscape of equally uninspiring federal buildings. Anyone driving past likely registered it only as a vague shape, probably assuming it was crammed floor-to-ceiling with miles of shelving, holding dusty, forgotten paper records…tax forms, census data, land deeds. The tedious detritus of bureaucracy. Just another quiet corner of the government machine, utterly devoid of interest.

They couldn't have been more profoundly wrong.

Beneath that deliberately boring exterior, hidden several levels below ground, shielded by layers of concrete and steel, lay the real operation. Within the fiercely guarded, compartmentalized world of Section M, it was known simply, almost reverently, as "The Vault." This wasn't some neglected, cobweb-draped basement filled with filing cabinets. It was a state-of-the-art labyrinth of reinforced pressure doors, humming server farms cooled by rushing air, and the cold, shadowless, sterile glare of secure laboratories. A hermetically sealed reality utterly divorced from the quiet, paper-shuffling offices accessible to the public upstairs.

Down here, in the hushed, pressurized depths, history wasn't merely something cataloged and stored. It was actively hunted, dissected, analyzed with cutting-edge technology, and sometimes, chillingly, weaponized. Section M's clandestine mandate was unique: to identify and neutralize threats hidden not in present-day intelligence chatter, but buried deep within the past. Anomalies, artifacts, ancient knowledge that could pose an existential danger the modern world never even suspected existed. The very air hummed with a low constant thrum, the sound of powerful climate control systems, banks of supercomputers processing unimaginable data streams, and the almost palpable intensity of dozens of highly focused individuals working in near silence on world-altering secrets.

Lab technicians in immaculate white coats moved with brisk, noiseless purpose through the brightly lit corridors, their eyes locked onto glowing screens displaying complex data visualizations or microscopic imagery. In sound-proofed linguistic labs, specialists hunched over fragile papyrus fragments or scanned high-resolution images of ancient clay tablets, their faces masks of concentration as they wrestled with syntax and semantics dead for millennia. Elsewhere, geospatial analysts pored over satellite imagery overlaid with historical maps, searching for subtle patterns, buried structures, or energy signatures that conventional archaeology would never detect. This subterranean complex was where cryptic clues from antiquity were meticulously translated into actionable intelligence for the precarious present day.

And right now, the laser focus of all this formidable machinery and expertise was directed at a relatively small, unassuming chunk of heavily oxidized ancient bronze resting on a sterile examination stage, bathed in the harsh, unforgiving glare of multiple high-intensity lab lamps. It was the fractured tablet recently unearthed during a fraught archaeological dig in Greece; the artifact that had triggered alarm bells deep within Section M and initiated this whole spiraling chain of events.

Dr. Evelyn Reed, Section M's chief linguist and arguably one of the best historical cryptanalysts in the world, stood before it. She was a sharp, intense woman in her late forties, whose pallor and the slight tremor in her hand suggested a diet consisting primarily of black coffee and pure adrenaline. She nudged her glasses further up her nose, her brow deeply furrowed as she stared intently at a bank of monitors displaying vastly magnified images of the tablet's surface. The strange, elegant, yet somehow menacing Greek script glowed starkly on the screens. Nearby computers whirred softly, running complex comparative algorithms, cross-referencing the symbols against vast databases of known epigraphy, attempting to make sense of characters and grammatical structures that hadn't been commonly used for nearly three thousand years.

Agent Marcus Thorne materialized silently in the laboratory doorway, leaning against the frame with an air of coiled energy. He was built lean and hard, radiating a quiet confidence that always seemed to border on impatience. His eyes, a startlingly pale grey, missed nothing. "Anything substantive yet, Evelyn?" he asked, his voice pitched low, clipped, cutting through the lab's low hum.

Evelyn let out a slow breath, tucking an errant strand of dark hair behind her ear, a habitual gesture when grappling with a particularly stubborn problem. "It's old, Marcus. Uncomfortably old. Older than almost anything securely dated we've ever encountered in this context. Current best estimate puts it 8th century BCE, possibly even pushing into the 9th. The dialect is brutal, highly localized, deeply archaic, riddled with forms that barely survived into the classical period. It's like trying to reconstruct a language from scattered whispers. And what little we can definitively translate..." She paused, tapping a gloved finger on a magnified, particularly complex ligature on the main screen. "It's... disturbing. Reads like some kind of apocalyptic prophecy, but not the usual vague Delphic pronouncements about harvests or border skirmishes. This language is dense, deliberately veiled, almost poetic in its obscurity, as if the author was consciously trying to hide the true, terrifying meaning behind layers of metaphor."

"Hiding uncomfortable truths is our stock-in-trade, Evelyn," Thorne replied flatly, unmoved. "Disturbing how?"

"The tone of it," Evelyn clarified, her voice dropping slightly, instinctively. "The sheer weight. It speaks of a great darkness gathering, some kind of catastrophic power rising in the East. The language is incredibly dramatic, overtly eschatological. You know, end-of-the-world stuff. We've managed to isolate recurring phrases; *'skotos apo anatolis* – shadow from the East' and *'kosmos klazomenos* – world broken or shattered'... This isn't just predicting a bad olive harvest or a minor dynastic squabble."

Thorne straightened from the doorframe, his focus visibly sharpening, the air around him seeming to crackle with sudden intensity. "The East? Could it be Soviet? Does any of this linguistic signature ping against known active projects? Codewords? We know they're pouring unprecedented resources into something big over there, something outside conventional arms development."

"We're running constant cross-references against every scrap of intel, every intercept, every rumor," Evelyn confirmed, gesturing vaguely towards the humming server racks visible through a reinforced glass wall. "But nothing concrete has popped yet. The language here... it's too symbolic, too mythological in its framing. Trying to link it directly to modern military-industrial jargon is like trying to nail Jell-O to a wall. We need more than just computational brute force. We need someone who doesn't just translate this stuff algorithmically, but feels it, instinctively understands the cultural nuances, the mindset of the era. Someone who lives and breathes archaic Greece."

Thorne's expression remained impassive, carved from granite, but Evelyn, who had worked with him for years, saw a flicker of reluctant understanding in his pale eyes. "So," Thorne said, his voice devoid of inflection, "you're saying the eccentric Professor Saint is our only viable play here?"

Evelyn nodded firmly, decisively. "Dr. Leon Saint. He's undeniably brilliant, unequivocally top of his field in classical philology and archaic epigraphy; although he can be notoriously difficult and operates entirely outside our usual circles. He knows these obscure ancient Greek dialects like most people know their own native tongue. If anyone on this planet can penetrate the layers of intentional obscurity and unlock what this tablet is really trying to warn us about, it's him."

***

Miles away from the sterile, fluorescent-lit, humming corridors of Section M's subterranean Vault, Dr. Leon Saint was blissfully lost in his own, very different world. His preferred natural habitat was not a secure lab, but either the towering, hushed maze of bookshelves in the University of Maryland's main research library, or the cozy, comforting chaos of his own home study. The latter was a large, high-ceilinged room perpetually overflowing with precariously stacked books, rolled-up historical maps leaning in corners, reproductions of ancient scrolls spilling off surfaces, and permeated by the wonderfully dry, slightly sweet scent of aging paper and old leather bindings. Leo, as his few friends called him, often felt he understood the faded words and fragmented thoughts of long-dead civilizations far better, and certainly more easily, than he understood the baffling complexities and unpredictable emotions of most living people. The gravitational pull of the past was his constant companion, his most demanding mistress.

That particular afternoon, warm spring sunlight streamed through the tall study window, illuminating dust motes dancing in the air and painting long, golden stripes across his cluttered mahogany desk. Leo sat hunched over a thick, illustrated volume on Minoan palatial architecture, completely engrossed, tracing the intricate floor plan of Knossos with a thoughtful finger. He was utterly oblivious to the mundane world outside his book-lined sanctuary. Which was precisely why the harsh, unexpected ring of his landline telephone made him jump. The beige relic balanced atop stacked journals violently pulled him back to the present. He rarely used the thing, preferring the quiet, controllable detachment of email for necessary communications.

With a distinct flicker of annoyance creasing his brow, he snatched the receiver off its cradle before the third ring. "Saint," he barked into the mouthpiece, making no effort to disguise his irritation at the interruption.

A crisp, cool, utterly no-nonsense male voice responded immediately, devoid of preamble. "Dr. Saint, this is Agent Thorne. I'm calling from a restricted government research facility. We've recently come across an artifact, something quite ancient and potentially very significant. Your colleague, Dr. Evelyn Reed, strongly recommended we contact you directly."

Leo's initial annoyance began to curdle into wary curiosity, one eyebrow arching slightly. "A government research facility?" he repeated, skepticism dripping from the words. He pictured grey men in grey suits dealing with grey bureaucracy. "What kind of artifact are we discussing?"

"Unfortunately, I cannot get into specifics over an unsecured line, Doctor," Thorne replied smoothly, his voice betraying no hint of frustration at Leo's tone. "But it's Greek. Ancient Greek. And it possesses characteristics that suggest it could be... important." Thorne deliberately let the word hang there, freighted with unspoken meaning, a carefully calibrated lure. "We were hoping you might be willing to consult. Strictly confidential, of course. We can arrange secure transport at your earliest convenience."

Leo hesitated, running a hand through his already untidy brown hair. He generally avoided entanglements with government agencies. Their agendas were opaque, their methods often clumsy, and their paperwork invariably soul-destroying. His books, his research, offered a much quieter, more predictable, and infinitely more rewarding kind of companionship. But... ancient Greek. Archaic, even, if Reed was involved. Something deemed important by people who likely didn't use the word lightly. The dedicated academic in him, the part that thrilled to the intellectual hunt, the scent of a genuine historical puzzle waiting to be solved, felt a distinct, undeniable tug.

"How much of my time are we potentially talking about?" Leo asked, attempting to maintain a reluctant tone, though he could already feel his resolve crumbling.

"Initial assessment and consultation? A day, perhaps two at the absolute most," Thorne responded quickly, smoothly, sensing the shift. "Naturally, all expenses will be covered, and a standard consultancy fee applies."

A day or two. It wouldn't completely derail his current work on Aegean trade routes. And the lure of a genuine, hands-on mystery emerging directly from the classical world... that was proving increasingly difficult to resist. His curiosity was a powerful force.

"Alright, Agent Thorne," Leo finally conceded, the intellectual excitement finally winning out, adding an unexpected touch of warmth to his voice. "You have my attention. Tell me when and where you need me."

***

The next morning, precisely at the arranged time, a plain, dark grey sedan that managed to scream 'government issue' despite its complete lack of markings slid to a silent, unobtrusive stop outside Leo's comfortable, slightly overgrown brick colonial home in the leafy suburbs. Agent Thorne stood waiting beside it, leaning against the passenger door. He looked exactly as Leo had pictured him from his voice. The sharp, dark suit was perfectly tailored, watchful grey eyes taking in everything. He radiated an aura of tightly controlled professional calm that somehow felt colder and more dangerous than overt aggression.

The drive itself was long, silent, and deliberately unremarkable. Thorne offered minimal conversation, volunteering no information about their destination, deflecting Leo's tentative questions with polite non-answers. They wound through a seemingly endless succession of anonymous office parks, past nondescript federal buildings identified only by cryptic acronyms, taking routes that felt circuitous and intentionally confusing. Leo quickly suspected the journey was designed more to disorient and impress upon him the layers of security than for simple transportation efficiency.

The real surprise came when they finally arrived, not at some imposing, high-security complex, but back at the utterly mundane Mid-Atlantic Regional Government Records Depository. Instead of heading towards the public entrance, however, Thorne guided him around the side of the building to a discreet, unmarked service door, swiped a keycard through a barely visible reader, and led him inside. Then they went down. Down several flights of sterile concrete stairs, and then into an elevator that descended smoothly, silently, for what felt like far too long.

The transition was abrupt and jarring. The warm, humid, pollen-thick air of the Maryland spring vanished instantly, replaced by the cool, dry, recycled air of The Vault, carrying a faint, almost imperceptible scent of ozone and sterilized metal. It felt like stepping through a portal into a different reality. Unnaturally quiet, hyper-controlled, humming with latent, unseen energy. They proceeded through a series of echoing corridors secured by heavy, electromagnetically locked doors. The only sounds were the soft click of Thorne's access card engaging each lock, the near-silent *'swish'* of the doors sliding open and shut, and the hard, assessing stares of the uniformed guards posted at intervals. These men and women looked immensely capable and like they wouldn't hesitate for a nanosecond to use the formidable hardware clipped securely to their belts.

Finally, Thorne opened one last door, this one leading into a brightly lit, spacious laboratory filled with advanced equipment Leo couldn't even begin to identify. And there it was.

Laying reverently on a sterile steel examination table, positioned directly beneath a focused array of powerful lamps, was the fractured bronze tablet. In this high-tech environment, it looked deceptively small, almost insignificant, yet it seemed to radiate a palpable aura of immense age, a static charge of ancient energy that prickled the hairs on Leo's arms.

Dr. Evelyn Reed stood beside the table, seemingly oblivious to their entrance, her entire being radiating intense concentration. She looked up as they approached, offering Leo a curt, preoccupied nod. "Dr. Saint. Thank you for coming on such short notice. Evelyn Reed, lead linguist on this project."

Leo barely registered her words or the offered handshake, his attention wholly, irrevocably captured by the object on the table. The sheer, undeniable antiquity of it, the immense weight of the centuries it had somehow survived, hit him with an almost physical force, stealing his breath for a moment. He automatically accepted the thin, white cotton gloves Evelyn offered and leaned closer, his eyes, expertly trained, immediately tracing the elegant, faded lines of the engraved script.

"Remarkable," he breathed, the word escaping him involuntarily. He carefully, gently ran a gloved fingertip along one of the fractured edges, feeling the cool metal beneath the fabric. "Utterly remarkable. The dialect is extraordinarily archaic... a fascinating, complex blend of early Attic forms, yes, but overlaid with something... older. Something more primal, possibly hinting at influences previously thought lost by this period. You're absolutely right, Dr. Reed, 8th century BCE feels conservative. This could easily push back into the late Geometric period, maybe even earlier."

"We've managed to translate isolated fragments, key phrases," Evelyn confirmed, gesturing towards several large printouts spread across an adjacent table, covered in handwritten annotations, highlighted sections, and complex grammatical charts. "But establishing the cohesive syntax, understanding the overarching context, is proving exceptionally difficult. "We keep circling back to these core phrases. 'Shadow from the East,' 'world broken,' 'power unleashed.' But the narrative thread connecting them, the specific nature of the warning, remains frustratingly elusive."

Leo spent the next hour utterly consumed, lost to the world outside the small circle of light illuminating the tablet. His mind dove deep, immersing itself in the linguistic nuances, the potential historical references, the very soul of the object. He compared the script mentally to dozens of other known inscriptions from the period, cross-referenced peculiarities of the dialect with obscure regional variations documented only in fragmented sources, and considered the specific historical and religious context of the Oracle of Delphi during that tumultuous era. Agent Thorne watched him silently from a corner of the lab, arms crossed, his stillness absolute, his patience seemingly infinite but his presence nonetheless a constant, low-level pressure at the edge of Leo's awareness.

Finally, Leo straightened up slowly, carefully removing the gloves. He pushed his glasses higher on his nose, his expression deeply thoughtful, his initial academic excitement now tempered with a dawning sense of gravity. "This isn't a standard Delphic prophecy," he stated, his voice quiet but firm. "It's not just foretelling some political upheaval or a coming plague or a military defeat. It feels... heavier. More profound. Weighted with genuine fear. The language structure, the grammatical choices, the deliberate use of ambiguous terms. It feels intentionally obscure, coded almost, designed to be understood only by initiates, perhaps. This recurring 'shadow from the East'... historically, in the 8th or 9th century BCE, that could theoretically point to several emerging powers or threats. The Assyrians, perhaps Phrygians, even nomadic incursions. But combined with the other fragmented warnings... the sheer intensity of the language used... I believe it's hinting at something far more specific than a geopolitical shift. Something perceived as fundamentally... dangerous."

Thorne pushed himself off the wall instantly, stepping closer until he was only a few feet away, his pale eyes locking onto Leo's, sharp and demanding. "Dangerous how, Doctor? Define dangerous. We have actionable intelligence, corroborated from multiple sensitive sources, suggesting this artifact might connect directly to a new, highly classified Soviet weapons program. Intel is thin, mostly whispers and defectors' rumors, but we know they're pursuing some kind of advanced energy technology. Something unconventional, based on principles we don't fully understand, something potentially... catastrophic on a global scale."

Leo's eyebrows shot up in genuine astonishment. "The Soviets? Using an ancient Greek prophecy, possibly from the Oracle of Delphi herself, as inspiration or justification for advanced weapons development?" The concept sounded utterly ludicrous, like the plot of a bizarre pulp novel or a conspiracy theory whispered in dark corners. It strained credulity to the breaking point. Yet... the unwavering conviction burning in Thorne's gaze, the stark, undeniable reality of the incredibly sophisticated, high-security laboratory surrounding him, the very existence of Section M itself. It all made outright dismissal impossible.

"We need to know precisely what this prophecy is truly warning about, Dr. Saint," Thorne pressed, his voice dropping, losing its earlier detachment, becoming hard as forged steel. "We need to understand, definitively, what this 'shadow from the East' represents in the context of the full text, and exactly how it could potentially 'break the world'. Can you decipher the complete message? Can you unlock its secrets? Will you help us?"

Leo looked from Thorne's intense, demanding face back to the silent, fractured bronze tablet resting on the table. The weight of three millennia seemed to press down on him. The ancient, elegant words, carved so long ago, seemed to whisper across the ages, pulling him inexorably out of his comfortable, predictable academic world and into something far more immediate, infinitely more complex, and potentially terrifyingly perilous. His quiet study, his beloved books, his carefully structured routines. They all felt suddenly flimsy, irrelevant, a million miles away. A thrill, sharp and unexpected, the thrill of discovery, mixed uneasily with a growing apprehension about the latent power these cryptic words might truly hold, tightened his gut.

"Yes, Agent Thorne," Leo heard himself say, his voice firmer, clearer than he expected. "Yes. I'll help."

Chapter Two

Nightingale's Song

Three weeks before Dr. Leon Saint was abruptly yanked from his comfortable academic cocoon into the unnerving world of shadows and secrets, Agent Seraphina Volkov was already navigating its iciest, murkiest depths. Tonight, the treacherous pool she swam in was the heart of East Berlin.

The wind slicing down the poorly lit, deserted streets felt like shards of glass against her exposed skin. It carried the ubiquitous, depressing stench of the city. Cheap lignite coal smoke lingering in the damp air, the smell of wet concrete and mildewed brickwork, and an undercurrent of something less tangible: stale fear and simmering desperation. It was late, well past the official curfew, pushing towards 02:00. The city felt hunched under a starless sky, grey and weary, collectively holding its breath beneath the suffocating weight of the Wall. The jagged scar that bisected streets, lives, and ideologies.

Sera moved with the practiced invisibility of a ghost, melting into the sparse, shuffling crowd near the Friedrichstrasse checkpoint. To any casual observer, or more importantly, to the perpetually watching eyes of the Volkspolizei and the ubiquitous Stasi informants, she was just another anonymous, exhausted worker heading home after a long, soul-crushing shift at some state-run factory. Her dark, usually tightly controlled hair was ruthlessly stuffed under a shapeless, scratchy wool cap. Her worn, grey overcoat was deliberately generic, identical to a hundred others moving through the dim light. She kept her gaze lowered, her posture slumped just enough to suggest fatigue, not defiance. Invisible. Non-descript. Utterly forgettable. That was the essential currency of survival in a city where paranoia was state policy and everyone watched everyone else.

Years spent playing the lethal game of Cold War espionage across hostile borders. Budapest, Prague, Warsaw, Moscow itself. These had honed her senses to an almost preternatural sharpness. Every flicker of movement glimpsed in a darkened apartment window above, every distant siren, every pair of headlights cutting through the oppressive gloom, every hushed, hurried conversation snatched from a shadowy doorway. Each registered, analyzed, categorized as potential threat or benign detail in milliseconds. She wasn't just trained in situational awareness; she was intrinsically wired for it, her nervous system perpetually thrumming at a higher frequency than ordinary people. It was a grim, draining existence, lived perpetually on the knife-edge, but navigating it, surviving it, beating the seemingly impossible odds. That brought a cold, fierce satisfaction few could ever comprehend.

Tonight's assignment had sounded deceptively simple on the encrypted briefing papers: extract a compromised Stasi informant before his handlers realized the full extent of his betrayal. But simple jobs had a nasty, often fatal, habit of turning sideways with blinding speed, especially here, in the nerve center of the East German surveillance state. The target was a physicist named Klaus Richter, a jittery, mid-level functionary who'd somehow gotten entangled in a highly classified Soviet research project based out near Minsk and now wanted out. Desperately. He claimed to possess technical data Section M needed with critical urgency. The exfiltration plan involved Richter slipping away from his apartment block and making his way towards a designated dead zone near the perimeter fence, shadowed by the ghostly, skeletal remains of the abandoned Teufelsberg listening station. A massive, defunct monument to earlier, cruder spy games looming just visible on the western horizon.

Sera subtly checked the cheap, utilitarian digital watch hidden beneath the frayed cuff of her coat. 02:17. Three minutes until the scheduled contact. She leaned against a damp, graffiti-scarred brick wall, letting the penetrating cold seep through her multiple layers of clothing. Her posture broadcast weary resignation, but beneath the drab coat, every muscle was coiled tight, every nerve ending alight, ready to explode into action instantly. Her gaze swept the street methodically. The narrow, garbage-choked alleyways opposite, the shadowed doorways of the crumbling tenement buildings, the rooftops silhouetted against the faint urban glow. Nothing seemed overtly out of place. No black sedans idling conspicuously. No unusual figures lurking. But in this city, normality itself could be the most dangerous camouflage. Complacency was a luxury agents like her couldn't afford; it got you captured, tortured, or buried in an unmarked grave.

A furtive flicker of movement in the mouth of the alley directly across the street. Right on schedule. Klaus Richter. He looked significantly worse than his grainy dossier photograph suggested. Gaunt, pale under the flickering sodium lamps, his eyes darting around with the frantic, trapped energy of a cornered animal. He clutched a battered, cheap fiberboard briefcase to his chest as if it were a life raft in a stormy sea; the critical intel was supposedly microfilmed and concealed within its lining. He radiated sheer, unadulterated terror, and rightly so. The Stasi's methods for dealing with perceived traitors were notoriously brutal and lethally efficient.

Richter took a hesitant, stumbling step out of the alley's concealing shadows, heading towards the pre-arranged pick-up point. A specific darkened doorway halfway down the block. Just as he reached the greasy cobblestones in the middle of the deserted road, headlights flared violently at the far end of the street. A black Volga sedan, the ubiquitous, menacing vehicle of choice for State Security, accelerated rapidly, tires screeching on the slick surface, spitting loose gravel. It slewed to a halt directly beside the frozen physicist. Before Richter could even react, two men erupted from the car. Nondescript in their ill-fitting suits and standard-issue haircuts, but their faces were hard, impassive, their movements radiating brutal efficiency.

Sera's blood turned to ice water in her veins. Compromised. The meet was irrevocably blown. Richter hadn't been careful enough, or someone else had talked.

There was no time for contingency plans. No time for careful assessment or strategic withdrawal. No time for thinking, only pure, hardwired reaction. Instinct, honed over countless dangerous operations, took over. In a single fluid motion, Sera melted back, deeper into the concealing shadows of her own alleyway, her right hand automatically finding the cold, reassuringly solid grip of the silenced Makarov pistol tucked securely inside her coat pocket. The mission parameters instantly shifted. Extraction just became an armed rescue. Or, more pragmatically, a recovery operation for the intel. She wasn't leaving Klaus. Or, more critically, his briefcase. In their hands.

Moving with a speed and absolute silence that belied her bulky disguise, Sera doubled back, slipping through a narrow, foul-smelling side passage choked with overflowing rubbish bins and discarded debris. She knew this warren of backstreets intimately, having scouted the entire neighborhood meticulously in the preceding days. She needed to circle the block, hug the shadows, avoid any direct confrontation until she understood the full picture. Her soft-soled boots made absolutely no sound on the grimy, uneven pavement. She needed eyes on the situation, needed tactical advantage. Needed high ground.

A rusty, skeletal fire escape clung precariously to the side of a nearby tenement building, offering a potential route overlooking the unfolding scene. Without a moment's hesitation, she reached up, grasped the cold, lowest rung, and swung herself upwards, ascending the structure with the fluid, economical movements of a practiced climber, ignoring the groan of protesting metal. Reaching the flat, gravel-strewn roof several stories up, she moved silently to the edge, peering cautiously over the crumbling parapet.

Below, the two Stasi agents were roughly manhandling Klaus into the back seat of the Volga. He wasn't resisting; he looked utterly paralyzed by fear, his face ashen. The briefcase lay discarded for a moment on the pavement before one of the agents retrieved it and tossed it onto the front passenger seat. The Volga's engine roared back to life, coughing out a plume of oily exhaust smoke. Taking a deep, steadying breath, Sera turned and sprinted lightly across the rooftop. Another fire escape, mirroring the first, offered a potential path down on the adjacent building, further down the street in the direction the Volga was likely heading. She descended it just as quickly, landing silently in the darkened alley below mere seconds after the black sedan pulled away from the curb, accelerating rapidly towards the city outskirts. Almost certainly towards a notorious Stasi interrogation center known euphemistically as 'Cafe Leila'.

She had to cut them off. Her mind raced, processing street maps stored in her memory, calculating speeds, predicting their most likely route out of the city. A disused, largely forgotten service tunnel ran beneath this section of East Berlin, emerging near the main autobahn entrance they'd almost certainly take to reach the facility quickly. It would be filthy, possibly flooded in sections, undoubtedly rat-infested, but it represented the fastest, most direct route to intercept.

Minutes later, coated in grime and smelling faintly of sewage, she emerged breathless from the tunnel's graffitied mouth into the cold pre-dawn air. The autobahn entrance ramp was just ahead, dimly lit. She needed wheels. Immediately.

Luck, or perhaps desperation, provided a battered, sputtering Trabant approaching her from behind on the road. The notoriously unreliable East German people's car, chugged along in the pre-dawn quiet, its two-stroke engine making a lawnmower-like racket. It was her only option. She stepped decisively into the road, holding up a hand, flagging it down. She flashed a set of impeccably forged East German identity papers at the startled, sleepy-eyed driver, simultaneously launching into a rapid-fire, plausible story about a sudden family medical emergency requiring immediate travel. A thick wad of Ostmarks pressed firmly into his hand sealed the deal.

"Autobahn entrance. Follow that black car!" she ordered, her voice sharp and authoritative, slipping quickly into the cramped passenger seat that smelled of stale tobacco and cabbage. "Drive. Fast."

The little Trabant whined in pathetic protest as the nervous driver, glancing uneasily at Sera's grim face, pushed the accelerator to the floor. The car vibrated alarmingly, weaving somewhat erratically through what little other traffic shared the road. Sera ignored the driver's muttered anxieties, her gaze fixed forward, scanning the road ahead, eyes peeled for the distinctive shape of the black Volga. Finally, she spotted it. Twin red taillights disappearing up the ramp leading onto the eastbound autobahn. "There! Follow them!" she urged, her voice low and intense.

The Trabant, bless its inadequate two-stroke heart, strained valiantly, but it was hopelessly outmatched. The Volga was faster, heavier, built for state security purposes, not puttering around the city. Sera knew instantly that a direct car chase was suicidal in this fragile tin can. She needed an equalizer. Something unexpected. Her eyes scanned the roadside ahead, not just for the Volga, but for any advantage. The road straightened ahead, no turns for miles. A direct chase was pointless. But then she saw it: a construction zone, running parallel to the autobahn, a swathe of churned earth and stacked concrete barriers. And up ahead, she noticed something else—the Stasi's Volga signaling to exit at the next ramp, leading directly off the main highway, past the construction site. A dangerous gamble, but the only one.

"Pull over here! Now!" she barked at the startled driver, pointing towards the darkened site entrance that lay before the exit ramp.

Before the Trabant had even fully shuddered to a halt on the gravel shoulder, Sera was out, moving fast, vaulting a low temporary fence into the shadowy construction zone littered with building materials and heavy equipment. Her eyes, already adjusted to the poor light, quickly found what she needed. A small, tracked Caterpillar crane, the kind used for lifting heavy concrete pipes, parked near a pile of gravel. Incredibly, defying all regulations but typical of late-night site security, the keys were still dangling invitingly from the ignition. Hotwiring it would have taken only seconds, but tonight, fortune offered a welcome shortcut.

She swung herself up into the cold metal cab, turned the key, and the powerful diesel engine coughed, then roared to life with a satisfying rumble, the sound thankfully masked somewhat by the constant drone of traffic on the nearby autobahn. With a lurch and a protesting grind of massive gears, she maneuvered the ungainly but powerful machine into motion. The crane's tracks chewed through the loose gravel and earth, cutting a direct path through the construction site, bypassing the winding autobahn. She aimed for the spot where the exit ramp would intersect with the main highway, a calculated gamble on timing.

The Stasi's black Volga, now slowed for the turn onto the ramp, was a perfect, unsuspecting target. The crane emerged from the construction zone, tracks churning earth, directly onto the shoulder of the exit ramp, just meters behind the sedan. The massive machine, a functional behemoth that dwarfed the car.

The faces of the two Stasi agents inside, momentarily illuminated in the crane's powerful, glaring work lights, registered comical shock quickly followed by disbelief and dawning alarm in their rearview mirror. No time to react. Treating the crane's heavy, articulated steel arm like a medieval battering ram, Sera swung it with calculated force, aiming for the Volga's rear quarter panel.

Metal screamed and buckled, safety glass exploded inwards. The heavy sedan, already turning, spun violently, its momentum combining with the crane's brute impact. It became a crumpled, screeching wreck, careening off the road and crashing sideways into the unforgiving concrete roadside barrier with a sickening, final crunch of metal on concrete. Before the dazed, likely injured occupants could even begin to react, Sera had killed the crane's engine. Silence. She jumped nimbly down from the cab, Makarov held steady and ready in her right hand, muzzle suppressor pointing forward. She moved swiftly towards the wreckage.

One agent, staggering dazedly out of the crumpled driver's side door, fumbling inside his suit jacket, clearly trying to draw his own weapon. Sera didn't hesitate. Two precisely aimed shots. Soft *phut-phut* sounds, barely audible puffs swallowed instantly by the night air and the traffic noise. The agent crumpled silently to the ground without a sound. The second agent was slumped unresponsive in the front passenger seat, either unconscious or worse from the violent impact. A quick check confirmed he wouldn't be a problem for anyone ever again.

She wrenched open the buckled rear door of the Volga. Klaus Richter stared up at her, his eyes wide with terror, shaking uncontrollably, but miraculously, physically alive and seemingly unharmed beyond minor cuts from the shattered glass. Sera quickly checked him for serious injuries, then hauled him unceremoniously out of the wreck, simultaneously reaching back inside to retrieve the precious, battered briefcase from the floor mats. The original extraction plan was shot to hell, buried under layers of unforeseen complications, but the primary objective was secured. The informant and his intelligence.

Hours later, safely back across the border in the comparatively bright, free-wheeling chaos of West Berlin, Sera delivered a still-trembling Richter and the vital briefcase to a waiting Section M reception team operating out of a nondescript safe house. The subsequent debrief was quick, clinical, efficient. The microfilmed technical data Klaus provided was, as suspected, even more critical and alarming than initial reports suggested, hinting at a major, potentially paradigm-shifting secret weapons project the Soviets were aggressively developing under extreme secrecy.

Later that day, as she methodically cleaned her Makarov, field-stripped her gear, and packed her sterile go-bag for the next inevitable, faceless assignment, a coded message chattered urgently from the secure telex machine in the corner of the operations room.

New file activated. Priority Designation: Alpha. Codename: Delphi Protocol. Primary operational partner assignment: Dr. Leon Saint, civilian consultant, historian. University of Maryland.

A rare, almost imperceptible, wry smile touched Sera Volkov's lips. An academic. A dusty professor specializing in dead languages. Thrown into the deep end with her.

This, she thought, holstering her cleaned weapon, was going to be... interesting.

Chapter Three

Moscow's Response

Moscow, KGB Headquarters, Lubyanka Square

Hours after Richter's Extraction

High within the imposing, grey granite edifice of the KGB Headquarters overlooking Lubyanka Square, a building whose very name evoked decades of fear and state power, Colonel Gregor Orlov stared impassively at the secure telex machine as it clattered out the final lines of the after-action report from Berlin. The air in his spacious, sparsely furnished office, tasted faintly of stale cigarette smoke and polished wood.

Failure. The word itself wasn't explicitly used, of course. Directorate S, the KGB's elite branch for external operations and assassinations, frowned upon such blunt, demoralizing language in official communications. But the subtext was brutally clear. Klaus Richter, the nervous little physicist privy to the highly sensitive initial feasibility studies for Project *Oko*, was gone. Vanished. Snatched from under the very noses of the supposedly vigilant East German State Security apparatus by a single, unidentified American operative: presumed female based on fragmented intercept chatter, preliminary designation 'Nightingale'. Who had then melted back into the decadent, chaotic mire of West Berlin like smoke dissolving in rain.

The collateral damage was equally galling: two experienced Stasi agents neutralized, a state security vehicle destroyed. A messy, amateurish, inefficient conclusion to what should have been a routine, almost trivial, intercept operation. Orlov felt a familiar flicker of cold contempt for the East Germans' habitual operational sloppiness, a disdain he quickly masked behind his usual carefully cultivated facade of icy control. Competence was rare; incompetence, endemic.

He took a slow, deliberate drag from his unfiltered cigarette, the harsh, strong tobacco doing little to ease the knot of tension coiling tightly in his gut. Losing Richter himself was merely inconvenient; the man was replaceable. Losing the *intel* the physicist carried, however preliminary, was potentially catastrophic. Especially given the persistent, almost unbelievable whispers circulating in the highest echelons about Project *Oko*'s theoretical power source. Whispers rooted in obscure historical anomalies, ancient myths, and classified research so sensitive only a handful of individuals were even aware of its existence.

The secure telephone on his vast, polished mahogany desk emitted a single, sharp, demanding buzz. Not the standard internal line, but the *direct* line. The one that bypassed all usual switchboards and cryptographic safeguards, connecting only to the highest, most feared, and seldom-heard authority within the entire Soviet state apparatus. The Centre of the Centre.

Orlov stubbed out his cigarette immediately in the heavy crystal ashtray, the movement precise, economical. He instinctively straightened his already immaculate uniform tunic and lifted the heavy Bakelite receiver, his posture automatically adjusting to reflect the absolute deference demanded by the caller. "Orlov," he stated, his voice perfectly modulated, betraying no emotion.

"Colonel." The voice on the other end was cold, metallic, utterly devoid of inflection or personality. It was a voice that carried the unmistakable, chilling weight of absolute, unquestionable power. The power of life and death over nations. "The... situation... in Berlin was... regrettable." The pauses were deliberate, each syllable a veiled threat.

"Unforeseen operational complications arose, Comrade Supreme," Orlov replied smoothly, his voice a carefully constructed neutral mask, automatically employing the required, almost reverential address reserved for this specific individual. "The American operative demonstrated unexpected skill and employed unconventional tactics."

"Skill becomes irrelevant when countered by adequate preparation and superior force," the cold voice stated flatly, dismissing Orlov's implied excuse. "Richter's knowledge, however preliminary, must now be considered compromised. However," the voice continued after a fractional pause, "another matter has arisen. Something potentially far more significant, requiring your... unique talents, Colonel."

Orlov remained silent, motionless, waiting. One did not prompt the Comrade Supreme.

"Our Hellenic station reports the recent discovery of a unique artifact during what they term 'unauthorized' excavations near Delphi," the voice continued, low and measured, each word precise. "A fragment of a bronze tablet, bearing an archaic inscription. Our contact there secured detailed photographs and high-quality rubbings before it ... disappeared into American hands. Preliminary analysis here in Moscow, based on those reproductions, attributes it with high probability to the Oracle herself, dating from the earliest period."

Orlov felt a distinct flicker of focused interest cut through his practiced impassivity. Ancient relics were usually the domain of archaeologists and museum curators, utterly insignificant to Directorate S, unless...

"Preliminary decryption of the recovered script," the voice stated, confirming Orlov's unspoken thought, "when cross-referenced with Directorate S's own deep archives on anomalous historical phenomena – files you know were foundational to the initial theoretical work on Project *Oko* – reveals an undeniable, and frankly unsettling, connection. The parallels are too precise to ignore. Specifically, Colonel, its references to a 'shadow from the East' align perfectly with certain documented energy signatures our research has pursued, and the prophetic terminology is strikingly consistent with our most classified theoretical models for controlled energy release." The line crackled faintly.

Orlov's grip tightened fractionally on the heavy receiver. Project *Oko*. 'The Eye'. It was the most deeply classified, most potentially transformative, most dangerous program currently active in the entire Soviet arsenal. Its success promised absolute strategic dominance, the power to reshape the global balance overnight. Its failure... or worse, its exposure... was unthinkable.

"The Americans," the voice went on, relentless, cold, "specifically their meddlesome historical threats unit, Section M, have, as predicted, already acquired the physical tablet fragment. Our monitoring of their secure facilities confirms its arrival approximately seventy-two hours ago. Intercepts of their internal communications indicate their top linguist has already consulted an external specialist. A civilian academic named Dr. Leon Saint. Historian. Based at the University of Maryland. Considered their leading expert in these archaic Greek dialects and epigraphy. A man who now knows too much."

"Saint..." Orlov committed the name instantly to memory. He visualized the type: *bespectacled, soft, naive*. Easily broken or manipulated. "And the American operative from the Berlin incident?"

"Agent Seraphina Volkov. Callsign 'Nightingale'," the voice confirmed. "She has been officially partnered with Saint for this operation. We anticipate imminent deployment, likely following leads suggested by the prophecy's text. Initial linguistic markers point towards Thracian regions, suggesting Bulgaria as a primary target area."

Bulgaria. Orlov knew the region intimately. He had connections there, assets cultivated over years. The terrain, the politics, the shadows...he understood them all.

"Your new assignment, Colonel Orlov," the voice stated, the words now sharp, absolute, leaving no conceivable room for discussion or refusal. "Priority Alpha. Effective immediately, you will assume operational command of all assets pertaining to this emerging 'Delphi' situation. Your objectives are as follows: Locate and monitor targets Saint and Volkov. Determine the full, precise nature and extent of the Delphic prophecy and its verified connection to Project *Oko*. Identify and secure any related artifacts or locations indicated by the text. Particularly the secondary component mentioned in our own fragmented historical sources, referred to as the 'obsidian lens' or 'heart stone'. Above all, Colonel, you will ensure that this knowledge, this potential power, remains exclusively under Soviet control. Failure," the voice added, the single word hanging heavy and cold as a death sentence in the silence, "is not an option."

A cold, fierce fire ignited deep within Orlov's controlled exterior. This wasn't just another assignment. This was a directive from the absolute pinnacle of Soviet power, entrusting him with a mission of paramount strategic importance. A chance to prove his worth, his ruthlessness, his indispensability. A chance to grasp real power.

"Understood, Comrade Supreme," Orlov replied, his voice crisp, precise, betraying nothing of the sudden, fierce ambition surging within him. "Consider it done."

He placed the receiver carefully back in its cradle, the decisive click echoing unnaturally loud in the imposing, silent office. He stood motionless for a long moment, gazing out the thick, reinforced window at the distant, onion-domed spires of the Kremlin piercing the grey Moscow sky. The Delphi Protocol. A mission handed down from the highest authority, bypassing layers of bureaucracy and rival departments. Let the Americans chase their ancient myths and academic theories. He, Gregor Orlov, would chase the tangible reality, the *power* promised by the conjunction of ancient prophecy and cutting-edge Soviet science. And he would crush, utterly and without hesitation, anyone or anything that dared stand in his way.

He reached deliberately for another cigarette from the silver box on his desk, his mind already rapidly mapping out logistics, selecting key personnel from his most trusted units, formulating contingency plans, anticipating obstacles. Even before the Comrade Supreme had disconnected, Orlov had mentally dispatched preliminary directives to his deepest networks: key European and Middle Eastern listening posts and antiquarian contacts were to be immediately alerted. Any whisper, any movement related to Delphic texts, Thracian artifacts, or unusual energy sources was to be reported directly, and with extreme prejudice towards any Western interference. Agent Volkov. Dr. Saint. The obsidian lens. Bulgaria. The hunt had begun.

Chapter Four

An Unlikely Partnership

The briefing room, located deep within the sterile, subterranean maze of The Vault, felt colder than the rest of the facility, both physically and metaphorically. It was a space stripped bare for ruthless efficiency: a polished steel table reflecting the harsh overhead lighting, uncomfortable ergonomic chairs designed for alertness rather than comfort, and blank, pale grey walls deliberately devoid of any distraction. One entire wall was dominated by a large, dark holographic display screen, currently inert but ready to project anything from real-time satellite feeds to meticulously rendered ancient maps at the flick of a switch. It emitted a low, almost subliminal hum, a faint thrum of latent energy that felt distinctly alien compared to the comforting, dusty silence of Leo Saint's book-lined study.

Agent Seraphina Volkov sat alone at the head of the steel table, nursing a thick ceramic mug filled with what smelled like brutally strong, almost burnt coffee. The institutional quiet didn't bother her; she was accustomed to long periods of solitary waiting, punctuated by bursts of intense activity. A specialized portable display terminal glowed softly in front of her, displaying the personnel file. Heavily redacted in parts of one, Dr. Leon Saint. The primary photograph showed a man likely in his late thirties or early forties, with a thoughtful, undeniably intelligent face, perhaps a little too soft around the edges, lacking the hard angles and watchful caution typically found in the world Sera inhabited. A neatly trimmed beard couldn't quite disguise a stubborn set to his jawline, but his eyes, magnified slightly by his glasses, looked far more suited to deciphering faded parchments than reading hostile intent in a crowded street.

The accompanying dossier detailed impressive academic credentials, fluency in a dizzying array of dead or obscure languages, and a shelf-load of scholarly publications on various aspects of ancient Greek history and culture. *Brilliant*, Sera conceded silently, scrolling through the list. *Undeniably brilliant in his specific sandbox.* But the crucial question remained unspoken: *Can he handle himself when things inevitably get messy? When the theoretical threat becomes terrifyingly real?* Her past experiences with academics thrust into fieldwork weren't encouraging; they tended to overthink tactical decisions, freeze under pressure, or worse, endanger the mission through naive idealism. Still, orders were orders, and the Delphi Protocol was clearly a high-priority directive.

The door slid open, and Agent Marcus Thorne strode in, carrying two more steaming mugs identical to hers. He moved with his usual purposeful stride, placing one mug directly across the table from Sera.

"Morning, Nightingale," he greeted, his tone crisp, professional. "Hope you managed to get some meaningful rest after the Berlin fireworks." For the briefest instant, Sera caught a flicker of genuine respect in his usually unreadable pale eyes. She'd pulled off a difficult extraction under extreme duress, even if the initial plan had gone completely sideways.

"Enough rest, Thorne," Sera replied curtly, taking a grateful sip of the fresh coffee. It was black, bitter, and scalding hot – just how she liked it. "So, this is our history expert?" she asked, gesturing towards the glowing tablet. "From the file, he looks like he'd be significantly happier digging through dusty scrolls than dodging actual bullets."

Thorne allowed himself a minuscule chuckle, a rare crack in his usual granite composure. "That's certainly where his head lives most of the time, alright," he admitted. "But Dr. Reed swears he's the sharpest tool in the box for this particular, highly specialized job. And right now, Professor Saint is the only one making any tangible headway decoding that damned tablet."

"Headway towards *what*, exactly?" Sera pressed, keeping her voice carefully neutral, devoid of inflection. She needed concrete facts, actionable intelligence, not just Thorne's operational gut feelings.

"Headway towards deciphering a prophecy," Thorne stated, his brief flicker of humor instantly evaporating, replaced by grim seriousness. "An ancient Greek prophecy that might be pointing directly at a new, highly unconventional Soviet weapons program. Something designed, we fear, to cause nightmares on a global scale." He leaned forward slightly. "That's where you come in, Sera. You're partnered with Dr. Saint on this. He's the brains, deciphers the ancient mumbo-jumbo, follows the historical breadcrumbs. You," Thorne paused for emphasis, "are the muscle. Keep him safe. Get him where he needs to go. Make damn sure he doesn't inadvertently walk into a minefield, literal or figurative."

Sera raised a skeptical eyebrow. "Muscle?" she queried, her tone dry. "Sounds suspiciously like babysitting duty, Thorne."

"Think of it as essential operational synergy, Nightingale," Thorne corrected smoothly, though his eyes held a subtle hint of warning. "You neutralize the immediate threats so he has the space to do his critical work. He finds the target on the map; you clear the path to get there."

Just as Thorne finished speaking, the briefing room door slid open again, and Dr. Leon Saint stepped somewhat uncertainly into the room. He blinked against the harsh, shadowless fluorescent lighting, clutching a worn, brown leather briefcase in front of him almost like a shield. He wore tweed trousers that looked permanently rumpled, a slightly wrinkled button-down shirt, and a tweed jacket that seemed molded to his shoulders from countless hours spent hunched over desks and library carrels. He looked utterly, profoundly out of his element. A creature of libraries and archives abruptly teleported onto the cold, sterile steel deck of a warship.

"Ah, Dr. Saint, welcome," Thorne said, stepping forward smoothly, projecting confidence, offering a firm handshake. "Agent Thorne. And this is Agent Volkov. She'll be your primary field partner on the Delphi Protocol assignment."

Leo turned, his gaze landing on Sera. He seemed momentarily surprised, perhaps having expected another man in a suit, but quickly masked it with polite, academic formality. He shifted his briefcase awkwardly to his left hand and offered Sera a slightly hesitant handshake. "Agent Volkov. A distinct pleasure." His voice was softer than Thorne's, cultured, with the precise diction of someone who cares deeply about language. "Please, do call me Leon. Or Leo, actually," he added, a quick, almost shy smile flashing unexpectedly across his face. "Most friends tend to."

Sera stood, her own handshake firm, brief, professional. A stark contrast to his softer, academic grip. Her eyes, sharp and assessing, quickly took his measure, noticing the clear intelligence flickering behind the slightly bewildered surface expression, the way his gaze kept drifting irresistibly towards the darkened holo-display, hungry for information despite his apparent discomfort. He might *look* like a harmless librarian tragically separated from his card catalog, but there was undoubtedly a sharp, analytical mind working diligently behind those glasses. Maybe not entirely hopeless after all.

"Sera," she replied curtly, releasing his hand. "Likewise, Leo." She instantly surmised Thorne's assessment wasn't far off; this man would definitely require vigilant watching out for in the field.

"Right," Thorne interjected briskly, taking charge and gesturing towards the holographic display unit. "Let's bring you both fully into the operational loop. Leo, Agent Volkov has received the preliminary background briefings, but perhaps you could walk us through your latest findings regarding the tablet's text?"

Leo visibly brightened, the invitation to discuss his work seeming to ground him instantly, replacing his awkwardness with focused energy. He placed his battered briefcase carefully on the steel table, snapping open the worn brass locks to reveal an interior crammed with notebooks filled cover-to-cover with meticulous handwritten notes, intricate sketches of linguistic symbols, and stacks of printouts heavily annotated in multiple colors of ink. He located a specific cable within the organized chaos and connected a portable Bernoulli Box databank to the display console. Instantly, a stunningly high-resolution, three-dimensional image of the fractured bronze tablet sprang to life, hovering ghostlike on the large wall screen.

"Okay," Leo began, stepping towards the display, his posture shifting, becoming more animated, the scholar firmly back in his element. "As Agent Thorne indicated, the tablet contains what appears to be a significant prophecy, attributed with high confidence to the Oracle of Delphi herself, likely dating from her earliest, most potent period. The language, as I noted yesterday, is incredibly archaic, characterized by dense symbolism and intentional ambiguity, making a direct, literal translation... challenging, to say the least. However, through comparative analysis and contextual reconstruction, I've managed to isolate several recurring phrases and critical keywords. The most significant, and potentially alarming, is this persistent reference to a *'skotos apo anatolis'*. Literally, a 'shadow rising in the East.'" He used a laser pointer integrated into his pen to highlight a specific cluster of elegantly carved Greek letters on the projected image.

"Now, historically speaking, within the geopolitical context of the 8th or 9th century BC, the concept of the 'East' could plausibly refer to several promising regional powers. The expanding Assyrian empire, perhaps Phrygian kingdoms in Anatolia, or even nomadic incursions from the steppes," Leo continued, warming to his subject, his voice gaining confidence. "But the accompanying phrases, fragmented though they are, speak of something far more catastrophic, something potentially world-altering. We find terms that translate roughly as 'song of destruction,' 'earth lamenting,' and the power to 'break the world' or 'shatter the foundations'. Taken together, especially when viewed through the lens of current geopolitical tensions and... certain other intelligence reports..." He glanced briefly at Thorne. "...well, the possibility that this ancient text refers prophetically to a modern, technologically advanced threat, however improbable it initially sounds, feels increasingly difficult to ignore entirely."

Sera listened intently, her face impassive, but her mind was racing, connecting Leo's words to the unsettling debrief of the physicist, Klaus Richter, back in Berlin. "Richter mentioned Project Oko was exploring... 'unconventional energy principles'," Sera said, her voice thoughtful. "He spoke of anomalies, localized tremors, and strange resonance effects the lead scientists were trying to harness, some of it apparently based on what he called 'rediscovered archaic theoretical texts' the KGB had supplied them. It sounded like crackpot science then." She leaned forward slightly, her focus sharpening. "So, this 'shadow' from the East in your prophecy, Leo... any specific clues in the text about the *nature* of this threat? The kind of power we're actually talking about?"

'Vibrations that shatter stone'..." Sera repeated, the phrase now hitting with the force of a hammer blow. "Richter's data detailed experiments aimed at creating 'focused harmonic waves' capable of 'structural disintegration at a distance.' He claimed they were trying to weaponize resonance." Her gaze met Thorne's. "Could this prophecy be describing precisely that – a directed sonic or resonance-based weapon?"

Leo's eyes widened slightly behind his glasses, his expression shifting from academic frustration to genuine surprise and grudging respect. "Resonance frequency weapons..." he conceded. "That's... remarkably astute, Agent Volkov. And yes, terrifyingly, it aligns. Not just with esoteric Delphic interpretations of sound and destruction, but with the very terms Richter used. It's theoretically possible, even within known physics. And our own broader intelligence chatter *has* indicated the Soviets are pouring unprecedented resources into something deeply unconventional, something that sidesteps traditional arms."

Thorne, who had been listening with still intensity, nodded slowly, his pale eyes hard. "Richter's information was fragmented, verging on the unbelievable. But coupled with an authenticated Delphic prophecy nearly three millennia old describing similar effects and pointing to the East... the pattern becomes difficult to dismiss." He turned to Leo. "Alright, Professor. This 'shadow,' this 'vibration weapon' – does your prophecy give us a location? Where is this power rising?"

Leo nodded, tapping commands into the console, bringing up another image. A rough map overlaid with notes. "There's more. Another cryptic clue, seemingly indicating a specific location. It's referenced poetically as 'the land where the sun god sleeps, and the ancient mountains weep tears of gold.' Pure metaphorical language, obviously. But cross-referencing this imagery with other fragmented Delphic texts, known Thracian mythology concerning sun cults, and regional geography and geology... the strongest candidate, by far, points towards ancient Thrace. Specifically, the Rhodope Mountains region, located in modern-day Bulgaria."

Sera's gaze sharpened instantly. Bulgaria. Deep behind the Iron Curtain. Politically sensitive, heavily surveilled, difficult terrain. This wasn't going to be a simple artifact recovery mission in friendly territory.

"Furthermore," Leo continued, clearly energized by the puzzle, pulling up another image. A careful sketch he'd made based on peculiar symbols recurring near the geographical references in the text. "The text explicitly mentions two more items or concepts linked directly to that location. It speaks of locating a *'kryptos ophthalmos. Hidden eye'* and finding a *'lithos astraskopos.* *Stone that sees the stars'*. More metaphors, undoubtedly, but I strongly suspect they refer to tangible objectives. Perhaps another related artifact, a specific hidden structure, or even a natural geological formation somewhere within the Rhodope range."

Thorne looked from Leo's earnest, slightly flushed face to Sera's cool, assessing expression, seeing the unlikely pairing clearly. "Then Bulgaria it is," he stated, his voice leaving no room for doubt. "Leo, you'll provide the essential historical context and linguistic navigation, interpreting the clues as we find them. Sera, you will accompany Dr. Saint, provide close protection security at all times, and handle all... operational aspects encountered in hostile territory. Your joint mission is codenamed Delphi Protocol: follow these ancient clues into Bulgaria, locate and identify this potential Soviet project, assess the nature and severity of the threat, and if feasible and necessary, neutralize it. Find out what the 'shadow' truly is, ascertain the meaning of the 'hidden eye,' and determine what the 'stone that sees the stars' has to do with it all."

Leo glanced instinctively towards Sera, a flicker of undeniable apprehension crossing his face. He was a historian, a decipherer of dead languages, not an intelligence operative or a soldier. Venturing behind the Iron Curtain on a clandestine mission guided by the riddles of a three-thousand-year-old prophecy felt profoundly, dangerously surreal.

Sera met his uncertain gaze steadily, her expression unreadable but conveying an aura of absolute, unwavering competence. She gave a single, almost imperceptible nod. The mission parameters were clear. The risks were high. The partner was unconventional. But the objective was critical.

This profoundly unlikely pair. The dedicated professor abruptly pulled from his quiet world of books and artifacts, and the hardened clandestine agent forged on the Cold War's unforgiving front lines. They were officially partnered, heading straight into the lion's den, guided only by the cryptic, millennia-old whispers of a long-dead oracle.

CHAPTER FIVE

The Istanbul Connection

Leaving the cold, sterile depths of The Vault felt like surfacing from underwater. Back in the mundane reality of suburban Maryland, Leo blinked in the sunlight, the cryptic phrases from the Delphi tablet. 'Shadow from the East', 'stone that sees the stars'. These echoed in his mind. Bulgaria seemed like the obvious next step based on the Thracian clues, but Thorne and Section M weren't ready to send them blindly behind the Iron Curtain just yet.

'One more lead first, Doctor Saint,' Thorne had said back in the briefing room, pulling up a grainy image on the holo-display. It showed a fragment of an obscure, Byzantine-era manuscript. 'This text references prophecies originating from Delphi, specifically mentioning unusual celestial phenomena linked to ancient Thracian sites. Sound familiar?'

Leo had peered closer. 'Yes, the language is similar... the symbolism...'

'The original manuscript resides in the Topkapi Palace library in Istanbul,' Thorne continued. 'But our sources indicate a known dealer in rare texts and antiquities, operating out of the Grand Bazaar, claims to possess *another* copy, or perhaps even related fragments dealing with the same prophecies. This dealer is known only as "The Scholar". Before we send you into Bulgaria chasing shadows, we need you to verify this manuscript in Istanbul. See if it corroborates your findings or offers any clearer clues about this "shadow" or the "stone".'

Sera had listened impassively, but Leo saw the strategic sense. Istanbul, a city straddling Europe and Asia, a historical crossroads teeming with secrets, was a logical place to hunt for obscure texts that might bridge the gap between ancient Greece and Thrace. It was also, she likely noted, relatively easier to access than plunging directly into Soviet-controlled Bulgaria.

And so, less than forty-eight hours later, Leo found himself stepping off a plane not in Sofia, but onto the bustling tarmac of Istanbul's Atatürk Airport. The air that greeted him was a world away from Maryland. A humid, hazy blend carrying the scents of diesel fumes, strong coffee, roasting chestnuts, unfamiliar spices, and the faint, briny zest of the Bosphorus Strait.

Sera moved beside him, already blending in seamlessly. She'd swapped her functional American clothes for looser trousers and a tunic-like shirt, a simple scarf covering her hair. She looked like any other European tourist, except for the watchful intensity in her eyes that never wavered. Their cover story was simple: Leo was an academic researching Byzantine-era trade routes, and Sera was his assistant and translator. Plausible enough for a city built on centuries of commerce and shifting empires.

Getting through customs was surprisingly smooth. They took a rattling yellow taxi through chaotic traffic towards Sultanahmet, the heart of the old city. Leo stared out the window, mesmerized. Istanbul assaulted the senses. The skyline pierced by the elegant minarets of ancient mosques, the sheer density of people crowding the streets, the riot of color in shop displays, the constant blare of horns and shouting vendors. Crumbling Byzantine walls stood beside grand Ottoman palaces, Roman columns peeked out from behind modern storefronts. History wasn't just studied here; it was lived in, layered thick like sediment.

'Try not to look *too* much like a wide-eyed tourist, Leo,' Sera murmured beside him, noticing his fascination. 'We need to blend in, remember? Low profile.'

'Right, right,' Leo mumbled, forcing himself to look less enthralled, though it was difficult. This city *breathed* history in a way few places did.

Their hotel was a modest establishment tucked away on a side street near the Hagia Sophia. Sera, true to form, did a quick, professional sweep of their adjoining rooms for bugs before giving Leo the all-clear.

'Okay,' she stated, dropping her bag onto the bed. 'Priority one is locating this "Scholar". The Grand Bazaar is massive, a maze. Finding one specific, likely secretive, book dealer won't be easy.'

'Thorne's intel packet mentioned the Scholar supposedly frequents the area around the Old Book Bazaar section, near the Beyazit Mosque entrance,' Leo offered, pulling out his own notes. 'Said he avoids the main tourist-heavy sections.'

Sera nodded. 'Good. Less chance of casual surveillance, but also harder for us to find him without asking too many questions.' She looked at Leo. 'Ready for sensory overload, Professor? The Grand Bazaar isn't like your university library.'

Leo grinned slightly, feeling a thrill of anticipation despite the underlying danger. 'Lead the way, Sera. Let's go find our Scholar.'

The entrance to the Grand Bazaar near the Beyazit Mosque wasn't just a doorway; it felt like stepping through a portal into another time. The relative quiet of the side streets vanished instantly, replaced by a dizzying, overwhelming cacophony of sound, color, and scent. The air inside the vast, arched passageways was thick with the mingling aromas of exotic spices, strong Turkish coffee, roasting meats, sweet perfumes, old paper, and the sheer press of hundreds of bodies.

Crowds surged through the labyrinthine corridors, a river of shoppers, tourists, and determined locals. Merchants called out from doorways hung with dazzling carpets, gleaming copperware, intricate jewelry, colorful lanterns, and mountains of Turkish delight. Their voices echoed under the high, vaulted ceilings, creating a constant, energetic hum. Sunlight streamed down in dusty shafts from high windows, illuminating the vibrant chaos below.

Leo's eyes went wide again, despite Sera's earlier warning. He couldn't help it. It was overwhelming, fascinating. A living museum, a thousand years of commerce compressed into one sprawling maze. He wanted to stop at every stall, examine every artifact, soak in every detail.

'Focus, Leo,' Sera murmured, her voice close to his ear, easily lost in the general din for anyone else. She moved through the crowd with a subtle, purposeful grace, her eyes constantly scanning, not lingering on the glittering distractions but assessing faces, noting shadowed alcoves, looking for anything out of place. Her hand stayed near the opening of her messenger bag. 'We're not here to sightsee. We need to find the Old Book Bazaar section.'

Following the signs overhead, written in both Turkish and English, they navigated deeper into the Bazaar's maze. They deliberately avoided the main, brightly lit corridors teeming with tourists and headed towards the older, quieter sections Thorne's intel had indicated. Here, the passageways grew narrower, the shops smaller and more specialized, the crowds thinning slightly. The scent of paper, leather, and dust began to overlay the more exotic aromas.

They entered the area known as the *Sahaflar Çarşısı*. The Old Book Bazaar. Stalls overflowed with books old and new, maps, prints, and stacks of brittle manuscripts tied with string. The atmosphere here was quieter, more studious, though the energy of the greater Bazaar still hummed around them.

'Okay,' Leo whispered, consulting his notes again. 'Thorne's intel said The Scholar keeps irregular hours, sometimes works from a small, unnamed stall near the back, sometimes meets clients in a nearby *han* or courtyard.'

'We'll check the stalls first,' Sera decided. 'Keep your eyes open for anyone matching the description. Older, maybe academic-looking, likely surrounded by rare texts.'

They began a slow, methodical search, browsing casually, trying not to look like they were searching for someone specific. Leo handled the browsing, his genuine interest in the old books providing perfect cover, while Sera watched their backs and observed the merchants. Several stalls fit the general description, run by elderly men surrounded by dusty volumes, but none felt quite right. None had the specific air of secretive knowledge Thorne's intel had hinted at.

Finally, tucked away in a poorly lit corner, almost hidden behind a towering, precarious stack of leather-bound volumes, they found him. It was less a stall and more a nook carved out of the surrounding shops, crammed floor-to-ceiling with books and scrolls in a dozen languages. Seated on a low stool behind a small, cluttered table, peering intently at a manuscript through a magnifying glass, was a wizened old man. His face was a roadmap of wrinkles, dominated by a pair of sharp, piercing dark eyes that seemed to miss nothing despite the thick lenses of his spectacles. He wore a simple tunic and a felt cap, but carried an air of ancient, perhaps cynical, wisdom. This had to be The Scholar.

Leo approached the stall cautiously, Sera hanging back slightly, observing. '*Merhaba*,' Leo began politely. 'Excuse me...'

The old man looked up slowly, his piercing gaze sweeping over Leo, then flicking to Sera, lingering for a moment before returning to Leo. He didn't smile. '*Evet?*' (Yes?)

'We were told...' Leo hesitated, unsure how to phrase the request without revealing too much. 'We are researchers... interested in ancient prophecies, specifically those originating from Delphi that might have connections to Thracian sites.'

The Scholar placed his magnifying glass down deliberately. He studied Leo for a long moment, his expression unreadable. 'Many are interested in such things,' he finally declared, his voice raspy, like dry leaves skittering across pavement. 'Knowledge of the old ways is rare. And valuable.'

'Indeed,' Leo agreed. 'We heard... that you might possess certain texts. Perhaps copies of, or fragments related to, Byzantine-era manuscripts discussing Delphic oracles and celestial events?' He tried to keep his tone purely academic.

The Scholar's eyes narrowed slightly. 'Who told you this?'

'Our research contacts mentioned your... reputation for acquiring rare documents,' Leo hedged.

A dry chuckle escaped the old man's lips. 'My reputation.' He gestured vaguely at the towering stacks of books surrounding him. 'I acquire many things. Texts pass through my hands. Some are genuine, some clever forgeries. Some hold wisdom, others only foolishness.' He fixed Leo with his sharp gaze again. 'What you seek... knowledge of prophecies... this is dangerous knowledge. Why do you look for it?'

Leo glanced back at Sera, who gave an almost imperceptible nod. Time to push gently. "We believe these ancient warnings may have relevance to... current events. Understanding the past to protect the future, you might say."

The Scholar considered this, stroking his thin, grey beard. "Protect the future? Or exploit the past?" He sighed. "Very well. Perhaps I have seen such fragments. Texts speaking of the Pythoness, of shadows from the East, of stones that mirror the heavens." His eyes held a shrewd glint. "But as I said, such knowledge is valuable. It comes at a price."

Sera stepped forward slightly, moving smoothly into the small space beside Leo. Her expression remained neutral, but her eyes held a sharp, assessing glint as she met The Scholar's gaze. "Prices can be discussed," she stated calmly, her voice low but carrying easily in the relative quiet of the stall. "But first, we need to know if the goods are genuine. You mentioned fragments... texts relating Delphi to Thrace, perhaps mentioning a 'shadow from the East' or celestial stones?"

The Scholar's piercing eyes shifted from Leo to Sera, taking in her quiet confidence, her subtle air of capability that contrasted sharply with Leo's academic demeanor. He seemed to re-evaluate them. "You speak plainly, girl," he rasped, a hint of grudging respect in his tone. "Good. I have no time for fools who chase myths without understanding the risks."

He slowly reached under his cluttered table and produced a flat, oilcloth-wrapped package tied with twine. He handled it with care, almost reverence. "I acquired this piece some years ago. From a... complicated estate. It purports to be a fragment of a commentary, Byzantine, perhaps 10th century, on earlier Delphic texts." He laid it carefully on the table, not yet unwrapping it. "It speaks of the Pythoness's darker prophecies, the ones concerning the *Thracian* cults and their connection to celestial power. It mentions the 'stone eye' that watches the stars, and the 'shadow' that sleeps in the East, waiting to awaken."

Leo leaned forward eagerly, his eyes glued to the package, but Sera subtly held him back with a slight pressure on his arm. "And does it offer any specifics?" Sera pressed gently. "Locations? Names? Anything that might help one... *understand* this shadow?"

The Scholar tapped a gnarled finger on the package. "Perhaps. There are obscure geographical references. Mentions of the Haemus Mons... the Rhodope range." He paused, his eyes shrewd. "But deciphering such texts requires expertise. Context. Cross-referencing." He looked pointedly at Leo. "Expertise like your friend here might possess. But accessing it... that is the price."

"And what is your price, Scholar?" Sera asked directly.

The old man named a figure in US dollars that made Leo's eyes widen slightly. It wasn't astronomical, but it was significant, far more than the value of a simple manuscript fragment.

Sera didn't blink. "That seems... high for a single fragment, however rare."

The Scholar shrugged, a barely perceptible movement of his thin shoulders. "The price reflects not just the parchment, girl, but the *knowledge*. And the risk involved in possessing it. Others," he added meaningfully, his gaze flicking momentarily towards the crowded alley outside the stall, "have inquired about similar texts recently. Dangerous men. Men with cold eyes and connections to the North."

Sera's expression remained impassive, but Leo saw her subtly shift her stance. The Russians or their networks? Already sniffing around here?

"We can meet your price," Sera said smoothly, reaching into her messenger bag. Leo expected her to pull out a wad of cash, but instead, she produced a small, high-quality photograph. It showed a detailed close-up of a rare, silver

Byzantine coin, the kind Leo knew would fetch a small fortune on the legitimate antiquities market, let alone the grey market The Scholar likely operated in.

"Or perhaps," Sera continued, placing the photo on the table, "you would prefer something more... unique? This coin, genuine 9th century, Thessalonica mint, extremely rare variant... is currently seeking a new home. A fair exchange, I think, for a look at your fragment."

The Scholar's eyes widened almost imperceptibly as he snatched up the photo, pulling his magnifying glass out again to examine the image with intense focus. His breathing grew slightly faster. Leo watched, fascinated by Sera's maneuver. Offering something potentially untraceable, highly valuable to someone like The Scholar, instead of cash that could be questioned.

After a long moment, The Scholar carefully placed the photo down, his eyes gleaming with avarice. "A very fine piece," he conceded, his voice losing some of its earlier rasp. "Yes. An exchange would be... acceptable." He looked from the photo back to them. "You may examine the fragment. Here. For one hour. Then, we conclude our business."

He carefully unwrapped the oilcloth, revealing several brittle, yellowed pages of parchment covered in dense Greek script. Leo leaned over instantly, his historian's heart pounding, pulling out his own reading glasses and a small notepad. The Greek was indeed Byzantine, referencing older sources, just as The Scholar had claimed. He scanned the text rapidly, his mind racing, absorbing the intricate details, the veiled allusions...

"Incredible..." Leo whispered excitedly, pointing to a passage, his voice hushed. "Sera, look here. This commentary explicitly links the legends of the 'stone that sees the stars' to a specific Thracian solar deity cult... one known primarily for its activity in the *Rhodope* region, not just near Delphi. And it mentions a hidden sanctuary by name. 'Belintash'. It calls it even older, more sacred than Tatul." He scanned further down the brittle page, his finger tracing the faded Greek letters. "And this part... fascinating... it speaks of needing to consult the 'keepers of the ancient lore' regarding the site's secrets... implying knowledge passed down outside of written texts. Possibly local folklore experts or guardians..." He looked up from the fragment, his mind buzzing. "Keepers of the lore... people who collect local folklore related to these sites..."

Sera subtly checked her watch. Their hour was passing quickly. "Anything else, Leo? Anything about the 'shadow'?"

Leo scanned the remaining fragments, his brow furrowed in concentration. "More symbolic language... difficult... but it connects the 'shadow's' awakening to a specific celestial alignment involving Lyra... the constellation Lyra... and warns against disturbing the balance..." He paused, pointing to another barely legible section. "Wait... this is different. It references an *even older* legend, pre-dating the Thracians. It talks about the 'first echo' of the shadow, not in Thrace, but further north... in the mountains near the ancient Dacian heartland... modern-day Romania. It mentions... 'unquiet earth' and 'whispers from below' in the Carpathian range. It's fragmented, obscure, but it hints that the source, or perhaps a key to understanding the *nature* of the shadow, might lie there." He looked up, his eyes wide with the implications. "Romania... before Thrace?"

"Time is up," The Scholar announced abruptly, already reaching to re-wrap the precious fragment.

Leo quickly finished scribbling his notes. As The Scholar re-wrapped the parchment, Leo looked up. "This mention of 'keepers of the old ways' in the Thracian context... is there anyone known today who studies these specific Thracian legends? Someone who collects the local folklore connected to the Rhodope sites?"

The Scholar paused, considering Leo's question, stroking his thin beard. "Folklore... superstitions..." he mused. "Most serious academics dismiss such things. However ..." A flicker of recollection crossed his face. "There *is* a professor at the university in Sofia. Ivan Dimitrov. A historian, but one known to have a... particular interest in Thracian mythology and the associated peasant beliefs of the Rhodope region. In fact," The Scholar added, his eyes narrowing slightly, "I recall hearing inquiries. Just whispers, you understand. That Professor Dimitrov himself was recently seeking information related to obscure Delphic texts and Thracian sun cults." Perhaps he could shed light on your specific interests, if you could persuade him to speak freely. Such men are often... cautious."

Leo absorbed this, filing Dimitrov's name away. A direct contact for the Rhodope clues. But the mention of Romania, of the 'first echo' of the shadow... that felt crucial, potentially more fundamental.

Sera nodded, then produced the actual silver Byzantine coin from her bag. The Scholar took it, his eyes gleaming, examining it closely before carefully tucking it away. The exchange was complete.

"Thank you," Sera said to The Scholar. "One last thing. These other interested parties you mentioned... the men with cold eyes... any idea who they were?"

The Scholar shrugged, already turning back to his manuscripts, the transaction concluded. "They spoke Russian," he replied dismissively. "Asked vague questions about Thracian power objects and prophecies. Seemed impatient. Official types, maybe, trying to look unofficial. I told them nothing of value." He waved a dismissive hand. "Now, go. And be careful chasing shadows, my friends. Sometimes, the shadows chase back."

Leaving the dim corner of the Old Book Bazaar, Leo and Sera melted back into the vibrant chaos of the Grand Bazaar, heading for the exit, the Scholar's final warning echoing in their ears.

"Well," Leo began once they were back on the bustling street outside, the noise of the city washing over them, "that fragment gave us Belintash in the Rhodopes, *and*

Professor Dimitrov in Sofia as a potential contact for the 'keepers of the lore'..."

"And it gave us Romania," Sera finished, her expression thoughtful as they walked briskly towards their hotel. "A potential origin point for the 'shadow'. Which lead do we follow first?"

Leo hesitated. "Dimitrov seems like the more direct link to the Bulgarian sites mentioned in the main prophecy. But this Romania reference... the 'first echo'... if the shadow *originates* there, understanding that might be key to understanding the whole threat."

Sera considered this, navigating them through a crowded intersection. "Agreed. The shadow itself is the primary target. Going straight to Dimitrov might lead us to the 'stone that sees stars', but it might not tell us what we're ultimately up against." She made a decision. "Okay. New plan. We follow the older clue first. Romania. See if we can find out anything about this 'first echo' in the Carpathians. Then, armed with whatever we learn, we head to Sofia and Dimitrov." She glanced at him. "More dangerous, maybe. Going off the map based on one cryptic reference. But potentially more important."

Leo thought of the cryptic prophecy, the ancient device it hinted at, the dangerous men with cold eyes The Scholar described, and his warning. Understanding the *source* felt right. He nodded. "Okay. Romania it is. How do we even start?"

"First," Sera stated, picking up the pace, "we get back to the hotel, check for surveillance, and figure out how to get across the border into Romania without attracting attention. Then we worry about finding legends in the Carpathian mountains."

CHAPTER SIX

The Unquiet Earth

The train rattled eastward through the flat plains of southern Romania, the landscape outside the grimy window a stark contrast to the vibrant chaos of Istanbul. Getting across the border from Turkey into Bulgaria, then immediately north into Romania under the guise of academic research into Roman Dacia had been tense, involving carefully planned movements, less-traveled crossings, and Sera's expertly crafted fake identification papers that spoke of meticulous preparation back at Section M. Leo found himself relying entirely on Sera's quiet competence, her calm professionalism a reassuring balm as she navigated bored or suspicious border guards while masking the constant undercurrent of danger he felt acutely.

Their destination was a remote region deep within the southern Carpathian Mountains, specifically the Bucegi range. An area Leo had pinpointed from cross-referencing the fragment's mention of the 'first echo' and 'unquiet earth' with geological surveys and ancient Dacian settlement maps. It was a wild, sparsely populated area, steeped in folklore and known for its dramatic, snaggle-toothed peaks and dense, ancient forests where shadows lingered long after sunrise. According to the fragmented text, this was potentially where the 'shadow' originated, the place where the earth itself held a dangerous memory.

As their hired car climbed higher into the mountains, the air grew cooler, sharper, scented with pine resin and damp earth. Another deliberately nondescript Dacia sedan arranged through one of Sera's discreet Section M channels. Paved roads, cracked and patched reminders of Ceaușescu's fading regime, gave way to gravel tracks littered with potholes, then rutted dirt paths winding through thick forests where sunlight struggled to penetrate the dense canopy. Villages became fewer and farther between, small clusters of weathered wooden houses clinging precariously to steep hillsides, smoke curling thinly from chimneys like whispered prayers. The sense of isolation was profound, almost suffocating. Civilization felt like a distant rumor.

"This is definitely off the beaten path," Leo commented again, looking out at the imposing, mist-shrouded peaks looming around them, feeling smaller and more insignificant with every mile.

"That's the point," Sera replied, her eyes constantly scanning the dense treeline, her posture alert. "The fragment mentioned 'unquiet earth' and 'whispers from below'. Sounds like phenomena you wouldn't find near a major city. Thorne's follow-up intel confirmed local legends about strange tremors and sounds focused around the ruins of an old Dacian sanctuary somewhere up here, near a place the locals apparently avoid. Marked on old maps only with symbols of dread or taboo."

Their immediate goal, however, wasn't the sanctuary itself, but a remote Orthodox monastery hidden even deeper in the mountains, a place whispered about even in historical footnotes Leo had unearthed. According to the scant information Thorne's team could dig up, this monastery housed an ancient library and was home to a handful of monks, including one elderly recluse, Father Nicolae, rumored to be the keeper of local legends and pre-Christian Dacian lore passed down through generations. If anyone knew about the 'whispers from below' or the sanctuary's secrets, it would be him.

Finding the monastery proved even more challenging than anticipated. The track shown on their faded map dwindled abruptly to an overgrown footpath choked with weeds and fallen branches. Leaving the car carefully concealed beneath camouflage netting in a dense thicket, they began the hike. Hours passed as they pushed through dense, silent forest, the only sounds the crunch of their boots on pine needles, their own ragged breathing, and the occasional cry of an unseen bird high in the canopy. The atmosphere grew thick, the trees seeming older, larger, their gnarled branches intertwined overhead like skeletal fingers blocking out the weak afternoon sun. Unease prickled along Leo's spine, a sense of being watched not by human eyes, but by the forest itself, ancient and wary of intrusion. He noticed Sera was also more tense than usual, her hand never straying far from the concealed Makarov beneath her jacket.

They stumbled into a tiny, impoverished-looking hamlet nestled in a high, shadowed valley. Barely half a dozen houses leaning together as if for support. Chickens scattered at their approach. When they stopped to ask an old woman, her face as wrinkled as a walnut shell, who was tending a few scrawny goats, about the location of the monastery, her reaction was visceral. She spat on the ground, crossed herself rapidly, and muttered urgently in Romanian about *'strigoi morți'*. The living dead. And the 'angry mountain that eats souls.' Pointing a trembling finger back the way they came, she insisted there was no monastery, only cursed ground, before gathering her goats and practically fleeing into her small cottage, slamming the wooden door shut behind her.

"Friendly locals," Leo remarked dryly, unsettled by the woman's genuine terror.

"Superstitious," Sera corrected, her voice tight, though her gaze lingered on the dark woods surrounding the seemingly deserted hamlet. "Or maybe they know something we don't. The legends spoke of spirits guarding the ruins. She seemed truly terrified. Let's keep moving, and stay alert."

The encounter cast a pall over the rest of their hike. The forest felt utterly silent, the shadows longer. Finally, late in the afternoon, utterly weary, they crested a ridge and saw it. Nestled in a seemingly inaccessible cleft between two towering peaks, almost invisible against the dark rock face, stood the monastery. It wasn't grand; it was small, ancient, built of dark, weathered stone that seemed to have grown organically from the mountain, looking more like a medieval fortress than a place of worship. A thin plume of woodsmoke rose from a single chimney, the only sign of life against the imposing backdrop of rock and darkening sky.

They approached cautiously, following a steep, winding path down towards the heavy wooden gate. The silence was absolute, almost watchful. The air felt cold, biting, despite the lingering autumn sun. Sera knocked firmly on the thick, iron-studded gate.

After a long moment that stretched Leo's nerves taut, a small viewing grille slid open with a rusty screech, and a pair of dark, deeply suspicious eyes peered out.

Sera replied calmly in fluent Romanian, her tone respectful but firm, explaining they were researchers studying regional history and pre-Christian folklore, seeking guidance from the learned monks within, specifically mentioning an interest in Father Nicolae's reputed knowledge of ancient Dacian traditions and legends surrounding the mountains.

There was another long pause, filled only by the sighing wind. Then, the sound of heavy bolts being drawn back echoed through the quiet air, and the massive wooden gate creaked open just wide enough for them to enter. A stern-faced monk, younger than the voice sounded but with eyes just as wary, stood just inside. He wore the simple black robes of Orthodox tradition, his beard long and untrimmed. He looked them up and down, his gaze lingering on Sera, perhaps surprised by her fluent Romanian, before giving a curt, dismissive nod.

"The Abbot will see you," he stated, his tone flat, unwelcoming. "Father Nicolae... does not often receive visitors. He prefers his texts to people." He turned abruptly and led them across a small, windswept stone courtyard towards the main monastery building, his sandals slapping softly on the worn flagstones.

The interior of the monastery was dark, cold, and smelled strongly of incense, beeswax, old parchment, and the sharp, metallic tinge of decay mingled with damp stone. Faded frescoes depicting stern-faced saints with hollow eyes peered down from the arched ceilings. It felt like a place utterly detached from the modern world, locked in centuries of prayer and isolation, guarding secrets it was reluctant to share. The young monk led them to a small, austere office where the Abbot, an older man with a neatly trimmed white beard and sharp, intelligent eyes that missed nothing, greeted them with formal, reserved politeness.

Leo, guided by Sera's prompts in low English, explained their academic interest in Dacian history, local legends surrounding the nearby mountains, and particularly any folklore related to unexplained natural phenomena. Tremors, strange lights, unusual sounds. Often attributed by locals to *strigoi* or other mountain spirits. He carefully avoided mentioning the prophecy, the sphere, or the Soviets, sticking to a purely historical inquiry.

The Abbot listened patiently, his fingers steepled, his expression unreadable. "Indeed," he said finally, his Romanian precise and educated, "this region is rich in such tales. The common folk cling to old beliefs, superstitions born of isolation and the raw power of these mountains. As for Father Nicolae..." The Abbot hesitated, stroking his beard. "He is our eldest brother. He came here many decades ago, seeking solitude from... a troubled world. He spends his days in prayer and in the study of texts even older than this monastery... texts concerning the ways of those who came before the Cross, before even the Romans."

"The Dacians?" Leo asked eagerly.

"And perhaps others even older," the Abbot acknowledged cryptically. "Father Nicolae rarely speaks of his studies, and as I said, he does not welcome disturbances. His connection is to the past, not the present." He looked from Leo's earnest face to Sera's quiet intensity. "But given your scholarly purpose, and perhaps," he added, a hint of shrewdness entering his eyes, "the... palpable urgency I sense in your visit, I will ask him if he will speak with you. Wait here."

The Abbot left them alone in the cold office. Minutes stretched into an eternity, the silence punctuated only by the distant chanting of unseen monks. Leo fidgeted, while Sera stood perfectly still, her senses alert, listening to the profound quiet of the ancient building. Finally, the Abbot returned, accompanied by the most ancient-looking man Leo had ever seen.

Father Nicolae was incredibly frail, thin as a bird, his back bent nearly double with age. His white beard flowed down over his black robes almost to his waist, thin and wispy like smoke. His skin was translucent, stretched taut over sharp bones. But his eyes, deep-set beneath bushy white eyebrows, were startlingly bright, sharp, and held an unnerving intensity, like burning coals in a dying fire. He carried a large, leather-bound book clasped in surprisingly strong, gnarled hands, its cover worn smooth by centuries of handling. He stopped just inside the doorway, his piercing gaze sweeping over Leo and Sera, seeming to penetrate deeper than mere physical appearance. He spoke directly to Leo, his Romanian voice thin but surprisingly clear, like dry leaves rustling across stone. Sera translated quietly.

"The Abbot tells me you seek knowledge of the 'unquiet earth' and the 'whispers'," the old monk stated, his eyes fixed on Leo with disconcerting focus. "Why do outsiders disturb the sleep of this mountain? What shadows do you bring with you?"

Leo, feeling strangely intimidated, explained again, carefully emphasizing their academic purpose, "We are historians, Father. We study ancient beliefs, how they shape the land and its people. We heard legends... about this area... phenomena linked to the sky, to the earth itself. The fragment we found in Istanbul mentioned..."

"Istanbul?" Father Nicolae interrupted, his gaze sharpening further, a flicker of something ancient and knowing in their depths. "You found a fragment? Describing... what precisely?"

Leo described the Byzantine text, the mention of the Dacian heartland, the 'first echo', the 'unquiet earth', and the 'whispers from below'.

The old monk listened intently, his head bowed slightly, his breathing shallow. When Leo finished, he was silent for a long moment, his eyes closed as if consulting some inner text. Then, he nodded slowly. "Yes," he whispered, the sound barely disturbing the air. "The *Chemarea Strābunilor*... the Calling of the Ancestors. Or perhaps... the Awakening of the Deep Ones." He opened his eyes, fixing Leo with that unnerving stare again. "The texts I guard speak of it. Not a shadow, as your Delphi text suggests, but a... presence. An ancient *energy* deep within the earth, tied to the movements of the stars, to cycles longer than human memory. The Dacian kings knew of it. They built their sanctuaries on the high peaks to watch it, perhaps even to commune with it... or appease it."

"Appease it?" Sera asked, her voice low, instinctively wary. "Was it considered dangerous?"

Father Nicolae nodded gravely, his frail body seeming to shrink slightly. "The energy waxes and wanes like the moon, but on a scale of ages," Father Nicolae continued, his voice barely a rustle. "When it is strong, the earth itself sings a dangerous song – not common quakes, but a *deep resonance* that can shatter rock and boil water in the deep springs. Strange lights, like captured auroras, dance on the peaks – colors not of this world. And the wind, it carries voices... the *şoapte*, the whispers. Some legends say they are the mountain spirits. Others," his voice dropped, his eyes holding a flicker of ancient dread, "say it is the raw voice of the earth-power itself... trying to warn. Or perhaps, in its own way, trying to *instruct* those who dared listen too closely."

"Warn? Instruct about what?" Leo pressed, leaning forward, the academic in him battling a primal unease.

"The old texts are fragmented, filled with allegory meant to shield the uninitiated," the monk replied, a trembling finger tracing a line in the ancient book he held. "They speak of cycles. Of a time when the energy swells, breaking its bonds, threatening to unleash a focused fury that could *reshape the land in fire and flood*. Some tales even recount how ancient priest-kings, in their hubris, sought not just to appease this power, but to *direct* it, to wield its shattering song. Their attempts, the scrolls hint, always ended in catastrophe – valleys incinerated, mountainsides collapsing – a raw, untamable force." He shivered. "They speak of guardians chosen to watch, of intricate rituals and sonic harmonies needed to maintain the fragile balance, lest the 'Deep Ones' – the very currents of this earth-power – fully awaken and unmake all."

"Can you guide us there?" Sera asked directly, cutting through the mythology to the practical need.

Father Nicolae looked hesitant, his ancient eyes clouded with worry. "It is not a place for outsiders, especially now. The mountain... does not welcome intrusion when it is restless. And it *has* been restless lately. More tremors than usual, deeper than before. Brighter lights reported on the peaks at night. Animals flee the high valleys. Even the *strigoi* seem uneasy." He shook his head slowly. "To go there now is to court disaster."

"We need to understand this energy, Father," Leo pleaded, sensing their window closing. "We believe it might be connected to a great danger threatening the world beyond these mountains. Something others seek to misuse."

The old monk studied their faces again, his ancient eyes seeming to weigh their sincerity against the potential sacrilege of revealing the mountain's secrets and the very real danger he perceived. Finally, he gave another slow, reluctant nod. "I cannot guide you myself; my legs are dust, my breath is thin. But I can show you the path on the old maps in our library. And I can give you a warning." He opened the heavy book he carried, its pages brittle and covered in archaic script interspersed with intricate astronomical diagrams. "The whispers... do not listen too closely. They can echo your own fears, your own desires, show you things that are not real, drive you mad. And the lights... they are beautiful, yes, hypnotic, but they can blind you to the true danger beneath your feet."

Father Nicolae spent a precious hour with them in the monastery's small, cold library, a room piled high with scrolls and manuscripts smelling of dust and ages. He carefully traced routes onto one of Leo's modern topographical maps using ancient landmarks noted in his texts. A crooked tree, a wolf-shaped rock, a spring that never froze. He pointed out the high valley where the ruined sanctuary lay hidden, marked on his older maps only by symbols Leo recognized as warnings or sacred ground designations. He also provided them with sturdy walking sticks and a small amount of dried fruit and hard bread from the monastery's meager stores, rations for a journey he clearly feared they might not return from.

Thanking the Abbot and the ancient Father Nicolae, whose final gaze held a profound sadness, Leo and Sera left the monastery just as the afternoon sun began to dip behind the high Carpathian peaks, casting long, skeletal shadows across the valley. They followed the barely-there trail indicated by the monk, plunging back into the vast, silent wilderness, the weight of the monk's warnings echoing upon them.

The hike to the cursed sanctuary was arduous, more difficult than the trek to the monastery. The path climbed steeply, often disappearing entirely amongst tangled roots and loose scree slopes that threatened to slide out from under them. The forest grew denser, the air colder, the silence deeper. That strange, watchful tension returned, thicker now, pressing in. Leo, despite his growing field experience, felt a primal unease creep up his spine, the old woman's fear and the monk's warnings echoing in his mind. Sera, too, was on high alert, her movements economical but her senses clearly straining, scanning the trees, listening intently to the silence that felt far from empty.

As twilight deepened, painting the sky in bruised shades of purple and grey, they experienced their first strange occurrence. A low, almost subsonic hum vibrated through the ground beneath their feet, brief but distinct, making their teeth buzz slightly. It wasn't like a typical earthquake tremor; it felt localized, rhythmic, almost... like the slow breath of something immense sleeping fitfully beneath them. The 'unquiet earth' indeed.

"Did you feel that?" Leo asked, pausing, his hand flat against a rough slab of rock, feeling the last of the vibration fade.

Sera nodded, her eyes scanning the darkening woods with heightened vigilance. "Yeah. Not natural." She pulled out her compass; the needle spun erratically for several seconds, refusing to settle, before finally quivering towards north again. "Magnetic interference too. Stronger than before. Something's definitely odd up here."

Later, as they navigated a narrow, exposed ridge using their flashlights, the forest falling away into deep, shadowed gorges on either side, they saw them. Faint, ethereal lights dancing silently between the distant, jagged peaks ahead of them. Not stars, not aircraft, not aurora. Pale green and blue lights that seemed to weave and pulse in the night sky, coalescing and dissipating like phosphorescent mist before vanishing as quickly as they appeared. They were beautiful, hypnotic, and deeply unnatural.

"Strange lights..." Leo breathed, mesmerized for a moment before remembering Father Nicolae's warning about being blinded. "What could possibly cause that?"

"Atmospheric phenomena? Piezoelectric effects from stressed rock? Gas vents reacting to the tremors?" Sera listed possibilities, her voice tight, her gaze fixed on the path ahead, refusing to be distracted by the display. "Or something else entirely, something the legends are trying to describe. Whatever it is, it fits. Let's keep moving. The sanctuary should be just over this next rise, in that high valley Father Nicolae marked."

They finally reached the ruins just before dawn, emerging onto a high, windswept plateau surrounded by even higher, forbidding peaks. The sanctuary was unlike anything Leo had seen, even Belintash. Built from massive, cyclopean blocks of dark, basalt-like stone not native to the immediate area, the remaining walls formed complex geometric patterns that felt alien, non-Euclidean. Strange channels, wider and deeper than those at the Thracian sites, were cut into the rock floor, converging on a central, heavily weathered stone altar that seemed to pulse with a faint residual energy. The air here felt charged, electric, the strange hum a constant vibration underfoot. And the acoustic properties were bizarre. Whispers seemed to echo from nowhere, the wind sighing through the stones sometimes sounded disturbingly like distinct, overlapping voices, nonsensical yet chillingly articulate ('whispers from below'). This place felt profoundly *wrong*.

While Sera, visibly uneasy, immediately began a thorough sweep of the perimeter, checking for threats, Leo approached the ruins with a mixture of dread and intense scholarly curiosity. He recognized motifs similar to Thracian designs but clearly much older, confirming Father Nicolae's words about pre-Dacian origins. The celestial alignments were undeniable, woven into the very fabric of the architecture. But there was something else... the subtle lines carved into the altar stone, and even more faintly within the deep channels that snaked across the floor, almost invisible unless the light hit them just right. He knelt, brushing away centuries of dust and grime. They weren't merely decorative. The lines formed intricate, repeating patterns, almost like waveforms, converging on focal points that corresponded with the altar and certain standing stones. "These look disturbingly like diagrams," Leo murmured, tracing a complex series of nested spirals and radiating lines. "Not just for energy flow, but perhaps for... harmonic amplification? Like ancient, lithic circuitry designed to gather, focus, and intensify telluric vibrations." The implications sent a shiver down his spine. He pulled out his camera, documenting everything, his mind already racing, trying to connect this terrifying potential to the Delphi prophecy and the device the sphere had hinted at in Crete.

As Leo knelt, absorbed in the strange carvings, Sera called out quietly from the edge of the ruins, her voice tight with alarm. "Leo, check this out. Now."

She pointed towards a small, sheltered area behind a collapsed wall. Partially hidden under some brush, glinting faintly, was a discarded piece of equipment. A modern, high-frequency geological sensor probe, clearly Russian-made, damaged as if dropped hastily or perhaps even overloaded by the ambient energy. Nearby lay a spent battery pack and crumpled Cyrillic-labeled ration wrappers, looking only a few days old.

"Soviets," Sera stated grimly, her hand moving to her weapon. "They've been here. Recently. Surveying the area. Why drop this? Did the energy interfere with it? Or were they disturbed?"

A deep chill ran through Leo despite the cold morning air.. "Looking for the same thing we are? The source? The 'shadow'?"

"Looks like it," Sera replied, her eyes scanning the surrounding rocks. "They're trying to understand this energy too. Which means this place is even more dangerous than we thought."

As if summoned by their words, the ground beneath them hummed again, stronger this time, the vibration sharp, almost painful. A section of the ruined wall near the central altar seemed to glow faintly with an internal blue light before fading, leaving dancing afterimages in their vision. The strange whispers intensified for a moment, swirling around them like unseen entities, carrying fragments of words in languages long dead.

Leo looked from the discarded Soviet tech – likely fried by the very energies it sought to quantify – to the faint, almost imperceptible thrumming he could now feel through the soles of his boots, to the intricate, wave-like carvings on the altar. An understanding clicked into place, terrifying in its implications.

"Sera... I don't think this energy is purely natural or geological," he stated slowly, his voice filled with a new, chilling certainty. "Father Nicolae spoke of 'deep resonance,' of the earth singing a 'dangerous song.' Those carvings, these channels... they're not just art or ritual pathways. They're schematics. This entire sanctuary... it feels like... ancient technology. A vast machine of stone and earth, designed to harness, amplify, and perhaps even *direct* those natural earth energies – those telluric vibrations – possibly amplified by precise celestial alignments."

He gestured towards the altar. "The Delphi tablet spoke of 'vibrations that shatter stone from afar,' of a power to 'break the world'. You theorized a resonance weapon, Sera. What if this... this is the primordial template for such a thing? The 'shadow' from the East the Oracle warned of... maybe it isn't just an allegorical power. Maybe it refers to the *knowledge* of how to reactivate or replicate this ancient, terrifying resonant technology. And," he added, the thought chilling him to the core, "judging by the hum, the Soviet interest, and the damage to their probe... maybe part of this ancient system is still... dangerously, unpredictably, semi-operational."

The pieces were falling into place. The prophecy wasn't just about a natural phenomenon; it was about controlling. Or being destroyed by. A form of power conceived millennia ago. And the Soviets, likely directed from Moscow, were trying to reactivate it or replicate it, starting here at one of the source points.

"Which means," Sera concluded, her gaze hardening, her hand tightening on her pistol, "that the device in Crete, powered by the sphere, is likely the main control mechanism, or the weaponized version derived from this older... template. We absolutely have to stop them from using it."

Their Romanian detour, prompted by a fragmented clue, had yielded a crucial insight into the fundamental *nature* of the threat they faced. It wasn't just geological power; it was ancient, potentially controllable, technology. Armed with this terrifying knowledge, they knew their next stop had to be Bulgaria, to find Professor Dimitrov and the path to Belintash and the sphere. The apparent key. Before the Soviets could use it to unlock catastrophe. They carefully concealed the Soviet probe. Evidence Section M would want. And prepared to leave the eerie, whispering sanctuary behind, the weight of their discovery heavy upon them, the charged silence seeming to press in as they turned away.

Retracing their steps from the plateau proved just as challenging as the ascent, especially now with the added burden of knowing what forces might be at play and who else might be interested. They moved cautiously back through the dense forest, the eerie silence feeling even more profound now, every rustle of leaves, every snap of a twig sounding like potential danger. They avoided the tiny hamlet entirely this time, taking a longer, more circuitous route back towards where they had hidden their car.

By late afternoon, they were finally back in the relative anonymity of the battered sedan, leaving the brooding peaks and unsettling legends of the Bucegi range behind them. Sera drove south, heading towards the Bulgarian border, while Leo organized his frantic notes from the monastery and the ruins, trying to synthesize the fragmented clues into a coherent picture. The weight of their discovery pressed down on them, urging them onward towards Sofia and their meeting with Professor Dimitrov.

Chapter Seven

Behind the Iron Curtain

Sofia, Bulgaria, early October 1986. Stepping off the aging Balkan Airlines Tupolev onto the tarmac at Sofia Airport felt like entering a different circle of hell compared to both the vibrant chaos of Istanbul and the brooding, ancient mystery of the Romanian Carpathians. The crisp autumn air carried the familiar Eastern Bloc scents: damp earth, low-grade coal smoke clinging to everything, the sharp note of cheap Bulgarian *Shipka* cigarettes. The sky seemed perpetually grey here, the sunlight thin and weak, as if reluctant to penetrate the iron curtain overhead. Leo clutched his briefcase tighter; the unsettling knowledge gained in Romania, the confirmation of Soviet interest, the bizarre energy phenomena, the sheer age and potential power of the 'shadow'. Adding a heavy weight to his steps. He tried consciously not to look like the complete fish out of water he felt, pulling the collar of his tweed jacket closer against a chill that had little to do with the weather.

Sera moved beside him with practiced, almost unnerving ease, a ghost slipping through the cracks in the drab reality of the state-controlled airport. Dressed again in practical, unremarkable clothes suitable for this side of the

Iron Curtain. Dark trousers, a plain blouse, a sturdy but unfashionable jacket. She looked like just another weary traveller. Only her eyes, constantly moving behind neutral sunglasses, scanning faces, noting the positioning of uniformed guards, clocking exits and potential chokepoints, betrayed the coiled alertness beneath the surface. The detour through Romania had yielded vital intelligence about the *nature* of the 'shadow'. Ancient technology, not just myth. But it had also confirmed the Soviets were actively investigating related phenomena. That meant the network Dimitrov had nervously alluded to, the one possibly directed from Moscow itself, was likely widespread and acutely alert. She'd reminded Leo on the short, rattling flight: keep quiet, follow her lead, *don't stare*. They were deep behind the curtain now, playing a dangerous game on Orlov's home turf, and any misstep could be fatal.

Their carefully forged Bulgarian visas, identifying them again as academics on a "cultural exchange" focused on Thracian archaeological links (a cover story feeling thinner by the hour), passed muster under the bored gaze of the passport control officer. The customs officials were equally listless and bureaucratic, stamping their passports with barely a glance, their movements mechanical, devoid of interest. Leo let out a breath he hadn't realized he was holding as they collected their minimal luggage – mostly Leo's research materials, maps, and notebooks crammed with cryptic symbols. Not to mention, Sera's nondescript duffel bag, which likely held more practical, and lethal, tools of her trade.

Their contact, Professor Ivan Dimitrov. The name provided by the Scholar in Istanbul and confirmed via a coded signal Sera sent back to Section M using sophisticated, disguised burst-transmission equipment. He was a historian at Sofia University. Known for his quiet fascination with Thracian folklore that bordered on the heretical in the eyes of the state-approved historical narrative, and a matching quiet disdain for the Zhivkov regime, he represented their best link to the 'keepers of the lore' mentioned in the Byzantine fragment. Thorne's people had quickly vetted him, confirming his suitability but also flagging the extreme risk he was taking. Meeting with undeclared Americans, especially after inquiries were likely flagged from Istanbul and perhaps Romania, could easily earn him a one-way trip to a State Security basement.

They found him waiting, exactly as arranged, in a dimly lit café near the university, tucked away on a cobbled side street that smelled faintly of boiled cabbage, diesel fumes, and damp decay. The café, with its stained tablecloths and single flickering fluorescent tube, felt like a relic from another era. Dimitrov was a bundle of raw, frayed nerves, thin and pale. He was chain-smoking pungent Bulgarian cigarettes, his eyes constantly darting towards the grimy windows and the scarred wooden door as if expecting the *Durzhavna Sigurnost* to burst in at any second. He stubbed out one cigarette in a chipped saucer already overflowing with butts and immediately lit another with trembling fingers as they approached his small table in the darkest corner.

"Dr. Saint? Agent... Volkov?" Dimitrov whispered, his voice a dry rasp barely audible above the clatter of cups from a hidden kitchen. He practically vibrated with anxiety, his slight frame seeming lost in his threadbare jacket. "It is... an honor, yes, but also a great risk. A very great risk for me to meet you here. You understand?"

"Professor, we understand completely the risk you're taking, and we appreciate it immensely," Leo replied, trying to project calm confidence he definitely didn't feel, consciously keeping his own voice low. He slid into the worn plastic chair opposite Dimitrov, the cold striking through his trousers. Sera, moving with silent efficiency, took the chair facing the door, her back literally against the peeling wallpaper, her posture relaxed but every sense clearly on high alert.

"We're here researching ancient Thracian culture," Leo continued, leaning in slightly, creating a small bubble of conspiratorial quiet amidst the café's low murmur. He drew on the information gleaned from the Istanbul fragment, omitting the Romania detour for now. "We have reason to believe certain legends, possibly connected to the sanctuary at Belintash or others in the Rhodope region, might relate to... significant historical events. The contact in Istanbul mentioned you are an expert in the folklore of that area, the stories the official histories ignore."

Dimitrov's haunted eyes flickered, a brief spark of academic curiosity warring visibly with his obvious, deeply ingrained fear. He inhaled a long, shaky drag from his cigarette, holding the smoke in his lungs for a beat too long. "Belintash... yes. A powerful place. And the Rhodopes..." He nodded slowly, a fine tremor running through his hand as ashes scattered onto the tabletop. "Folklore, you say? Not the approved narrative from the Academy of Sciences?" There was a hint of bitterness in his tone.

Sera leaned forward slightly, her movements economical, her gaze steady and surprisingly reassuring on Dimitrov. "Sometimes, Professor, the real truth hides in folklore, doesn't it? We're interested in stories about ancient sites connected to sun worship, celestial events... perhaps local legends mentioning a 'hidden eye' or a 'stone that sees the stars'?" She delivered the keywords gently but precisely.

Dimitrov flinched almost imperceptibly, his eyes darting towards the door again. He nervously crushed his half-smoked cigarette in the overflowing ashtray. "Those terms... yes, they echo certain... obscure tales from the Rhodope region. Dangerous tales, some might say." He glanced around the nearly empty café again, assuring himself the only other patrons were two old men engrossed in a game of backgammon. "The mountains... they are soaked in myths, Dr. Saint, Agent Volkov. More secrets than stones. Filled with tales of hidden tombs, forgotten sanctuaries carved directly into the living rock... Places the government prefers people forget about, places they actively discourage exploring."

He paused, lowering his voice even further, forcing Leo and Sera to lean closer. "One place... Tatul village. You know it? South, towards Kardzhali. There is a prominent rock sanctuary nearby, very old, Thracian for certain, but possibly built on something even older. Dedicated to the sun, or perhaps something *represented* by the sun. The locals... they have stories. Old wives' tales, the authorities call them. They speak of rocks that 'weep' when the seasons change. Water trickling down mineral-rich faces, glittering like golden tears in the sun." He shivered slightly, despite the stuffy air in the cafe. "They say the place feels... watchful."

"Tatul," Leo repeated, quickly jotting the name in his small notebook, his academic instincts momentarily overriding his caution. Belintash was mentioned in the fragment, the ultimate goal perhaps, but Tatul was a specific local lead, maybe an intermediary step or related site mentioned in Dimitrov's extensive folklore collection. "That sounds... very promising. And potentially linked to Belintash?"

"Linked by energy lines, some legends claim," Dimitrov whispered, lighting yet another cigarette. "Invisible paths of power connecting the high places. But these are just stories..."

Their meeting was necessarily brief, wrapped in layers of palpable caution. Dimitrov confirmed Tatul was the most accessible major sanctuary potentially linked to the Belintash legends and provided a rough, hand-drawn map marking it and the nearby village, along with names of a couple of potentially helpful, though equally cautious, contacts further south. A village elder, a local museum curator. Who knew the Tatul area well. He stressed repeatedly, his voice trembling slightly, the need for absolute discretion. "The *Durzhavna Sigurnost*, the State Securit y... Orlov's people... they have ears everywhere now. Since that business with the tablet in Greece... they are watching all academics with Thracian interests. Foreigners asking about old ruins, especially after inquiries were likely flagged from Istanbul and perhaps Romania... it attracts dangerous attention. Be invisible."

They paid for their untouched coffees and left the café separately, Leo first, trying to look like a preoccupied academic, Sera lingering a few minutes longer before melting back into the city's subdued rhythm. The weight of a hundred unseen eyes pressed against Leo's back, his paranoia intensifying after the Scholar's and Dimitrov's stark warnings. The grey anonymity of Sofia suddenly felt menacing.

Sera, however, seemed completely unfazed as she met him near their rented car. A dull grey Renault, deliberately chosen for its ubiquity and ability to blend in, arranged via Section M's skeletal local assets. She slid behind the wheel, her driving smooth and efficient, navigating Sofia's wide, slightly crumbling socialist-era boulevards and occasional potholes with practiced skill. Leo consulted Dimitrov's map, trying to reconcile the hand-drawn lines with the official, state-approved road atlas spread across his lap, the discrepancies already highlighting the gap between official narratives and local knowledge.

As they drove south, leaving the grey concrete sprawl of the capital behind, the landscape gradually transformed. Flat, cultivated plains gave way to rolling hills patchworked with fields, then the dramatic, forest-clad peaks of the Rhodope range rose before them, majestic and imposing under the vast Bulgarian sky. Small villages, clusters of sturdy stone houses with red-tiled roofs, clung to the valleys, smoke curling lazily from chimneys. The air grew cooler, cleaner, scented sharply with pine and damp earth, a welcome change from the city's smog.

"Stay sharp, Leo," Sera instructed quietly, her eyes constantly scanning the road ahead, the sparse traffic, and the rearview mirror. "Dimitrov was right to be scared. We're deep in their territory now. Assume every car, every person leaning against a wall, could be trouble."

Leo nodded, tearing his gaze away from the rugged, breathtaking beauty of the mountains. It was easy to get lost in the scenery, to forget the human danger lurking just out of sight. "Belintash seemed like the main target from the Istanbul fragment," he mused, thinking aloud. "And Dimitrov mentioned it too. Why do you think he emphasized Tatul first?"

"Could be a known site they use as a reference point, somewhere easily accessible to start," Sera replied thoughtfully, expertly downshifting for a steep curve. "Or maybe Tatul holds its own piece of the puzzle, a necessary step before Belintash makes sense. Or," she added grimly, her knuckles momentarily white on the steering wheel, "maybe Tatul is where the Soviets *expect* anyone following Dimitrov's research to go first. A honeypot. We treat it as a potential trap until proven otherwise."

They reached the Tatul area late in the afternoon. The village itself was tiny, a cluster of stone houses seemingly untouched by time, nestled quietly in a valley below a striking, rocky ridge. A few dogs barked half-heartedly at their Renault's approach, and an old man smoking a pipe watched them pass with expressionless eyes. They checked into the only guesthouse, a small, clean but basic stone building run by a stern-faced old woman whose gaze lingered on them with undisguised curiosity mixed with a healthy dose of suspicion. Foreigners, especially Americans, were clearly a rarity here.

Wasting no time, eager to investigate before darkness fell completely, they headed up the rough track leading towards the Tatul rock sanctuary. The site sat perched high on the ridge, a dramatic collection of massive, strangely shaped megalithic rocks silhouetted against the spectacular afternoon sky. The place radiated an undeniable aura of antiquity, a raw, ancient power that seemed even older than the Thracians who had clearly carved into its surfaces millennia ago. It felt simultaneously sacred and profoundly alien.

A familiar thrill pulse through Leo, the instincts of the historian momentarily overshadowing the fear of the reluctant spy. His eyes shone as he began examining the intricate carvings, the strange channels cut into the rock, the deliberate, almost astronomical arrangement of the stones. "Incredible," he murmured, pulling out his camera and notebook, already lost in the puzzle. "The weathering suggests immense age..."

While Leo lost himself in the details of the ancient site, Sera kept watch, her senses heightened by the exposed location and Dimitrov's warnings. A few locals ambled nearby on the lower slopes, mostly shepherds guiding their flocks home as dusk approached. But something else caught her attention. A plain, dark Lada sedan parked on a nearby overlook, partially hidden by a cluster of stunted pine trees. Two men sat inside, seemingly engrossed in a newspaper even as the light failed, but their stillness felt wrong. Too patient. Too watchful. It might be nothing, a coincidence. But Sera's instincts, honed by years of survival in hostile territory, screamed otherwise. They weren't alone.

"Find anything interesting?" Leo asked quietly, looking up from a peculiar disc-shaped carving that resonated with solar symbolism he'd seen in texts.

"Maybe," Sera replied, her voice low and carefully neutral, her gaze fixed on the distant Lada. "Company. Just keep looking like a fascinated professor for now. Let them think we're harmless academics."

As the sun began its final descent, painting the sky in fiery shades of orange and purple and casting long, dramatic shadows across the ancient sanctuary, Leo pointed excitedly towards the highest cluster of rocks. "Sera, look at this alignment! See how that central stone, the one shaped almost like an altar, lines up perfectly with that distant mountain peak? And these symbols..." He traced a series of precise markings cut deep into the stone surface, barely visible in the fading light. "They look like star charts. Constellations. Similar to Belintash, maybe this whole sanctuary functions as an observatory, a 'stone that sees the stars'."

Suddenly, a smooth, cultured voice spoke directly behind them, startlingly close in the quiet mountain air, making them both jump.

"Fascinating theories, Professor. Truly fascinating."

They spun around. A man stood just a few feet away, impeccably dressed in well-cut civilian clothes. Charcoal trousers, a crisp white shirt, a tailored blazer. That still somehow screamed authority and precision. He was handsome in a sharp-featured, predatory way, with piercing blue eyes that held no warmth, only cold calculation and a disturbing hint of amusement. His smile was polite, almost charming, but utterly unsettling. Behind him, standing silently, their earlier pretense dropped, were the two men Sera had spotted in the Lada. Their postures were rigid, alert, hands held near concealed weapons beneath their drab jackets.

"Colonel Gregor Orlov," the man declared, extending a perfectly manicured hand towards Leo, his smile widening slightly, revealing perfect teeth. "Bulgarian Ministry of Culture, special attaché for historical preservation. It appears," he added, his gaze flicking briefly towards Sera, taking in her alert stance with cool appraisal before settling back on Leo, "that we share a deep interest in the rich, and sometimes... surprising, history of ancient Thrace."

Colonel Gregor Orlov's smile didn't reach his piercing blue eyes, which held the flat, assessing coldness of polished steel. The air, thick with the scent of herbs and ancient dust, suddenly felt charged, brittle. Sera resisted the urge to shift into a more combative stance; his men were positioned too well, blocking any easy retreat back down the path. This was controlled, deliberate intimidation theatre.

Leo, taken aback, adjusted his glasses nervously. "Colonel Orlov? We weren't expecting... anyone official up here."

"Ah, the Ministry works in mysterious ways, Dr. Saint," Orlov continued, his smile practiced, almost surgical in its precision. Despite the cooling mountain air, a thin sheen of perspiration gleamed on his brow. Not from heat, but from the effort of climbing the plateau in his precisely tailored suit. "Especially when matters of national heritage... potentially significant discoveries... are concerned. The Ministry takes a particular interest in sites that might attract... undesirable foreign attention."

His pale blue eyes, sharp and calculating, settled on Sera. She'd instinctively shifted her stance, weight balanced evenly, one hand hovering near her hip where her messenger bag concealed her weapon. Years of training screamed at her; these men were operatives, not bureaucrats. The way they moved, how they'd positioned themselves to control the high ground, the practiced efficiency of their arrival... KGB, certainly. Possibly First Directorate.

"Our interest is purely academic, Colonel," Sera stated, her voice level, controlled, matching his tone exactly. "We're here following historical references. Nothing more."

"Of course," Orlov nodded, though skepticism flickered in his eye. Taking a measured step closer, just enough to crowd their space. "Nevertheless, I must insist on proper coordination. These mountains hold many secrets - some best left undisturbed. Others..." His gaze briefly tracked Leo's notebook before returning to Sera. "...require proper handling by those with appropriate authority."

Leo felt the weight of the moment, the subtle threats layered beneath polite words. He clutched his notebook tighter, acutely aware of the celestial carvings they'd been studying just moments before. How much had Orlov seen? How much did he already know?

"Your concern is noted, Colonel," Leo interjected, trying to defuse the tension. "We have no intention of disturbing anything. We're simply documenting"

"Documentary work," Orlov cut in smoothly, his smile never wavering, "must follow proper channels. I suggest you return to Sofia. Submit your preliminary findings through the Ministry. We can arrange guided access to approved sites."

The message was clear: leave now, or face consequences.

Sera remained silent, reading the tells - the tension in his shoulders, the way his hand hovered near his side. Orlov was sizing them up, calculating. A predator masking intent with professional courtesy.

"Perhaps we could continue this conversation somewhere more comfortable," Orlov suggested, his voice dropping slightly. "Over dinner in Sofia, perhaps. The Ministry maintains excellent hospitality for visiting scholars. I insist."

It wasn't an invitation - it was an order disguised as one.

Leo and Sera exchanged a glance - the briefest acknowledgment of their precarious position. They were outnumbered, on foreign soil, facing an adversary who clearly knew more than he was revealing. The ancient stones of Tatul suddenly felt less like a sanctuary and more like a stage for something far more dangerous than academic research.

"Your hospitality is appreciated, Colonel," Sera finally responded, knowing refusal would only raise more suspicion. "We'll certainly consider your offer as we finalize our field notes."

Orlov's smile widened fractionally - a cat that had just cornered its prey. "Excellent. I look forward to our future collaboration." He turned to his men, speaking rapid Bulgarian. They immediately moved to flank him as he began his descent from the plateau.

Just before disappearing down the path, Orlov paused, looking back. "A word of caution, Dr. Saint, Ms. Volkov. These mountains can be treacherous after dark. Many have lost their way pursuing shadows that were never meant to be found."

With that, he was gone, the sound of his footsteps fading into the gathering dusk.

Chapter Eight

Tatul's Shadow

Leo and Sera stood frozen on the rock plateau, the dust kicked up by Orlov's departing Lada settling slowly in the twilight air. The sudden silence that rushed back in was oppressive, contrasting sharply with the serene beauty of the sunset painting the Rhodope peaks in vivid hues of orange and deep purple. The ancient sanctuary, which had felt mysterious and exciting just minutes before, now seemed ominous, its weathered stones whispering silent warnings under the dying light.

Leo let out a shaky breath he hadn't realized he was holding, the cold mountain air doing little to calm the frantic hammering of his heart against his ribs. His hands felt clammy. Orlov's cold, calculating eyes and smoothly delivered, veiled threats had been far more unsettling than any contentious academic debate he'd ever experienced. This wasn't a disagreement over footnotes; it felt like a genuine threat to his life.

"Ministry of Culture," Sera repeated finally, breaking the tense silence. Her voice was low, tight with controlled anger and rapid professional assessment. She spat the words out like they tasted foul. "Right. The tailored suit that cost more than a year's salary for most people in this country, the perfect English with just that hint of Moscow polish, the well-drilled goons trying to look casual... That man has 'KGB' written all over him, probably First Chief Directorate, or GRU special projects at the very least. High-level, dangerous, and definitely not interested in historical preservation".

"No doubt about it," Leo agreed, running a shaky hand through his hair. The adrenaline from the encounter was starting to wear off, leaving him feeling exposed and deeply worried. "That wasn't a casual chat. Dimitrov warned us about 'Orlov's people'. He knew our names, knew where we were staying down in the village. He was waiting for us up here. How could he possibly know?"

Sera scanned the surrounding hillsides again, her gaze sharp and calculating even in the gathering twilight, searching for any glint of binoculars or unnatural stillness in the deepening shadows. "Easy enough if he has the resources, Leo. Airport surveillance likely flagged us the moment we landed. Tracking the rental car wouldn't be hard. Leaning on local informants in the village... hell, maybe even Dimitrov's phones are tapped back in Sofia. We have to assume they've been watching us since we stepped off the plane, maybe even before. His 'offer' of assistance..." She snorted derisively, a harsh sound in the quiet air. "That was an offer to put a leash on us, control our movements, see exactly what we found, and likely arrange a convenient 'accident' once we outlived our usefulness".

"And the warning," Leo added, recalling Orlov's final, chilling words about 'unhealthy interest' from 'outsiders'. "He was telling us to back off, or else face the consequences".

"Or more likely," Sera corrected grimly, turning to face him, her expression hard in the dim light, "he was telling us he *knows* we're not just academics. He suspects we're after something specific, something *he* wants too. Perhaps, the 'stone that sees the stars,'? He was sizing us up, testing our cover story, seeing how we'd react under pressure. And," she added, her voice hardening further, "he probably assumes we have the Delphi tablet fragment with us, or at least detailed copies".

She took a deep breath, the cold air seeming to center her. "Which means our 'cultural exchange' cover is effectively useless now, at least with him and his network. He'll be watching our every move, reporting back to Moscow. He might let us do the initial legwork, follow the clues, but he'll be right behind us, waiting to step in when we find whatever it is we're looking for".

A wave of fresh anxiety washed over Leo, cold and sickening. "So, what do we do now? He knows we're interested in Tatul, in the celestial alignments... He might even guess we spoke to Dimitrov".

"Which means we don't waste another second here," Sera stated decisively, already turning towards the track leading down the ridge. "We got the confirmation we needed. This place fits the clues, the star alignments spotted are real.

But the *real* prize, according to the Istanbul fragment and Dimitrov's hesitant confirmation, is likely Belintash, or perhaps information held by Dr. Anya Petrova in Plovdiv. Orlov was probing, trying to see if we'd reveal those names. We didn't. That gives us a small edge, maybe our only edge, for now".

She started moving back towards the track leading down to the village, her pace slower now that the adrenaline was fading. "We stick to the plan Dimitrov gave us. Head south to Plovdiv, try to connect with Dr. Petrova. She's our best bet for information on Belintash. But we do it *fast*, and we assume Orlov's men are already scrambling to figure out our next move, maybe even setting up surveillance on Petrova already. From here on out, Leo," she glanced back at him, her eyes intense, "we're not just researchers operating under flimsy cover; we're active targets in hostile territory. Everything just got exponentially more dangerous".

Leo nodded, the full weight of their situation settling heavily upon him. This wasn't a historical puzzle anymore. It wasn't even just espionage. It was a deadly chase, a race against a ruthless, high-ranking Soviet intelligence officer for stakes that felt terrifyingly real, potentially world-altering based on the translation of "Light of Annihilation". He looked back one last time at the ancient stones of Tatul, now dark, imposing silhouettes against the last vestiges of the twilight sky, feeling like he'd crossed an invisible line, leaving his old life irrevocably behind. There was no turning back to his quiet library now. He was in Sera's world, a world of shadows, immediate danger, and constant vigilance. He hurried after her down the darkening path towards the village and the uneasy sanctuary of the guesthouse, the quiet confidence she projected, even now, a small, essential anchor in the sea of uncertainty that threatened to overwhelm him. Whatever came next, they would have to face it together.

CHAPTER NINE

The Hunted

Back in the cramped, slightly musty room at the Tatul guesthouse, the air felt thick with unspoken tension and the lingering undertone of adrenaline. The encounter with Colonel Orlov on the rock plateau had stripped away any lingering illusion that this was just an academic field trip with unusual stakes. The game had fundamentally changed; the board was smaller, the pieces fewer, and the opponent was revealed to be ruthless, well-informed, and dangerously close.

"He's no Ministry pencil-pusher," Sera stated flatly, pacing the short length of the room like a caged panther, her body tight, her expression grim. Her movements were tight, controlled, but Leo could sense the coiled energy beneath the surface, the professional assessing the new, heightened threat level. "He knew our names, knew we were here at this specific guesthouse. That wasn't a coincidence, Leo. That was a calibrated warning shot across our bow".

Leo, hunched over his notebooks at the small, rickety wooden table, nodded grimly, running a hand over his face. The unsettling smoothness of Orlov's questioning, the cold calculation devoid of any real warmth in his eyes... it had chilled him more than the sharp mountain air outside. "I felt it too," he admitted, rubbing his temples where a headache was starting to throb. "His interest wasn't just professional curiosity about Thracian history. It felt... predatory. Possessive. Like he was sizing us up, deciding whether we were useful idiots or obstacles to be removed". The memory made his stomach clench.

"Exactly," Sera agreed, stopping her pacing to fix him with an intense gaze that seemed to pin him to the spot. "We have to assume they're watching us constantly now. That Lada outside the sanctuary earlier? Just the tip of the iceberg, I guarantee it. They'll have assets all over this region if he's as high-level as I suspect". She took a deep breath. "We need to get ahead of him, figure out the next clue. Belintash or Petrova. Before he slams the door shut".

She paused, her mind clearly processing options. "The contacts Professor Dimitrov mentioned... the curator in Plovdiv, Dr. Petrova, seemed the most promising lead from the Istanbul fragment regarding Belintash, right? The direct academic connection?"

Leo flipped through his notebook, scanning the hastily scribbled notes from their tense meeting in the Sofia café and comparing them with the details from the Istanbul fragment. "Right. Dr. Anya Petrova at the Plovdiv Regional Archaeological Museum. Specializes in Thracian artifacts, particularly from the Rhodope region. Dimitrov thought she might have insights into local legends, unpublished findings... maybe point us towards sites related to the 'hidden eye' or the 'stone that sees the stars'". He tapped the page. "She seemed like the most direct route to Belintash".

"Plovdiv," Sera mused, crossing her arms. "Logical next step geographically too. What was the other contact Dimitrov mentioned? The backup?"

"Someone more... discreet," Leo continued, checking his notes again, the code name feeling strange on his tongue. "Back in Sofia... there are other avenues. People who deal in information, antiquities... outside official channels. They have... extensive 'connections' and could potentially offer help finding things quietly." Leo frowned slightly. Dimitrov also warned that dealing with such people would be extremely risky. Unpredictable, he said.".

Sera filed the warning away mentally. Such shadowy contacts were always a last resort. "Okay. Plovdiv first. Trying to double back to Sofia to chase those kinds of shadowy contacts feels wrong, especially now. Orlov's network is almost certainly watching Dimitrov, and anyone connected to him. Let's pursue the academic angle with Dr. Petrova. It's cleaner, hopefully less likely to be directly compromised already."

"Agreed," Leo stated, though a part of him felt a strange pull towards the mystery of the Sofia contact. "Petrova is the logical path. While you figure out the logistics of getting us there without Orlov's entire security apparatus breathing down our necks, I'll dive deeper into these symbols again. The 'hidden eye'... it could be literal, like a carving, or symbolic, maybe a specific type of rock formation aligned with the stars? And the 'stone that sees the stars'... it still feels strongly linked to astronomy, maybe an artifact made of meteorite, or obsidian, like some ancient mirrors used for scrying..." He trailed off, already losing himself back in the historical puzzle, the familiar comfort of research a welcome antidote to the fear Orlov had instilled.

As Leo became absorbed in his notes, Sera moved quietly to the window, carefully drawing aside the thin, floral-patterned curtain just enough to peer out at the quiet village street below. The same dark Lada she'd spotted earlier near the sanctuary was still parked down the road, partially obscured by a dilapidated farm cart piled high with hay. Two men sat inside, motionless, attempting to look inconspicuous but failing miserably in the small, watchful village. Professionals didn't nap quite so rigidly on surveillance duty.

"They're still there," she confirmed, her voice a low murmur that barely disturbed the quiet room. "Patient bastards. Or maybe just waiting for instructions. We need to shake them cleanly before we make a move towards Plovdiv. Can't lead them straight to Dr. Petrova's doorstep".

"Any brilliant espionage ideas?" Leo asked, glancing up from his books, a hint of nervous energy still flickering in his eyes despite his focus on research.

A faint, almost mischievous smile touched Sera's lips, a rare sight. "It's been a while since I had to get creative in this part of the world," she admitted. "The game hasn't changed much, though. Just the players. I might have a few old tricks up my sleeve. Requires a bit of acting on your part. Just try to look like a hopelessly lost, slightly incompetent tourist tomorrow morning, okay? Think you can manage that?"

Leo sighed. "Sadly, Sera, I suspect that won't require much acting at all".

The next morning played out like a carefully choreographed, if slightly clumsy, dance. Leo left the guesthouse first, clutching a large, unfolded map and affecting an air of academic distraction bordering on bewilderment. He wandered through the small village square, pausing to examine the faded frescoes on the wall of the local church with exaggerated interest, occasionally consulting his map with a theatrical frown and turning it upside down. Playing the part Sera had assigned him perhaps a little too enthusiastically.

Meanwhile, Sera slipped out a back delivery entrance, her appearance subtly altered. Hair tucked under a different, plainer headscarf, a pair of oversized, slightly smudged sunglasses hiding half her face, carrying a local string shopping bag instead of her usual messenger bag. She moved through the narrow, winding back alleys, silent and purposeful, looping around towards the dusty lot that served as the village's bus stop, staying in the shadows cast by the stone walls.

From a vantage point behind a stack of empty wooden crates smelling faintly of chickens, Sera watched the square. As predicted, two men detached themselves from the shadows near the Lada and began casually tailing Leo, trying to look inconspicuous but moving with a stiffness that screamed 'security detail' to her trained eyes. One paused to light a cigarette, cupping his hands against a non-existent wind; the other pretended to study a faded communist party notice board with intense interest. *Sloppy*, Sera thought. Or maybe just overconfident. Good.

Leo, playing his part, seemed oblivious, continuing his 'sightseeing' tour towards the bus stop, occasionally stopping to consult his map again with a perplexed air. Sera waited until the watchers were fully focused on Leo, anticipating his move onto the waiting bus. Then, she slipped from her hiding place, moving quickly and blending seamlessly with a group of local women heading towards the same bus, pulling her headscarf lower. She bought a ticket from the driver, boarded, and took a seat near the rear window, keeping her face turned away, seemingly engrossed in the contents of her string bag.

A few minutes later, just before the ancient bus driver growled and slammed the folding doors shut, Leo hurried aboard, looking slightly flustered and out of breath, giving a believable performance of a tourist almost missing his connection. He spotted Sera, gave no sign of recognition beyond a brief, almost imperceptible dip of his head that confirmed the watchers hadn't followed him onto the bus, and took an empty seat a few rows ahead.

"Did you... uh... notice anyone paying undue attention back there?" Leo asked quietly several minutes later, leaning back slightly as the bus rumbled and backfired its way out of the village onto the main road.

"Two of them," Sera confirmed, her voice barely audible over the engine noise and the chatter of other passengers. "Stuck out like neon signs. Pretty sure their focus was entirely on Professor Saint, the lost tourist. I think we lost them in the shuffle getting on board. Doesn't mean they won't have alerted patrols further down the road, or have assets watching the stations in Plovdiv, though. We stay vigilant".

The journey to Plovdiv took several dusty, bumpy hours. The landscape shifted from the rugged, pine-clad mountains to rolling hills dotted with vineyards basking in the autumn sun and fields of drying tobacco leaves hanging in sheds. Leo buried himself in his research, trying to make sense of Thracian star charts and solar symbols, the rhythmic, jarring motion of the old bus surprisingly conducive to concentration after the tension of the last few days. Sera remained watchful, her gaze constantly scanning fellow passengers. A suspicious man reading a newspaper too intently? A woman whose shoes looked too expensive for local travel? Vehicles they passed on the road, the landscape flashing by, alert for anything out of the ordinary, her hand never far from the small pistol concealed beneath her jacket.

They arrived in Plovdiv, Bulgaria's second city, a place with a palpable sense of history far deeper than Sofia's grey conformity. Here, ancient Roman ruins stood very close to each other with colorful, slightly dilapidated Ottoman-era houses boasting ornate wooden balconies, all interweaved against the stark, utilitarian lines of drab communist concrete blocks. An amphitheater, a stadium. The air felt different here. Busier, more complex than the capital, vibrant with street life, yet still carrying an undercurrent of watchfulness, a feeling that eyes observed from shadowed windows.

Following Sera's lead, navigating the winding, picturesque but potentially confusing streets, they found a small, unassuming hotel tucked away on a cobblestone side street in the historic Old Town, recommended by Dimitrov as being relatively free from official scrutiny. Before they even put their bags down, Sera insisted on doing a thorough sweep of the room, pulling out a small, sophisticated electronic detector Leo hadn't seen before. He watched, fascinated and slightly unnerved, as she methodically ran the device over the walls, checked behind pictures, lamps, and inside the bulky telephone receiver, unscrewing the mouthpiece to examine the wiring. Only when she was completely satisfied the room was clean did she nod, slipping the detector back into a hidden pocket in her bag.

"Okay. Clear for now," she announced, the tension easing slightly from her shoulders. "Standard procedure, but necessary. Let's plan our next move".

Leo consulted his notes again, spreading them out on the small, scarred table. "Dr. Anya Petrova. Professor Dimitrov mentioned her office is at the Plovdiv Regional Archaeological Museum, not far from here. Maybe we try to make contact first thing tomorrow morning? Go through official channels, present our academic credentials?"

Sera shook her head immediately, her expression thoughtful but firm. "Tomorrow is definitely too late. Orlov knew we were heading south from Tatul. He's smart enough to figure out Plovdiv, and Dr. Petrova is the obvious next step for anyone researching Thracian sites. He'll already have alerted his local network. Watching the museum, watching known experts like Petrova... it's standard operating procedure. Walking in the front door tomorrow morning is asking for trouble, practically announcing our arrival". She paused, considering, tapping a finger against her chin. "We need to approach her carefully. Tonight. Unofficially. Away from the museum, away from prying eyes".

Leo looked hesitant. "Tonight? How? We don't even know where she lives, do we?"

"Leave that to me," Sera replied, a determined glint returning to her eyes. She pulled out her own detailed map of Plovdiv and began studying the layout of the Old Town near the museum, marking potential approach routes, noting alleyways, blind corners, and possible escape paths. "There are always ways, Leo. You just have to know how to look".

While Sera focused on the tactical details, Leo returned to his notes, hoping to find some obscure historical connection, some specific detail about Thracian artifacts from Belintash that Dr. Petrova might recognize. Something that could act as a subtle code, verifying her trustworthiness or giving them leverage if things went wrong. The clock was ticking. Orlov was out there, hunting them, his network spreading like invisible threads through the ancient city. And the secrets hinted at by the Delphi prophecy felt both closer and infinitely more dangerous than ever. Their quiet infiltration of Plovdiv was about to begin.

Chapter Ten

The Cautious Curator

The Plovdiv Regional Archaeological Museum was housed in a grand, slightly faded building from the late 19th century, its neo-classical stone facade standing in somewhat awkward proximity to newer, uglier concrete structures from the communist era. Inside, the air was cool and smelled faintly of dust, floor polish, and the indefinable scent of antiquity. High ceilings amplified the echoing footsteps on the worn marble floors. Display cases filled with impressive Thracian pottery, intricate gold treasures gleaming under spotlights, and ancient weaponry lined the somewhat sparsely populated halls. Under normal circumstances, Leo would have been itching to explore every exhibit, captivated by the tangible connection to the past. Today, however, the silent artifacts were just background noise, obstacles between him and their target: Dr. Anya Petrova.

They approached the main information desk, a heavy, dark wooden counter presiding over the entrance hall like a judge's bench. Behind it sat a stern-looking woman with iron-grey hair pulled back in a severe bun, her lips pursed in disapproval at the world in general. She was knitting, the rhythmic *click-click-click* of her needles the loudest sound in the immediate vicinity. She looked up as they approached, her expression suggesting interruptions were a personal affront.

Leo summoned his most earnest, slightly bumbling academic charm. A persona Sera was quickly learning he could adopt with surprising, almost concerning, effectiveness. "Excuse me," he began politely, offering a tentative smile. "*Dobar den*. We were hoping to have a brief word with Dr. Anya Petrova? We are visiting researchers..."

The woman's knitting needles paused mid-click, suspended in the air like accusatory fingers. Her gaze sharpened as she gave them a slow, deliberate once-over, lingering perhaps a moment too long on Sera's practical, travel-worn clothes which contrasted with Leo's slightly rumpled but still identifiable academic attire. "Dr. Petrova?" she repeated, her tone laced with skepticism, implying that Dr. Petrova was far too important for unscheduled, foreign visitors. "She is a senior researcher here. A very busy woman. Do you have an appointment?" Her Bulgarian was crisp and formal.

"Ah, no, unfortunately not," Leo admitted sheepishly, inwardly cursing their lack of time for formalities. "But Professor Ivan Dimitrov, from Sofia University?" He let the name hang in the air, a calculated gamble, watching her reaction closely. "He suggested we speak with her, if she had a moment. Our research concerns Thracian solar cults, particularly in the Rhodope region, and he felt Dr. Petrova's unparalleled expertise would be invaluable."

At the mention of Dimitrov's name, the woman's stern expression softened, just a fraction. A flicker of recognition, perhaps mixed with caution, entered her eyes. "Ah, Ivan Dimitrov. Yes, I know Professor Dimitrov. A respected scholar, though... unconventional in his views." She seemed to mentally reclassify them from 'annoying tourists' to 'potentially legitimate, if perhaps slightly suspect, academics'. She pursed her lips again. "Dr. Petrova is in her office. Second floor, Room 214. But I tell you, she *is* very busy this morning. Important Ministry deadlines."

"We understand completely," Leo assured her with another polite smile. "We promise not to take up much of her time. We would be grateful for even just five minutes."

"Second floor, 214," the woman repeated, gesturing vaguely towards a wide, imposing marble staircase before returning her attention pointedly to her knitting, the clicking resuming its steady rhythm, dismissing them.

They climbed the creaking wooden stairs of the grand staircase, their footsteps echoing slightly in the high-ceilinged corridor of the upper floor. Administrative offices lined the hall, most doors closed. Room 214 was tucked away at the far end, somewhat isolated. The door itself, bearing a simple plaque with "Dr. A. Petrova," was slightly ajar, revealing an office that looked less like a workspace and more like an archaeological dig site in miniature had collided with a university library. Books were piled precariously on every available surface. Desk, chairs, floor, windowsills. Papers overflowed from battered filing cabinets, threatening to spill their secrets. Display cases along one wall held fragments of pottery, bronze tools, and small, intriguing artifacts labeled in meticulous handwriting. Maps. Ancient and modern. Were pinned haphazardly to the walls between shelves sagging under the weight of academic journals.

Behind a massive, cluttered oak desk, almost obscured by stacks of folders, sat a woman who looked to be in her late fifties. Silver-streaked hair was loosely pinned up, stray strands escaping around a face that was intelligent, lined with concentration, and framed by sturdy reading glasses perched on her nose. She was engrossed in examining a large shard of pottery under a desk lamp, turning it carefully in her hands, oblivious to their arrival. This had to be Dr. Anya Petrova.

Leo knocked gently on the open doorframe, the sound startlingly loud in the quiet concentration of the office. "Dr. Petrova? Forgive the interruption."

She looked up, her initial expression one of sharp annoyance at being disturbed, her focus clearly broken. But as she took in Leo's academic appearance. The slightly rumpled tweed, the briefcase, the earnest expression. And Sera's quiet, watchful presence beside him, the annoyance quickly shifted to professional curiosity, overlaid with a hint of wariness.

"Yes? Can I help you?" she asked, her voice carrying a note of authority despite its quietness. Her eyes, sharp and intelligent behind the glasses, assessed them both quickly.

"I'm Dr. Leon Saint, from the University of Maryland," Leo explained, stepping just inside the doorway, careful not to disturb any precarious piles. "And this is my research colleague, Ms. Volkov. Professor Ivan Dimitrov in Sofia suggested we might impose upon your expertise, if you could possibly spare a moment."

Dr. Petrova raised a quizzical eyebrow at the mention of Dimitrov but gestured towards two chairs half-buried under stacks of journals and excavation reports. "Professor Dimitrov, you say? Yes, I know Ivan well. A good man, passionate about his work. Please, come in, sit down. If you can find the chairs, that is." Her tone was dry, a hint of humor lurking beneath the surface, but her eyes remained watchful.

Leo and Sera managed to excavate the chairs, perching somewhat awkwardly amidst the comforting chaos of decades of dedicated research. Leo, surrounded by the tangible fragments of the past, felt a little more grounded. He briefly outlined their supposed project. Thracian sun worship, potential connections to regional geology, a specific interest in local legends surrounding celestial phenomena. Carefully weaving in the keywords they needed answers for, monitoring her reactions. Dr. Petrova listened intently, her sharp eyes occasionally flicking towards Sera, who sat quietly, absorbing the atmosphere, her stillness a counterpoint to the office's clutter.

"Ah yes, the solar cults," Dr. Petrova said finally, leaning back in her chair, tapping a pen against her cluttered desk. "The Rhodope Mountains are indeed fertile ground for such research. The Thracians had a deep reverence for the sun, as you know. Its power, its cycles... it permeated their worldview. Many shrines, megalithic structures, rock formations... Tatul, of course, is the most famous example, though perhaps becoming too much of a tourist curiosity these days."

"We visited Tatul yesterday," Leo confirmed, keeping his tone purely academic. "Quite an extraordinary site. The astronomical alignments were remarkable, especially considering the presumed age."

A subtle shift occurred in Dr. Petrova's expression. A flicker of caution, perhaps, or maybe a deep weariness entered her eyes. She'd likely dealt with intrusive officials or crackpot theorists before. "Tatul is... significant. And well-known, perhaps too well-known, as I said. Subject to much... official interest." She fixed Leo with a direct gaze. "What specifically about the site captured *your* interest, Dr. Saint? Beyond the general alignments?"

Leo chose his words carefully, sensing he was being probed. "Mainly the potential celestial alignments, as I mentioned. The precision is startling. And we came across some unusual local folklore in preliminary research regarding rather poetic terms like a 'hidden eye' or a 'stone that sees the stars'. We were wondering if you'd encountered similar, perhaps unpublished, references in your own extensive research connected to other sites in the Rhodopes?"

Dr. Petrova's eyes narrowed slightly behind her glasses. She placed her pen down deliberately on a stack of papers. "Those are... rather specific, and unusual, terms, Doctor. Not typical academic phraseology for Thracian mythology, as I'm sure you know. Where did you encounter such phrases?" Her voice was polite, but the underlying question was sharp: *Who are you really?* She looked from Leo to Sera, her gaze lingering on Sera for a moment, clearly recognizing that Sera was more than just a "research colleague." She wasn't just an academic; she clearly had sharp instincts honed by navigating the political complexities of her field in this regime.

Sera decided it was time to step in, her voice calm, respectful, but direct, meeting Petrova's sharp gaze evenly. "We understand they might sound strange, Dr. Petrova. Our research occasionally touches upon less... conventional interpretations. Following obscure threads, apocryphal texts, local stories that perhaps haven't been fully investigated by mainstream scholarship."

Dr. Petrova studied Sera for a long moment, assessing her quiet confidence, her unwavering gaze. Leo could almost see the internal debate playing out on her face. Professional caution warring with scholarly curiosity, perhaps layered with a deep-seated distrust of official channels and anyone who might represent them. Finally, she seemed to reach a decision. She sighed, a sound that seemed to carry the weight of years spent protecting fragile history from clumsy politics.

"Look," she stated, lowering her voice conspiratorially and leaning forward slightly across the mountainous terrain of her desk. "You must understand the context here. Certain historical sites, certain *artifacts* unearthed in this country ... they attract unwanted attention. Official attention. Especially when foreigners take an interest." She glanced towards the closed door, almost instinctively. "Our Ministry of Culture," she added, a hint of bitterness creeping into her tone, "can be exceedingly... protective. Sometimes, it feels less like preservation and more like... state possession, aimed at controlling the narrative, burying inconvenient truths."

Leo exchanged a quick, knowing glance with Sera. *Orlov*. His influence, his methods, reached even here, intimidating genuine scholars into silence.

"We understand completely, Doctor," Leo responded smoothly, hoping he sounded sincere and not like just another official trying to extract information. "And we have no wish to cause any difficulties, diplomatic or otherwise. Our interest is purely academic, historical."

Dr. Petrova hesitated again, her gaze searching their faces, then seemed to commit, perhaps sensing a shared frustration with bureaucratic interference. "There are always whispers," she continued, her voice barely above a murmur now, forcing them to lean in closer. "Old tales, passed down in the mountain villages for generations, stories you won't find in the approved publications from Sofia. Stories of hidden chambers beneath the well-known sanctuaries, sacred objects with... unusual properties attributed to them."

She leaned closer still, the academic passion momentarily overcoming her caution. "Forget Tatul for a moment; it is too exposed. There is another site, Belintash. Higher, more remote, possibly even older. Local legends there speak explicitly, repeatedly, of a 'stone eye'. Some say a rock formation, others claim a carving. That aligns perfectly with certain constellations during specific nights of the year. And," she added, her eyes gleaming with academic excitement despite the risk, "there are associated stories, very persistent ones, of a nearby spring whose water is said to... *shimmer*, almost like liquid light, especially under moonlight. Or liquid gold, depending on which village tells the tale."

Belintash. The name resonated, matching the Istanbul fragment. 'Stone eye.' 'Sees the stars.' Liquid light. It fit. This was it.

"Dr. Petrova," Sera interjected, her voice low and persuasive, sensing the importance of the moment. "We aren't here to stir up trouble for anyone, least of all you or Professor Dimitrov. We are simply trying to understand the truth behind these specific legends. Any further details you could provide about Belintash, any unpublished maps, excavation notes, related findings... it would be invaluable to our research, and kept in the strictest confidence."

Dr. Petrova looked from Sera's intense gaze to Leo's earnest expression. She seemed torn, the ingrained habit of caution battling the academic desire to share hidden knowledge, to potentially validate these old, dismissed legends. The lure appeared to be winning. "Alright," she finally nodded slowly, making up her mind. "Belintash is notoriously difficult to access, and only superficially excavated decades ago. Funding was pulled, officially due to 'instability', unofficially... perhaps they found something they didn't want known. But there are some unpublished monographs gathering dust in the archives here, some speculative papers from the original survey team... I can tell you what I know. I might even have sketches." She paused, her expression serious again. "But you *must* be discreet. Extremely discreet. The Rhodopes guard their secrets jealously. And if anyone connected to the Ministry asks, this conversation never happened. Understand?"

Just as she reached for a large, dusty folder buried under a pile of papers on her desk, a sharp, authoritative knock rattled the doorframe. The sound was loud, intrusive, instantly shattering the fragile bubble of shared confidence.

They all looked up, startled.

A tall, squarely built man in a severe dark suit stood in the doorway. His face was impassive, expressionless, his eyes cold and assessing as they swept over Leo and Sera before settling heavily on the curator. He radiated an aura of menace that had nothing to do with cultural preservation.

"Dr. Petrova," the man stated, his Bulgarian clear but carrying the unmistakable clipped tones of State Security officialdom. "Colonel Orlov requires your immediate presence. A car is waiting downstairs."

Dr. Petrova's face went deathly pale, her earlier academic excitement vanishing instantly, replaced by raw, undisguised fear. She looked helplessly from the menacing figure in the doorway to Leo and Sera, her eyes wide with panic. "I... I must go," she whispered, her hands trembling slightly as she pushed her chair back.

The man gave Leo and Sera a single, dismissive nod, his gaze lingering just long enough. Cold, knowing, threatening. To convey that their presence, their conversation, had been duly noted, before turning his full attention back to Dr. Petrova. He held the door open, waiting.

The message couldn't have been clearer: *Orlov knows*. And his reach was long.

CHAPTER ELEVEN

Running Blind

The appearance of Orlov's heavy in Dr. Petrova's office doorway wasn't just a warning shot; it was a grenade tossed into their carefully constructed plans, the pin already pulled. His cold, assessing eyes swept over them, lingering for a fraction of a second too long on Sera, a silent acknowledgment of her perceived role, and she knew instantly: playtime was over. Their academic cover, already flimsy, was shredded. They were unequivocally blown.

"We need to leave," she murmured urgently to Leo, her voice barely a breath, her hand subtly gripping his forearm beneath the table, pulling him back towards the hallway even as he stammered a hasty, inadequate thank you to the terrified Dr. Petrova, whose face had gone the color of old parchment. "Now. Not casually. *Now.*"

Leo, though his mind was still buzzing with the implications of Belintash and Petrova's confirmation, caught the sudden, sharp edge in Sera's voice. The unmistakable tone of imminent danger she reserved for moments when things went critical. He didn't argue. He pushed back his chair, the legs scraping loudly on the stone floor, nearly tripping over a stack of archaeological journals in his haste. They practically bolted from the office, moving swiftly down the corridor, ignoring the curious glances from a museum staffer carrying a tray of artifacts who frowned at their unseemly hurry.

"They'll expect us to use the main entrance and staircase," Sera muttered as they reached the grand landing, her eyes darting left and right. "Too obvious. Too many potential bottlenecks." She steered him sharply towards a narrower, less conspicuous side corridor she'd clocked on their way up; plain, unmarked doors, likely leading to service areas or storage. Her senses were screaming, every shadow seeming to hold a waiting threat, every distant footstep potentially belonging to another of Orlov's men.

They slipped through an unmarked wooden door, finding themselves in a dingy, dimly lit service stairwell that smelled strongly of damp plaster, stale cigarette smoke, and harsh disinfectant. They descended quickly, their footsteps echoing unnervingly in the narrow, concrete space, the sound magnified, making them feel terrifyingly exposed. Bursting out onto the ground floor into a cluttered corridor behind the main exhibit halls with stacks of packing crates, rolled-up carpets, discarded display stands. They headed for a side exit that Sera had noted earlier. A heavy, paint-chipped metal door used for deliveries, currently propped slightly open with a rubber wedge.

Glancing back through a connecting archway towards the museum's main hall, Sera caught a glimpse of Orlov's henchman escorting a pale Dr. Petrova towards the front entrance, his hand firmly on her elbow. He hadn't followed them directly, there was no need. He knew they were here; he'd seen them. Reinforcements would already be moving into position outside, alerted by radio, ready to seal the exits.

They slipped out the side exit into a narrow, garbage-strewn alleyway running behind the museum, the sudden transition from the museum's cool, quiet dignity to the alley's noise, heat, and fetid smells jarring. Overturned bins overflowed, stray cats scattered. Sera grabbed Leo's hand again, pulling him along at a near run over the broken pavement.

"Did you see if they took Petrova with them?" Leo gasped, stumbling slightly on a loose brick, struggling to keep up with Sera's urgent pace.

"Yes, looked like it, but she's not our primary problem right now," Sera replied grimly, risking a quick glance over her shoulder as they rounded a sharp corner onto a slightly wider, busier street lined with small shops. "They know we talked to her. That's enough. They know we're onto something significant."

Confirming her worst fear and what she had just stated, a black Lada sedan of identical make and model to the one Orlov had used at Tatul, peeled around the corner at the far end of the street; its engine roaring, accelerating rapidly towards them.

"They spotted us leaving the alley!" Leo exclaimed, his voice tight with panic, his eyes wide.

"Run!" Sera commanded, reacting instantly, yanking him bodily off the street and into the sudden, overwhelming chaos of a bustling open-air marketplace that spilled out from a nearby square. Stalls overflowing with colorful textiles, pyramids of gleaming produce, fragrant spices piled high in sacks, caged birds chirping frantically, and shouting vendors provided instant, albeit temporary, cover. Sera plunged into the throng, weaving expertly between shoppers haggling loudly, pushcarts laden with goods, and stray dogs scavenging for scraps, pulling Leo inexpertly in her wake. He stumbled, bumping into people, murmuring apologies, the sudden shift from quiet museum to desperate flight triggering a surge of adrenaline that left him breathless and disoriented. The smells of roasting meat, strong coffee, unwashed bodies, and exotic spices filled the air, thick and confusing.

"Where are we going?" he panted, narrowly dodging a collision with a stout woman carrying a basket piled high with fresh bread that smelled heavenly despite their predicament.

"Anywhere but here! Anywhere they lose line of sight!" Sera shot back, her eyes scanning ahead, searching for an escape route through the dense river of people. "We need to break contact, lose them completely, then get out of Plovdiv fast. Belintash is our only solid lead now, and Orlov knows we likely got the name from Petrova. He'll try to cut us off, block the roads south."

She spotted a narrow, shadowed passage barely wide enough for one person, promising darkness and anonymity. "This way!" She pulled Leo sharply left, out of the main flow of the crowd, into the sudden cool darkness of the passage. She pressed him flat against the damp, moss-covered stone wall as heavy footsteps pounded past the entrance to the passage, followed by angry shouts in Bulgarian. They were Orlov's men, frustrated at losing Sera and Leo in the market's confusion.

"Close," Sera whispered, straining her ears, listening intently as the footsteps hesitated, then receded slightly down the main market street. They'd likely overshot their hiding spot. "Okay, move. We can't stay here." She pointed upwards. A rickety, rust-streaked fire escape clung precariously to the side of the taller building, ascending into the bright sunlight above the shadowed alley. "Up. Quickly. Rooftops are better than alleys."

Sera went first, scaling the protesting metal ladder with practiced agility, testing each rung before putting her full weight on it. Reaching the first landing, she leaned down, offering a steadying hand to pull Leo up the awkward first few rungs. He scrambled after her, his inappropriate dress shoes slipping on the rusty metal, his heart pounding like a drum against his ribs, the height making his head swim. They climbed higher, emerging onto the searing terracotta tiles of the rooftop, the sudden brightness making them blink. Below them, muffled shouts echoed from the street as Orlov's men realized their mistake and began searching the alleyways.

"Across there!" Sera pointed to an adjacent building, its roof slightly lower but tantalizingly close, separated by a dizzyingly narrow gap that dropped three stories to the alley below. "It leads towards the older part of town, Kapana, the Trap district. More alleys, more chances to disappear if we can make it."

Leo hesitated, staring numbly at the gap. It looked wider than it probably was, the alley pavement terrifyingly far below. Sera didn't wait for him to find his courage. She took a short running start and leaped, landing lightly, cat-like, on the dusty tiles of the other roof. "Come on, Leo! Don't think, just move!" she urged, her voice sharp but low.

Taking a deep breath, closing his eyes for a fraction of a second, Leo followed, launching himself across the gap with more desperation than grace. He landed heavily, stumbling, arms windmilling, but managed to stay upright. They scrambled across several more interconnected rooftops, a frantic, high-altitude escape through Plovdiv's historic, uneven skyline. Leaping narrow gaps, scrambling over low parapets, dodging laundry lines strung between chimneys. Before finding another, slightly sturdier fire escape leading down into a blessedly quiet, deserted alleyway paved with ancient, uneven cobblestones several streets away from the market.

Sera quickly scanned the alley, then peered cautiously onto the main street. Seeing a battered yellow taxi approaching, she stepped out and hailed it, rattling off instructions in clipped, fluent Bulgarian to the surprised, mustachioed driver, urging him towards the city's sprawling industrial outskirts on the Maritsa riverbank.

"Where now?" Leo asked, sliding onto the worn vinyl seat, trying to catch his breath, adrenaline still making him shake uncontrollably.

"Somewhere Orlov won't expect us to go," Sera replied, keeping a close watch on the streets behind them through the taxi's dusty rear window. "We need transportation that won't be easily traced. Public transport is out. Too many checkpoints. Our rented Renault is undoubtedly being watched, probably already found back in Tatul." She seemed to run through a mental checklist, ticking off options. "I have a contact here. Met him years ago on another job. Not exactly reputable," she admitted with a grimace, "but he owes me a favor. And, more importantly, he deals in untraceable vehicles. The kind that disappear."

The contact operated out of a grimy auto repair shop in a sprawling industrial district near the freight yards, a place that smelled overwhelmingly of stale oil, welding fumes, and cheap cigarettes. He was a burly, taciturn man named Boris, with grease permanently ingrained under his fingernails and a face that looked like it had absorbed, and possibly delivered, too many punches in dimly lit bars. He grunted a monosyllabic greeting at Sera, gave Leo a brief, incurious glance, and after a swift, low-voiced negotiation involving a thick wad of US dollars Sera produced, he wordlessly pointed them towards an older, battered-looking beige Moskvich sedan parked in the back lot amongst rusting automotive corpses.

As Sera checked the engine, which turned over with a surprisingly healthy, throaty rumble despite the car's derelict appearance, Boris leaned against a stack of worn tires, wiping his hands on an oil-stained rag. His gaze, surprisingly sharp, flicked to the street beyond the grimy workshop entrance. "These Rhodope Mountains," he said, his voice a low rumble, "they are my home. Some guests... they bring trouble that echoes long after they're gone." He looked pointedly at Sera. "That Lada that tailed your taxi here? Too clean, too new for local business. Be careful who's watching your back trail, little bird. Some shadows in these hills have very long teeth."

He then gave a curt nod towards the Moskvich. "She's ugly, but she's solid. Keep her off the main highways if you can. Better for your health."

It was dented, the paint faded and peeling, but the engine was sound. It was perfect, completely anonymous, and utterly forgettable.

They drove out of Plovdiv, heading south again, back towards the rugged Rhodope Mountains and the promise of Belintash, the tension in the small, stuffy car thick enough to cut with a knife. Sera drove with focused intensity, her eyes constantly flicking between the road ahead and the rearview mirror, while Leo tried, unsuccessfully, to relax his clenched jaw, every nerve ending tingling with residual fear. Every passing truck, every distant glint of sun on metal felt like a potential threat; every shadow seemed to hide an observer.

Just as they began to allow themselves a sliver of hope that they might have actually slipped the net this time, headlights flared aggressively in the rearview mirror. A black Lada, appearing seemingly out of nowhere on the winding mountain road, was closing the distance fast.

"Damn it!" Sera cursed under her breath, slamming her foot down on the accelerator, the Moskvich's engine protesting with a weary whine. "They found us again! How the hell are they doing it?"

"How?" Leo exclaimed, twisting frantically in his seat to look back at the pursuing vehicle. "Is there a tracker on this car? Or the one we rented? Are they tracking *us* somehow?"

"Could be," Sera answered grimly, her knuckles white on the steering wheel as she expertly navigated a tight curve. "Could be a transponder hidden on us, our gear... or Orlov just has eyes everywhere, informants in every village reporting unfamiliar cars. Doesn't matter now. Hold on!"

The Moskvich, though surprisingly sturdy, was no match for the heavier, more powerful Lada in terms of speed or handling, especially on these treacherous, winding mountain roads with their sheer, unforgiving drop-offs. Sera pushed the older car to its absolute limits, tires squealing in protest on the sharp curves, the engine whining like a tortured animal, the smell of burning oil filling the cabin. The Lada stayed glued to their tail like a predator, occasionally bumping their rear bumper or trying to force them towards the steep cliffs that lined the road. This wasn't just pursuit; they were actively trying to force a crash, disable them, capture them alive.

Sera expertly navigated a dizzying series of hairpin turns, downshifting violently, using her superior driving skills and knowledge of physics to momentarily gain a few precious yards, the tires throwing up gravel. But the Lada, driven with ruthless precision, was relentless. As they came around another blind curve, tires protesting, Sera suddenly slammed on the brakes, the Moskvich fishtailing wildly on the dusty asphalt. A massive, recently felled pine tree lay directly across the narrow road, completely blocking their path. Its fresh, sappy scent filled the air. A deliberate, inescapable roadblock.

"We're trapped!" Leo cried out, bracing for impact against the dashboard.

Before the Moskvich had even fully stopped skidding, the black Lada screeched to a halt directly behind them, boxing them in against the fallen tree. Two men burst out, AK-74s already drawn and leveled, moving with practiced military precision. One of them bellowed in harsh Russian, "Get out of the car! Hands where we can see them! Now!"

Sera glanced at Leo, her eyes hard as flint, filled with a cold, deadly resolve. "This isn't over," she muttered through clenched teeth. Then, in one explosive, unpredictable movement, she kicked open her driver's side door, using it as a shield as she lunged out, firing her Makarov pistol even before her feet hit the dusty ground, the silenced *phut-phut* barely audible over the pounding in Leo's ears.

The lead agent, caught completely off guard by her speed and raw aggression, stumbled back, firing wildly, his shots kicking up puffs of dust near Sera's feet. The second agent swung his assault rifle towards Sera. Leo, reacting purely on instinct and terror, scrambled out the passenger side, his eyes darting around for a weapon, anything. He spotted a heavy, jagged rock by the roadside and grabbed it, though he had no clear idea what he intended to do with it.

The second agent saw Leo emerge, registered him as a secondary threat, hesitated for a split second, then swung his rifle back towards the more immediate danger...*Sera*. That fractional hesitation cost him dearly. Just as he raised his weapon towards Sera again, a deafening shotgun blast echoed from the dense pine forest beside the road, the sound shockingly loud in the mountain quiet. The agent staggered as if punched by an invisible giant, a dark, blossoming stain spreading rapidly across his chest, before collapsing face down onto the asphalt without a sound.

Sera, having already disarmed her initial attacker with a swift, brutal combination of kicks and chops that left him groaning on the ground clutching his wrist, spun towards the tree line, her own pistol tracking the source of the unexpected shot, ready for another threat.

Standing at the edge of the woods, almost hidden by the deep shadows of the pines, was the burly, grease-stained figure of Boris, their Plovdiv car contact. A smoking, double-barreled shotgun rested easily in his large hands.

"Looked like you might need a little help, little bird," Boris stated, his voice gruff, a grim, humorless smile cracking his weathered face.

"Wasn't expecting backup," Sera replied, lowering her pistol slightly but remaining wary. How had he found them?

"Figured those types might still be sniffing around after you left my shop," Boris shrugged, stepping out from the trees. "Saw them follow your taxi. Took a shortcut through the hills. Don't like KGB thugs causing trouble in my mountains." He gestured with the shotgun further up the blocked road, towards the ridge line barely visible through the trees. "Belintash. It ain't far now, maybe two kilometers, just beyond that ridge. Go. Now. I'll clean up this mess here. Make sure they don't follow." The implication of "cleaning up" was chillingly clear.

Sera didn't waste time arguing or asking questions. She trusted Boris's timely intervention, whatever his motives. She grabbed Leo's arm, pulling him from his stunned state. "Come on! Move!"

They scrambled over the massive trunk of the fallen pine tree, leaving the sounds of Boris dispassionately dealing with the remaining, wounded agent behind them. They plunged into the dense woods, running uphill towards the ridge, the ancient, enigmatic rocks of Belintash looming somewhere in the near distance, promising answers. And almost certainly, more danger.

CHAPTER TWELVE

Plateau of the Ancients

Belintash felt profoundly different from Tatul. Older, yes, but also wilder, rawer, imbued with a palpable sense of untamed, ancient power that Tatul, perhaps due to its greater accessibility and previous excavations, lacked. The air at this higher altitude was thin and sharp, biting at their exposed skin, carrying the clean, resinous scent of pine needles warmed by the sun and the hint of damp earth after a recent rain. Immense rock formations, carved and scoured into fantastical shapes by millennia of wind, rain, and ice, jutted towards the clear, deep blue Bulgarian sky like the fossilized bones of forgotten titans. Weather-beaten pine trees clung stubbornly to the steep slopes, their roots gripping tenaciously into shallow pockets of soil between massive slabs of grey, lichen-streaked stone. A profound, almost unnerving silence hung over the place, broken only by the sigh of the wind whistling through rock crevices and the distant, lonely cry of a hawk circling on thermal currents high overhead. It felt utterly remote, powerful, and deeply secret. A place where the veil between worlds might feel thin.

Leo and Sera, lungs still burning from their desperate scramble through the dense woods after the roadblock confrontation, stood at the edge of the sprawling rock plateau, catching their breath and taking in the extraordinary scene. Even after the frantic escape and the violence they'd just witnessed, Leo couldn't suppress a shiver of pure awe that ran down his spine. This was it. He *knew* it.

"This place..." he breathed, his voice husky, eyes wide as he scanned the bizarre, almost unearthly landscape. "It's incredible. More than the legends hinted at, more than Petrova described. You can almost *feel* the history here, like static electricity prickling the air." He felt dwarfed by the scale, by the sheer, crushing weight of antiquity surrounding them.

Sera, ever practical, was less interested in the palpable atmosphere, though even she seemed subtly affected by the site's stark grandeur. Her gaze, sharp and focused, swept the surrounding hillsides, the dark tree line encircling the plateau, the winding, barely visible track leading up to the sanctuary from the valley below. "Our friend back there bought us some time," she stated quietly, scanning methodically for any sign of movement, any unnatural glint of metal or misplaced shadow. "But Orlov won't give up that easily. He's obsessed. They'll be coming, maybe from a different direction. We need to figure this out, find whatever the 'stone' is, and fast."

Leo nodded, forcing himself to refocus, pulling out his battered notebook and pen, the familiar tools of his trade feeling slightly inadequate in this vast, ancient setting.

"Okay. Right. The clues from the prophecy, the Istanbul fragment, and Dr. Petrova. The 'hidden eye' and the 'stone that sees the stars'... Petrova mentioned the eye aligns with constellations, possibly a rock formation." He started moving carefully across the uneven rock surface, his eyes searching, scanning the bizarre shapes, the natural depressions, the man-made carvings. "Let's look for formations, specific carvings, anything that looks like an eye or has a clear, undeniable connection to the sky."

They began exploring the vast rock plateau, a natural stage set amidst the towering peaks. Sera moved with cautious alertness, checking sightlines, noting potential ambush points, her senses straining for any hint of their pursuers, while Leo became absorbed in examining the strange carvings and unique geological formations scattered across the site. The surface of the rock was pocked with odd, basin-like depressions, some filled with stagnant rainwater reflecting the sky like murky mirrors. Intricate networks of shallow channels snaked across the plateau, possibly for channeling liquids during ancient rituals. Water? Blood? And everywhere, symbols were carved into the stone. Spirals, sun-discs, crosses within circles, patterns that seemed even older and more abstract than those at Tatul, hinting at a deeper, perhaps more disturbing, past.

Reaching the highest point of the sanctuary, a relatively flat expanse of rock commanding a breathtaking panorama of the surrounding Rhodope mountains stretching away in hazy blue waves, Leo stopped suddenly, pointing excitedly towards the cliff edge facing east. "Sera, look at this! Over here!"

He indicated a peculiar natural formation in the rock face just below the main plateau level. A large, almost perfectly oval depression, weathered smooth by time and elements. The surrounding rock contours created an uncanny effect, like a massive, stylized eye gazing toward the eastern horizon. Watching. Waiting for the sun and key constellations to rise.

"Could that be it?" Leo wondered aloud, excitement rising in his voice, quickening his breath. "The 'hidden eye'? The symbolism is almost too perfect."

Sera joined him, studying the formation critically. It was striking, undeniably eye-like in shape and orientation. "It's possible," she conceded, her tone cautious. "It certainly fits the poetic language of the prophecy. But what about the 'stone that sees the stars'? Is it this entire platform? Or something else?"

Leo moved closer to the rock 'eye', kneeling carefully on the weathered stone to examine its surface more closely. He noticed something he hadn't seen from further back. A series of small, precisely drilled holes scattered around the upper perimeter of the oval depression, almost like markings on a celestial dial or sightlines. They seemed far too regular, too deliberately placed, to be mere weathering or natural erosion. He pulled his trusty compass from his pocket and consulted the laminated star charts he'd hastily copied from his research materials.

"These holes..." he muttered, his brow furrowed in concentration, measuring angles with his compass, comparing the positions of the holes to the star charts. "They're not random. Definitely not. They seem to align perfectly with the rising points of specific stars, major constellations... look, that one matches Sirius, that cluster aligns with the Pleiades... maybe even planets, at different times of the year. Dr. Petrova mentioned this site might be older than Tatul. What if its primary purpose wasn't just worship, but precise celestial observation? Tracking cosmic cycles?"

"You two work fast for folks who look like they belong in a library."

The gruff, familiar voice, startlingly close behind them, made them both spin around, Leo letting out a small yelp of surprise, Sera instinctively reaching for the Makarov beneath her jacket. Leaning casually against a nearby weathered boulder, looking as solid and immovable as the rock itself, shotgun slung comfortably over his shoulder, was Boris, their Plovdiv car contact, a wry expression on his face, though his eyes were watchful. He looked slightly winded, but otherwise unfazed by his earlier violent intervention.

"Boris!" Leo exclaimed, relief mixing overwhelmingly with surprise. "How did you... how did you get here so fast? And past..." He gestured vaguely back the way they had come.

"Know my way around these mountains better than the goats do," Boris stated with a dismissive shrug, pushing himself off the rock. He spat onto the ground. "Saw the roadblock mess from higher up the ridge. Figured those KGB snakes wouldn't give up easy, and you might need pointing in the right direction again after your run through the woods." He glanced back towards the track below. "Besides," he added, his expression hardening slightly, "I told you I don't like those types throwing their weight around here. Bad for business. Bad for Bulgaria."

"You saved our lives back there," Sera acknowledged, lowering her hand from her weapon, offering a curt, respectful nod. Even she seemed slightly surprised by his reappearance. "We owe you. Again."

Boris waved a dismissive hand, clearly uncomfortable with the thanks. "Just evening the odds. Forget it. So, what have the ancient rocks been telling you scholars?"

Leo quickly explained their theory about the 'hidden eye' formation and his discovery of the drilled holes aligning with stars. "We think this whole place might be the 'stone that sees the stars'," he concluded, gesturing around the vast rock platform. "Some kind of incredibly ancient observatory, far older than Stonehenge maybe."

Boris nodded slowly, his gaze sweeping over the rock plateau with a familiarity born of long experience, his eyes lingering on the 'eye' formation. "Could be. My grandfather, his father before him... they knew stories. The old ones, the ones before the Thracians even... they knew things about the stars, about the earth, things we've forgotten. There's a local story, one the fancy professors down in the city always laugh at, of course..." He lowered his voice slightly, glancing around as if the rocks themselves might be listening. "They say that on certain nights, special nights when the moon is dark and the stars are just right. Maybe the solstice, or when Lyra is highest. This whole rock up here... it *shines*." Not reflected light, but like the stone itself gathers starlight, drinks it in. Some say the 'eye' formation reflects the heavens then like a perfect mirror, showing visions... things hidden from the normal world."

"Reflects the heavens... gathers starlight..." Leo murmured, his eyes gleaming, his mind racing. "A mirror of starlight... Boris, could the 'stone' be literal after all? Not the entire platform, but something *on* it? Or hidden *in* it? Something that collects or focuses the starlight aligned by those holes?"

Just as the implication of Boris's words began to sink in, a faint but distinct sound drifted up from the valley below, cutting through the high mountain silence. The unmistakable sound of straining vehicle engines, multiple engines, laboring up the rough track towards the sanctuary.

Sera tensed instantly, her head snapping up, her gaze locking onto the access track far below. "Trouble," she stated, her voice low and urgent, all trace of academic curiosity vanishing, replaced by cold, hard readiness. "And lots of it."

The sound grew rapidly louder, echoing off the surrounding rocks, amplifying in the clear mountain air. Dust plumes rose from the track below, visible now even from their high vantage point. Two... no, three black Ladas were speeding towards Belintash, bouncing violently over the uneven ground, kicking up stones. Orlov hadn't given up. He hadn't been delayed for long. He'd called in reinforcements, and they were heavily armed.

"They're here," Sera declared flatly, pulling her Makarov from its holster, the metallic click loud in the sudden tension. "And they brought friends."

Boris hefted his shotgun, checking the breach. "Looks like the welcoming party's starting early."

"We need to get off this plateau!" Leo urged, his earlier awe replaced by rising panic, scanning the surrounding cliffs desperately. "Is there another way down? A hidden path? Quickly!"

Boris nodded grimly towards the far side of the rock platform, away from the approaching track and the main ascent path. "There's an old shepherd's trail over there," he said, pointing towards a barely discernible notch in the cliff edge. "Starts steep, gets dangerous further down, easy to miss if you don't know exactly where it is. Might be our only chance to lose them in the rocks and forest below."

Just then, the first Lada screeched to a halt in a cloud of dust at the base of the main path leading up onto the rock sanctuary. Doors flew open, and Orlov emerged, flanked by several heavily armed soldiers in drab Bulgarian army fatigues, their AK-74s held at the ready. He looked furious, his movements stiff, his eyes burned with cold, obsessive determination as he spotted them silhouetted against the sky on the high plateau.

"Move!" Sera commanded, grabbing Leo's arm and pulling him towards the far edge of the plateau where Boris was already heading for the hidden trail.

Orlov raised his hand, barking orders in sharp Russian. His men began spreading out, fanning across the base of the rocks, starting their ascent, weapons raised and ready.

The chase was on again, this time on sacred ground.

Chapter Thirteen

Cornered on Sacred Ground

"Go!" Sera yelled again, her voice sharp, cutting through the sudden tension, giving Leo a firm shove towards the narrow fissure in the rock face that Boris had indicated was the start of the perilous shepherd's path. "Boris, get him moving! Don't wait for me!"

As Leo stumbled onto the treacherous trail, his feet scrambling for purchase on the loose scree, followed closely by the shotgun-wielding Boris who gave him a rough, encouraging push forward, Sera spun back towards their rapidly advancing pursuers. Orlov and his uniformed soldiers were already scrambling onto the main rock platform, spreading out efficiently, weapons glinting menacingly in the late afternoon sun. There was no time for finesse, no chance for subtlety now. This was about survival.

Sera dropped instantly into a low crouch behind a jagged, weathered boulder that offered minimal cover, the rough stone biting painfully into her knees through her thin trousers. She brought her Makarov up smoothly in a two-handed grip, steadying her breathing despite the adrenaline flooding her system. She sighted down the barrel, acquiring the lead soldier as he clambered awkwardly over a rock ledge, exposing himself for a split second. She squeezed off two quick, controlled shots. The silenced *phut-phut* was almost lost in the wind, but the impact was immediate. The soldier yelped, clutching his shoulder as he stumbled backward with a surprised cry, momentarily disrupting the disciplined advance of the soldier behind him.

Return fire erupted immediately. The angry, distinctive cracks of multiple AK-74s echoing sharply off the ancient stones, the sound shockingly loud after the plateau's deep silence. Chips of rock exploded near Sera's head with violent force, spraying her with stone dust and forcing her to duck lower behind the inadequate cover of the boulder. Bullets whined past like angry hornets, ricocheting wildly off the hard rock surfaces in unpredictable directions.

"Keep moving, Leo!" she shouted back towards the cliff edge, hoping her voice sounded calmer than she felt, hoping he couldn't hear the fear trying to claw its way up her own throat. Fear was a luxury she couldn't afford right now; it dulled reflexes, caused mistakes. *Focus*, she told herself. *Isolate targets. Create openings.*

Using the uneven terrain of the rock sanctuary, the scattered boulders, the shallow depressions, the sudden changes in elevation to her advantage, Sera shifted position rapidly, rolling behind another cluster of weathered stones, bullets kicking up dust where she had been a second before. She popped up just long enough, exposing herself minimally, to fire again, two more shots aimed at center mass, forcing two more soldiers advancing up the main path to dive frantically for cover behind smaller rocks, momentarily halting their progress. Orlov himself had taken position behind a larger, table-like rock formation further back. From there he directed his remaining men, his voice sharp with Russian commands. Bullets flew around him, but he seemed unfazed. She noted with grudging respect how he gestured decisively, barking orders with practiced authority. The man was experienced. Disciplined. Driven by something beyond mere duty.

Sera needed to break their formation completely, create chaos, buy Leo and Boris more time on that treacherous path below. Faking a retreat towards the opposite side of the plateau, she scrambled backwards, deliberately drawing their fire towards a different section. Two of Orlov's soldiers took the bait. Younger men, less experienced, eager to impress their Colonel. They surged forward from cover, trying to outflank her perceived position, rifles spitting short bursts. A classic, but often fatal, mistake.

Sera burst from behind a low stone outcrop where she'd actually taken cover, catching them completely exposed on the open rock face, silhouetted against the sky. Two precise shots from the Makarov. Two solid hits, center mass. The soldiers crumpled without a sound, collapsing onto the ancient stone like puppets with their strings abruptly cut. That left Orlov and only one remaining conscious soldier, who now looked considerably less confident, his eyes wide as he glanced nervously between Sera and his downed comrades.

Orlov's face, previously a mask of cold command, twisted into sheer fury. He emerged from behind his cover, ignoring the potential danger, his service pistol held low and steady in his right hand, advancing deliberately, almost suicidally, towards Sera's position, limping heavily but his movements filled with menace. The remaining soldier moved cautiously, scrambling to Orlov's right, rifle raised, trying to create a crossfire, clearly reluctant but obeying his Colonel's unspoken command.

Sera knew she couldn't win a protracted shootout against a rifle at this range, especially with her escape route narrowing. She was outnumbered, technically outgunned, and her backup was currently occupied trying not to fall off a cliff. She needed to end this fast, decisively.

With a sudden, explosive burst of speed she hadn't known she still possessed after the long chase and the tension, she didn't retreat. She charged *towards* Orlov, firing her Makarov on the run. Her shots went wide, kicking up stone chips near his feet, but the sheer audacity of the move, the unexpected aggression, made Orlov instinctively hesitate for a critical fraction of a second. She closed the distance rapidly, ignoring the pistol now aimed directly at her chest, and pivoted, delivering a vicious, disabling side-kick to Orlov's knee.

Bone crunched audibly over the wind. Orlov roared, a raw sound of agony and surprise, his pistol clattering away onto the rock as his leg buckled completely beneath him, sending him sprawling onto the unforgiving stone surface, his face contorted.

CORNERED ON SACRED GROUND   155

The last soldier, startled by Sera's charge and Orlov's sudden collapse, swung his AK-74 around, trying to track her sudden, close-quarters movement. No time to aim her own weapon, no room to maneuver. Sera's hand closed around a loose chunk of heavy granite lying conveniently near her feet. Fist-sized, jagged, ancient. With a grunt of desperate effort, she hurled it underhand with all her strength. The rock spun end over end, catching the soldier squarely on the side of the head, just above the temple, with a sickening, hollow thud. His eyes rolled back in his head, and he collapsed, rifle clattering beside him, unconscious before he hit the ground.

Silence descended abruptly, broken only by the whistling wind and Orlov's harsh, pain-filled gasps. He was already pushing himself up, ignoring the shattered knee, his face contorted in agony and pure hatred, reaching with his good hand for his dropped pistol lying just out of reach. Sera didn't give him the chance to recover it. She lunged forward just as he lunged clumsily towards the weapon. Sidestepping his desperate, pain-fueled grab, she fluidly reversed her Makarov in her grip and brought the heavy steel butt down hard against the side of Orlov's head with brutal, focused force.

He staggered back, a guttural cry tearing from his throat, his hand flying instinctively to his face. Dark, arterial blood seeped instantly between his fingers. Sera froze for a split second, seeing the horrifying extent of the damage her blow had inflicted. It wasn't just a knockout blow. Where his left eye should have been, there was only a mangled, bloody ruin. The impact had been devastating, irreparable.

A wave of bile rose in her throat, hot and acrid, quickly suppressed by years of training and the immediate need for survival. No time for reaction, no time for regret. Despite the grim satisfaction of neutralizing the immediate threat, she knew reinforcements wouldn't be far behind; Orlov wouldn't have come with just these men.

"Leo! Boris!" she yelled, her voice hoarse, turning and scrambling desperately towards the cliff edge where the hidden shepherd's path began. She found them maybe twenty feet down the treacherous trail, Leo pale-faced and wide-eyed, clinging to the rock face, Boris steadying him on the narrow, crumbling ledge.

"What happened up there?" Leo asked, his voice shaky, seeing the blood spatters on Sera's jacket.

"Orlov's out of commission. Permanently, maybe," Sera replied grimly, deliberately omitting the gruesome details. The image of Orlov's ruined eye was burned into her mind, an unwelcome addition to her collection of violent memories. "Let's *move*. Now! Before more company arrives!"

The shepherd's path was barely a path at all, more like a series of precarious, crumbling footholds winding steeply down the sheer rock face. Shale fragments shifted treacherously under every step, threatening to send them plummeting into the forested gorge hundreds of feet below.

Boris led the way, his bulk surprisingly nimble, his knowledge of the terrain their only lifeline, pointing out loose rocks and safer places to grip with terse grunts. Sera brought up the rear, fatigue trembling through her muscles with each careful step down, constantly glancing back up towards the plateau, expecting more soldiers to appear silhouetted against the sky at any second.

After twenty minutes of heart-stopping, leg-trembling descent that felt like hours, Boris stopped abruptly just below a dense overhang. He reached out, pushing aside a thick curtain of ancient, gnarled ivy clinging tenaciously to the rock face beside the barely discernible trail.

"Hold on," he muttered, peering into the absolute darkness behind the leaves. "That's... strange. Never noticed this before."

Hidden behind the ivy was a narrow fissure in the rock, barely shoulder-width, almost perfectly concealed from anyone not specifically searching for it. It looked like a natural crack, perhaps widened by water erosion over centuries, but there was something about the way the edges were subtly worn smooth, almost polished in places, that suggested it might be more than that. It clearly led somewhere...deep into the blackness within the mountain.

"What is it?" Leo asked, breathless, his academic curiosity momentarily overcoming his fear as he craned his neck to see past Boris.

Boris shrugged, his expression puzzled, running a hand over the smooth rock edge. "Could be an old mine shaft, maybe Thracian silver prospectors. Or maybe... a tomb entrance? Hard to say. Like I said, I've scrambled all over these slopes since I was a boy, never seen this opening before."

Sera approached cautiously, pulling out her heavy-duty flashlight again and shining its powerful beam into the fissure. The beam seemed to be swallowed by darkness after only a few feet, revealing nothing but damp, black rock descending steeply. A draft of cool, slightly metallic-smelling air flowed out, carrying the faint scent of deep earth and something else... something indefinably ancient and still.

"The 'hidden eye'... maybe it wasn't the rock formation on the plateau," Leo whispered, his voice filled with sudden, dawning excitement, connecting the dots. "Maybe it was *this*? A hidden entrance? Leading to the 'stone that sees the stars'?"

Sera considered their rapidly diminishing options. Going further down the exposed shepherd's path felt like suicide; Orlov's reinforcements, alerted by the gunfire or lack of radio contact, could already be swarming the area above and below. Staying put was impossible. This hidden passage... it was a huge, unknown risk, plunging them blind into the mountain's depths, but it might be their only chance of evasion.

"Orlov's friends won't take long to find that shepherd's trail," she stated decisively, her tactical mind made up, nodding towards the fissure. "They'll expect us to continue down the trail. This is passage is unexpected and might be our best bet. Let's see where it goes."

Boris, trusting his mountain instincts over logic, nodded grimly and squeezed his considerable bulk into the narrow opening first, disappearing into the blackness. Sera followed immediately, her flashlight beam cutting into the oppressive darkness, her pistol held ready. Leo took one last, nervous glance back up the cliff face towards the silent plateau above, then took a deep breath and plunged into the fissure after them. The sunlit, dangerous world disappeared behind him as he descended into the unknown depths within Belintash.

Chapter Fourteen

Into the Mountain's Heart

The air inside the hidden passage was instantly cooler, heavier, pressing in on them after the sun-warmed, wind-swept air of the plateau. It smelled ancient, primal. Damp stone and ancient, packed earth filled the air with mineral scents. But there was something else, a faint acidity that made Leo's throat prickle. Old blood, maybe. Or deep ore veins that had never seen sunlight. Boris, moving with surprising agility for his considerable size, located a cleverly disguised section of the thick ivy curtain near the entrance and carefully pulled it back into place, plunging them into near-total darkness. The faint sounds of the wind whistling over the plateau above were instantly muffled, replaced by an echoing, subterranean silence and the faint rustle as Boris concealed their entry point from anyone following the now-exposed shepherd's path below.

"Not many know this way," Boris whispered again, his voice hushed and distorted, echoing strangely in the confined space, making Leo jump slightly despite himself. "Old shepherds, maybe, used it to shelter from sudden mountain storms generations ago. Mostly, it's forgotten now, swallowed by legend, part of the mountain's deeper secrets. Be careful where you step; the footing can be treacherous, slick with seepage."

Sera nodded grimly, clicking on her heavy-duty flashlight without a word. Its powerful, focused beam sliced through the oppressive blackness, revealing a narrow, rough-hewn passage descending steeply into the mountain's heart. The walls weren't smoothly carved but looked almost clawed out of the rock, though centuries of water seepage had smoothed some edges. They moved in single file. Sera took point, her light dancing ahead, probing shadows and checking the uneven floor. Leo followed close behind, avoiding the slick, weeping walls that felt unnaturally cold. Boris brought up the rear, shotgun ready, his bulk filling the narrow passage. Water trickled down the rock face in places, the steady *drip-drip-drip* sound echoing eerily in the profound quiet, amplifying the sense of isolation and descent into the unknown, into the literal bowels of the earth.

Leo ran a gloved hand along the cold stone wall, his earlier fear momentarily eclipsed by the thrill of discovery, the palpable sense of stepping into utterly untouched history. "Incredible," he breathed, his voice barely a whisper but still sounding loud in the confined space. "This feels... untouched. Like stepping back thousands, maybe tens of thousands of years into the mountain's core."

"Eyes open, Leo," Sera cautioned, her voice low but sharp, cutting through his academic reverie. Her own flashlight beam methodically swept the path ahead, checking the low ceiling for loose rock formations and the floor for sudden drops or pitfalls. Her Makarov pistol was still held ready at her side, clutched loosely but prepared for instant action. "We don't know what we're walking into down here. Or who else might have used this passage over the centuries."

The passage followed natural fault lines in the rock, twisting unpredictably through the stone. It widened occasionally into damp alcoves where pale, sightless spiders clung to the walls. Then it would narrow again, forcing them sideways, their clothes scraping against cold rock. Several minutes of silent progress brought them deeper, their breathing and dripping water the only sounds. Then the tunnel opened abruptly into a small, circular chamber. The air was less damp here but still carried that metallic scent. Sera played her flashlight across the walls and stopped. Primitive carvings covered every surface from floor to ceiling, intricate and surprisingly well-preserved.

"Look!" Leo exclaimed, stepping forward eagerly past Sera, his voice filled with unsuppressed awe as he brought his own smaller flashlight beam to bear on the nearest wall, illuminating the dense patterns. "These symbols... they're Thracian, certainly, related to motifs at Tatul, but cruder, much older somehow. Maybe pre-Thracian? Neolithic, even? The style is so raw... so powerful..."

The carvings depicted strange, elongated, almost skeletal figures with stylized suns or stars for heads, dancing under complex patterns of constellations and crescent moons. There were intricate geometric shapes. Spirals, concentric circles, meanders, labyrinthine patterns. Interwoven with what looked like depictions of shamanistic rituals or sacrifices involving animals (bulls, stags, serpents) and celestial bodies. It was a raw, visceral art, utterly alien in its worldview yet echoing motifs found across ancient Europe, hinting at shared, deeply buried beliefs about cosmic power and earth energy. The detail was astonishing, preserved perfectly by the stable underground environment.

Boris, who had remained quiet, observing Leo's excitement with a neutral, almost bored expression, pointed a thick finger towards one prominent carving near the center of the chamber wall. A large solar disc with dozens of rays emanating outwards towards small, kneeling figures making offerings. "The sun," he stated, his voice unusually subdued, hushed in this enclosed space. "They worshipped the sun god here, long, long ago. Or maybe the sun was just a symbol for... something else. My grandfather used to say places like this... deep in the rock... they feel holy. But a dangerous kind of holy. Powerful."

As Leo began to examine the carvings more closely, running a gloved finger gently over the deep grooves, tracing the lines, Sera's more practical gaze swept the chamber methodically. She noted the chamber's size, the single entrance they'd used, and then spotted a darker shadow against the far wall, almost lost in the uneven contours of the rock. Another opening, much narrower than the one they'd entered through, looking barely wide enough for a man to squeeze through. She moved towards it cautiously, shining her light inside.

"Another passage here," she reported back quietly, her voice tight with readiness. "This one seems to go down, steeply. Can't see where it leads."

Before they could investigate further, Leo let out a small gasp of discovery. He gestured towards a large, flat stone set almost perfectly into the center of the chamber floor, directly beneath the prominent sun carving on the wall above. The stone was unnaturally smooth, clearly polished by time or human intention, and carved deeply into its center was a single, stylized eye, remarkably similar in design to the large oval formation they'd seen on the plateau above.

"The 'hidden eye'," Leo whispered, excitement making his voice tremble as he knelt beside the stone. "I think *this* is what the prophecy meant. Not the formation outside, but this symbol, marking the true way forward." He looked around the chamber, at the dead-end passage they hadn't taken, at the narrow one Sera had found. "This marks the path... But where's the 'stone that sees the stars'? It must be further in."

As if summoned by his words, Boris, who had moved silently closer to the narrow, downward-sloping passage Sera had found, let out a low whistle of astonishment. A faint, almost ethereal blue glimmer emanated from the opening, casting strange reflections in his wide eyes as he peered down into the darkness below.

"Down there," Boris breathed, his voice hushed with a mixture of wonder and apprehension. He squinted into the darkness below. "*Svetlina*... light... I think... I think I see it. Something's glowing."

The passage beyond was steeper than it looked, descending sharply into the mountain's deeper depths, the staleness in the air growing stronger. Sera went first without hesitation, her powerful flashlight beam probing the darkness below, checking the precarious footing, her pistol held ready. Leo followed close behind, his heart pounding with anticipation, excitement warring with a deep sense of foreboding. Boris carefully brought up the rear, his shotgun awkward in the tight space. The air grew noticeably colder as they descended, and the faint blue glimmer grew steadily stronger, resolving into a soft, pulsing light source somewhere far below and ahead.

Finally, after another ten minutes of careful descent down the narrow, winding passage, it opened abruptly into a much larger cavern. It wasn't vast like some natural caves, but it felt significant, ancient, the air utterly still and heavy with unspoken energy. And in the exact center of the smooth, dark stone floor, resting on a natural pedestal of rock that seemed to have been deliberately shaped and smoothed, was an object that stole their breath away.

It was a perfect sphere, perhaps ten inches in diameter, crafted from what looked like flawless, jet-black obsidian. Its surface was polished to a mirror finish, reflecting the beams of their flashlights in distorted, swirling patterns, making the cavern seem to warp around it. It seemed to drink the surrounding darkness, absorbing the light, yet at the same time, it radiated a faint, inner luminescence of its own. A pulsing, deep blue light, like a captured star, that seemed to emanate from its very core. It felt ancient beyond comprehension, powerful in a way that defied explanation, and utterly, disturbingly alien.

"The stone that sees the stars," Leo whispered, his voice barely audible, filled with a profound reverence that bordered on fear. He moved involuntary closer, captivated, reaching out a trembling hand as if drawn by an unseen force, needing to confirm its reality.

***

Miles above, on the windswept surface of Belintash, Colonel Gregor Orlov clawed his way back from a vortex of searing agony. The world was a blinding, nauseating blur; the place where his left eye *had been* pulsed with a white-hot torment that threatened to shatter his disciplined mind. He felt fumbling hands – a field medic, his own shaking with fear.

"The trauma kit! Stim-pack! *Now!*" Orlov's command was a raw rasp, barely more than a snarl. He shoved the medic's clumsy attempt to apply a fresh bandage away from the ruined socket, his face a mask of contorted fury and agonizing humiliation. The American agent... Volkov... she would endure a universe of suffering for this. But first, the prize. He *would not* be denied.

INTO THE MOUNTAIN'S HEART

The sharp sting of a high-dose syrette rammed into his thigh cut through the pain like a scalpel, a jolt of chemical fire that brought a brittle, hyper-alert clarity. Adrenaline surged, a welcome tide chasing back the encroaching darkness. He gripped the edge of a makeshift command table – a map case unfolded across two ammunition boxes near the parked Ladas – and dragged himself upright. Waves of dizziness still threatened to pull him under, but his iron will, now supercharged by the combat drug and a volcanic rage, held them at bay. His mission. Volkov. The sphere.

His remaining men were scrambling, disorganized, their discipline fractured by the brief, brutal firefight and the quarry's vanishing act over the cliff edge.

"Report!" Orlov snarled, the word tearing from his throat. He fixed his one good eye on a subordinate officer hovering nervously nearby, the man visibly intimidated by his Colonel's mangled appearance and the raw, simmering rage radiating from him.

"Comrade Colonel," the officer stammered, his gaze skittering away from Orlov's bloodied bandage, "Units Three and Four are securing the plateau perimeter, as ordered. Unit Two... they attempted the shepherd's path. It is dangerously unstable, Comrade Colonel. A treacherous descent. No visual contact with the targets below."

"Fools! Incompetents!" Orlov slammed his fist onto the map case, a fresh wave of agony lancing through his head, which he brutally suppressed. "They didn't simply evaporate! They found another way – down, or *in*! That hidden passage the peasant tracker spoke of... Search the cliff face where Volkov staged her ambush! Every crack, every fissure! I want them found!"

He paused, taking a ragged, deliberate breath that shuddered through his battered frame, the stimulants fighting a losing battle against the true extent of his injuries, but his resolve was a shield of ice. His gaze, sharp and chilling, pinned the subordinate officer. "Bring them to me. *Alive.* I need to know what they've discovered down there, before they meet their... inevitable and instructive end."

Despite the grievous wound that would have crippled a lesser man, Colonel Orlov's fanaticism burned brighter, hardened by the pain and the fury of near-defeat. He would regroup. He would adapt. He would reclaim the initiative. The meddling Americans and their local accomplice would not escape him. The obsidian sphere, the key to unimaginable power, was close. He could almost feel its energy pulsing from deep within the mountain like a siren call. And he would drag himself through the very bowels of the earth if necessary to claim it for the Soviet Union, and for the glory he knew awaited.

***

Back in the hidden cavern, deep within the mountain, Leo's trembling fingers brushed against the obsidian sphere's impossibly smooth, cool surface. A faint, almost electric hum seemed to vibrate up his arm, a tangible connection to something ancient, powerful, and utterly unknown. They had found it. The stone that sees the stars. But standing here, in its silent, pulsing presence, a profound sense of foreboding mingled with the thrill of discovery in Leo's mind. This felt less like an ending and more like the beginning of something far more profound, and perhaps, far more dangerous than any of them could comprehend.

Chapter Fifteen

The Awakening Sphere

The instant Leo's trembling fingers brushed against the obsidian sphere's impossibly smooth, cool surface, the cavern changed profoundly. A low, resonant hum filled the air, escalating rapidly, vibrating not just in their ears but deep in their chests, a physical pressure against their sternums that felt like a giant heartbeat awakening within the mountain. The faint blue light pulsing lazily within the sphere intensified dramatically, flaring outwards like a miniature blue sun igniting in the subterranean darkness. Lines of pure energy, like captured lightning rendered in impossible blues, violets, and flickers of white, began to trace intricate, complex geometric patterns across the sphere's polished surface. Patterns Leo instantly recognized mirrored the strange, ancient carvings he'd seen on the chamber walls back up the passage, but now alive, moving, shifting. The sphere wasn't reflecting their flashlights anymore; it was generating its own brilliant, otherworldly light, a light that felt ancient and startlingly potent.

"Leo, get back from that thing!" Sera commanded sharply, instinctively taking a step back herself and raising her

Makarov, her knuckles white, her training screaming at her about uncontrolled energy sources. Boris muttered a hasty prayer in Bulgarian behind her, crossing himself rapidly, his eyes wide with superstitious awe.

But Leo couldn't move, couldn't breathe, rooted to the spot, utterly mesmerized. The light emanating from the sphere wasn't harsh or blinding.t was a deep, celestial blue, intense yet strangely beautiful, humming with barely contained power that felt both terrifyingly ancient and impossibly advanced. It sang in his bones. The strange carvings etched into the cavern walls themselves responded to the sphere's awakening, glowing softly with the same ethereal blue light, lines of energy connecting distant symbols, turning the dark, hidden chamber into a breathtaking, almost sacred space filled with shifting constellations of light and shadow. It felt like standing inside a living star map, the air thrumming with tangible potential, the very rock seeming to hold its breath.

"Incredible..." Leo breathed, oblivious to the potential danger, his academic mind overwhelmed by the sheer wonder of the discovery. He felt a strange pull, a sense of connection to the sphere, almost as if it recognized him, or the knowledge he carried. "It's... it's responding... activating..."

As they stared, captivated and momentarily paralyzed by the spectacle, Leo felt wonder while Sera and Boris felt wary apprehension. Boris shifted his weight nervously near the passage entrance. The shifting, hypnotic light made him uneasy. His heavy boot caught on a loose flagstone embedded in the cavern floor, a stone that looked no different from any other. A distinct mechanical *click* echoed sharply through the chamber, loud and incongruously mundane amidst the resonant hum of ancient power.

With a low grinding sound that vibrated through the floor, startlingly smooth for something presumably untouched for millennia, a section of the cavern wall directly behind the sphere's pedestal slid silently, seamlessly inwards, revealing a hidden alcove bathed in a soft, internally generated white light. An image shimmered into existence on the smooth stone at the back of the alcove. A map, projected with startling clarity and detail.

It wasn't a map of Bulgaria, or even the Balkans. This map depicted the familiar, unmistakable basin of the Mediterranean Sea, its coastlines rendered in fine, glowing blue lines against the dark stone. Major landmasses were outlined, but details were sparse, except for one location. Pulsing brightly upon the projected map, like a beacon in the darkness, pinpointed by a narrow beam of soft blue light now emanating steadily from the obsidian sphere itself, was the island of Crete. Below this glowing point, seemingly drawn from the same light source, ancient Greek letters formed, sharp and clear as if freshly carved: **ΛΑΒΥΡΙΝΘΟΣ**.

Labyrinthos. The Labyrinth.

"Crete?" Leo whispered, his voice choked with disbelief, his mind reeling, trying to reconcile the impossible image before him with millennia of myth and academic debate. "The Labyrinth? Minos... the Minotaur... Daedalus... the heart of Minoan civilization... But those are legends... stories... Aren't they?" His academic skepticism battled with the undeniable reality of the glowing map pointing the way.

"Looks less like legend and more like precise directions now, Professor," Sera cut in grimly, her training kicking back in, her eyes narrowed, her focus snapping instantly back to tactical reality. She took a mental snapshot, memorizing the projected image and Crete's location relative to other landmarks. The light show was already beginning to fade, having delivered its core message. The map flickered, the carvings on the walls lost their ethereal glow, the resonant hum lessened, stepping down to a low hum, as if the device, having shown them the next step on their perilous journey, was now returning to a state of watchful standby.

Harsh shouts erupted from the passage they'd entered through. Running footsteps echoed closer, growing louder. Flashlight beams stabbed into the cavern, cutting violently through the fading blue glow and blinding them. "They're in here! Spread out! Find them!" It was Orlov's voice, raw with fury and undeniable pain, amplified by the cavern acoustics, much closer than they'd dared to imagine. He'd found them, navigating the hidden passages with ruthless speed, his reinforcements right behind him, undeterred by the earlier confrontation on the plateau.

"They're right behind us!" Boris exclaimed, his face paling, hefting his shotgun automatically, the heavy *thump* of the weapon reassuring in the sudden return of imminent threat. "Time to go! Back the way we came. Quickly!" Sera made the decision instantly, grabbing Leo's arm and pulling him away from the pedestal. The map projection was already vanishing. Their next destination was Crete, the Labyrinth, but that knowledge meant nothing if they didn't survive the next five minutes. Escape first, analysis later.

Orlov, the crude bandage hastily wrapped around his head partially covering his ruined eye socket, burst into the chamber, his remaining eye blazing with manic energy and possessive fury. He was flanked by the handful of soldiers who had survived the earlier confrontation on the plateau, their faces grim, their AK-74s held at the ready, sweeping the cavern. Their flashlight beams swept the chamber, momentarily fixing on the glowing obsidian sphere and the open, now-darkening map alcove. They paused for only a split second, clearly stunned by the implications, but it was the head start Leo, Sera, and Boris desperately needed.

They scrambled back into the narrow, descending passage they'd emerged from minutes earlier, Boris taking the lead again, his bulk surprisingly agile in the tight space, his knowledge of the tunnels their only hope in the oppressive darkness. Gunfire erupted behind them almost immediately. Orlov's men weren't hesitating this time, orders likely overriding any awe or caution they might have felt. Bullets sparked angrily off the stone walls inches from their heads, ricocheting wildly down the narrow corridor with terrifying velocity, the sharp cracks echoing deafeningly in the confined space like cannon fire. Chips of rock rained down, stinging their faces and hands.

The passage twisted and turned, a confusing, natural maze leading ever deeper into the mountain. Sera brought up the rear, pausing occasionally at turns, bracing herself against the rock, to fire a few carefully aimed shots back towards their pursuers' bouncing flashlight beams, not aiming to kill but to slow them down, forcing them to take cover, buying Leo and Boris precious seconds. The air quickly filled with choking dust raised by the bullet impacts and the sharp, acrid smell of cordite, burning their throats and making their eyes water.

"There! Another way!" Boris yelled over the din of gunfire and ricochets, his voice strained, pointing towards a small, easily missed opening low down on the tunnel wall ahead, partially hidden by a curtain of pale, dripping stalactites that looked like stone icicles. "This looks different! Newer maybe? Might lead back towards the other side of the mountain, closer to where we came down!"

Sera didn't question him. She squeezed through the narrow opening first, emerging onto a steep, rocky slope in what seemed to be a different cave network. Wider passages, damper air, heavy with the smell of sulfur and mineral deposits. Mercifully quiet for now. Leo tumbled through after her, face grime-streaked but determined, clutching his satchel protectively. Boris emerged last and quickly pulled loose rocks down to partially obscure the opening, just as Orlov's men reached the junction behind them.

"They went this way!" Orlov's distinctive voice boomed from the darkness behind the makeshift rockfall, filled with rage. "After them! Don't let them escape! I want that sphere!" The sounds of them starting to clear the opening followed, punctuated by angry curses in Russian.

Leo, Sera, and Boris half-slid, half-ran down the rocky slope, the sounds of renewed pursuit echoing from the tunnel opening above and behind them, closer now. They plunged into a bizarre section of dense underground forest. Not trees, but thickets of strange, pale, faintly bioluminescent fungi clinging thickly to the walls and floor, some reaching shoulder height, nourished by unseen water sources, casting a faint, sickly green, underwater-like glow. They used the strange, rubbery growths and towering, moisture-slick rock pillars as cover, stumbling over unseen roots and slick patches of mossy stone. The terrain was treacherous, uneven, and visibility was limited to the bouncing beams of their flashlights cutting through the faint fungal glow and the oppressive darkness. Adrenaline, raw and potent, was the only thing keeping them moving forward into the unknown depths.

They could hear Orlov's men crashing through the subterranean landscape behind them, their heavier boots slipping on the slick surfaces, their shouts getting closer again, echoing strangely in the fungus-dampened, enclosed space. Sera knew they couldn't keep running like this; they were losing ground on this difficult, alien terrain, and her injured leg was screaming in protest, threatening to buckle. They needed to create a real diversion, something significant to buy them more time, maybe even block the pursuit entirely.

"Boris," Sera panted, stopping for a second behind a thick, slimy fungal pillar, scanning their surroundings rapidly in the bouncing beams of their flashlights, assessing angles and structural weaknesses. "These tunnels...are they stable *here*? This whole place feels ready to collapse."

Boris glanced up at the low ceiling, visible between the grotesque fungal growths, covered in ominous-looking cracks and loose, dripping rock formations, some heavy with calcite deposits. "Mostly," he grunted, catching his breath, wiping sweat and grime from his face. "But some parts... not so much. This section feels... *heavy*. Like it's holding its breath. Why?"

Sera pointed her flashlight beam upwards, towards a section of the ceiling directly above the narrowest part of the path their pursuers would *have* to take to follow them. A precarious-looking overhang heavy with loose rocks, debris, and large chunks of crystalline calcite. "Think we can bring that down?"

Boris's eyes followed her gesture. He peered up, assessing the tons of rock hanging above the chokepoint. A slow, grim smile spread across his face, visible even in the dim green light, showing stained teeth. "With the right encouragement?" he replied, his voice a low growl of destructive enthusiasm. "*Da*. Definitely. Give the bastards a Bulgarian welcome."

Chapter Sixteen

Descent into Chaos

"Right, let's give them something to remember us by," Boris growled, determination hardening his features. He immediately began scrambling nimbly up the slippery slope towards the base of the precarious rock overhang Sera had identified, his earlier exhaustion seemingly vanished, replaced by focused, destructive energy. Sera was right behind him, moving with surprising speed despite the throbbing pain in her injured leg. Adrenaline was a powerful, if temporary, anesthetic. Leo stayed low near the entrance to the next narrow fissure, covering their rear with his small flashlight, his beam nervously probing the darkness back the way they'd come, listening hard for the tell-tale sounds of pursuit. Scrambling boots, muffled curses. Over the frantic pounding of his own heart.

The shouts of Orlov's men were definitely getting closer now, echoing eerily through the strange subterranean forest of glowing fungi. Their flashlight beams danced through the pale, ghostly growths just a hundred yards back. They didn't have much time before their pursuers reached this chokepoint.

Boris ran expert, calloused hands over the base of the massive rock formation supporting the overhang, testing for weaknesses. "See here?" he directed, pointing his flashlight beam towards a series of deep, natural cracks near the bottom, almost hidden by fungal growth. "Natural fault line. Runs right through this section, which looks ready to go. If we can dislodge this big wedge-boulder here... should trigger the whole damn thing."

Sera assessed the situation quickly, her tactical mind calculating angles and potential impact zones. The overhang was massive. Easily dozens of tons of rock, ancient debris, and thick slabs of fungal growth held precariously in place only by the geometry of the lower boulders. Bringing it down wouldn't be easy, or quiet, but the potential payoff was worth the risk. Blocking the passage completely, buying them significant time. She spotted several large, loose-looking boulders near the base, seemingly wedged just tightly enough to provide the key structural support. "Those look like the keystones," she confirmed, pointing. "If we can lever those out..."

"My thought exactly," Boris grinned savagely, pulling a sturdy, 24 inch steel pry bar from the canvas pack hanging from his belt loops. Apparently standard, if unofficial, equipment for wandering his treacherous home mountains. "Good old-fashioned physics. Strong back, long lever."

Working together frantically, leveraging Boris's brute strength and Sera's focused energy, they jammed the chisel-end of the pry bar deep into the cracks around the largest wedge-boulder, finding grip against the main rock face. They positioned themselves carefully, needing maximum force but also a clear escape path. The shouts from their pursuers were alarmingly close now; flashlight beams danced wildly through the pale fungal growths only yards away from the entrance to this section of the cave. They could hear boots slipping on the damp rocks, harsh commands echoing clearly now.

"Ready? Heave!" Boris grunted, throwing his considerable weight against the end of the bar. Sera added her own strength, muscles straining, her teeth gritted against the pain in her leg as she pushed alongside him.

Stone scraped loudly against stone, the sound grating and amplified in the enclosed space. The massive boulder shifted, perhaps an inch, maybe less, but it was enough to dislodge a shower of dust and small pebbles from the overhang far above.

"Almost... Again!" Sera urged, repositioning the pry bar slightly for better leverage. "Harder! Now!"

They heaved again, putting every ounce of strength into the effort. This time, the boulder groaned, a deep, protesting sound from within the rock, scraped violently against its neighbors, and then suddenly gave way with a loud *crack*, tumbling ponderously down the slope with a heavy crash that echoed through the cavern like a thunderclap. Almost immediately, a series of deeper, sharper cracking sounds echoed rapidly from high above. The entire overhang shuddered visibly in their flashlight beams. More dust and larger rocks rained down around them.

"It's going! Run!" Sera yelled, grabbing Boris's arm and shoving him hard towards Leo and the fissure escape route.

They scrambled away, slipping and sliding on the damp rock, just as the overhang gave way completely. With a deafening, grinding roar that shook the entire cavern, shaking stalactites loose from the distant ceiling, tons upon tons of rock, ancient debris, and slabs of pale fungi crashed down onto the narrow path below, sending up a massive cloud of thick, choking dust that instantly obscured everything in billowing grey fog. The ground trembled violently beneath their feet as if in a major earthquake, threatening to shake them off balance. The sounds of pursuit abruptly cut off, replaced by panicked, terrified shouts from *behind* the newly formed wall of rubble, followed by an echoing, stunned silence broken only by the rumble of settling rock.

"Think... *cough*... think that'll slow them down?" Leo asked breathlessly, coughing heavily, his lungs burning from the thick, harsh dust that billowed into their escape passage.

"Slow them? It likely buried half of them under several meters of rock," Sera replied grimly, catching her breath, already assessing their next move, wiping layers of dust from her face. "For a while, maybe, it stops them cold. But," she added, her voice hardening, "it also tells anyone else Orlov has exactly where this tunnel system leads, and that we're still alive. Let's not stick around to find out if they have another way around or decide to blast through."

Boris nodded, his face streaked with grime but wearing a look of grim satisfaction at the destruction they'd wrought. "This way. Quick now." He ducked into the narrow fissure they'd spotted earlier. "There's another cave system nearby. Very old. We used it as kids for exploring, telling ghost stories about the *samodivi* – the wood sprites. Twists like a drunken snake, easy to get lost if you don't know it, but I know a way out. Leads towards the surface, other side of the mountain, if the passages haven't collapsed over the years since I was last here."

He led them through the echoing chaos left by the rockfall, the air still thick with choking dust, plunging into the narrow fissure that seemed barely wide enough to squeeze through. This new network of caves was tighter, more confusing, and felt distinctly older, damper than the passages leading into the sphere chamber. They navigated by the bouncing beams of their flashlights, the darkness absolute between the dancing circles of light, relying entirely on Boris's mountain-bred instincts and fading childhood memories. Leo felt completely disoriented, the twisting tunnels making his head spin, trusting blindly as Boris guided them through tight squeezes that scraped their clothes, sharp turns that led into black voids, low-ceilinged crawls over slick mud, and across unseen subterranean streams that gurgled eerily nearby in the pitch darkness. Sera moved behind Leo, occasionally putting a steadying hand on his back, her own movements hampered slightly by her injured leg but still remarkably quiet and alert.

After what felt like an eternity lost in the black, silent depths, navigating by touch as much as sight, feeling the oppressive weight of the mountain above them, they saw a faint grey light filtering from ahead. Fresh air, cool and carrying the damp, clean scent of rain and pine needles, flowed towards them, a welcome relief from the stale, mineral-heavy cave air. With a final scramble over slick, algae-covered rocks, they stumbled out of a concealed opening, hidden almost perfectly behind the thundering, white curtain of a waterfall cascading down a high, moss-covered cliff face into a deep, churning pool below. They were back in the outside world, blinking in the unexpected, diffuse grey daylight of a cloudy afternoon, the roar of the waterfall deafening, effectively covering the sound of their exit.

Boris didn't pause to admire the view or catch his breath. He immediately started moving away from the waterfall at a relentless pace, pushing through dense, dripping undergrowth, leading them into thick forest. For several more miles, he circled back, deliberately crossed streams, used rocky terrain to hide their tracks. Employing all the woodcraft he knew to obscure their trail. Until they finally reached a small, secluded valley hidden deep within the folds of the mountains. Tucked away against the treeline, built into the slope itself and almost invisible until you were right upon it, was a lonely cabin. It was roughly built from unpeeled logs, chinked with mud and moss, but looked sturdy, a thin ribbon of smoke curling faintly from a squat stone chimney, blending into the overcast sky.

"It's not much," Boris said, his voice rough with exhaustion as he pushed open the heavy, creaky wooden door. "My grandfather built it for hunting trips, long ago. Nobody comes up here much now. Too remote. But it's safe. Safer than anywhere else in these mountains right now. We can rest here, get warm, figure out what comes next."

Inside, the cabin was basic but surprisingly clean and dry. A large, crudely built stone fireplace dominated one wall, radiating welcome warmth, a small fire already crackling merrily within its depths. Boris must have had it prepared, or had sent word ahead somehow. A couple of simple wooden cots built into the walls were covered with thick, woven wool blankets, and a rough-hewn table with a few sturdy log stools stood in the center of the single room. Animal pelts hung on the walls, providing insulation and a rustic decoration. Boris immediately moved to the fireplace, adding more wood from a neat stack nearby, while Sera, despite her obvious weariness and the throbbing in her leg, instinctively made a quick circuit outside, checking the perimeter, scanning the treeline, her operational security instincts still on high alert even in this seeming sanctuary.

Leo, feeling utterly drained, his body aching in places he didn't know existed, every muscle screaming from the unaccustomed exertion and terror, simply collapsed onto one of the cots, the rough wool blanket feeling like the finest silk. The adrenaline finally ebbed away, leaving him with bone-deep exhaustion and the chilling memory of the strange energy in the sphere chamber and Orlov's relentless, fanatical pursuit. He closed his eyes, the warmth from the fire slowly seeping into his chilled limbs.

Later, huddled near the crackling fire, wrapped in the thick blankets, they shared a simple but incredibly welcome meal of tough smoked sausage, hard local cheese, dense black bread, and potent plum brandy (*rakia*) that Boris produced from a hidden cache beneath the floorboards. The silence was heavy at first, each lost in their own thoughts, processing the chaos they had survived in the mountain's depths. The crackling fire and the sound of rain beginning to drum softly on the cabin roof were the only sounds.

"So," Leo finally asked, breaking the silence, his voice hoarse, the *rakia* burning a welcome path down his throat. "Crete. The Labyrinth. That's where the map, the sphere... pointed. That's where the prophecy leads next."

Sera nodded, carefully examining the makeshift bandage on her leg in the firelight. Boris had provided some antiseptic herbs and cleaner bandages. It needed proper cleaning and maybe stitches, but it wasn't actively bleeding now. "That map was specific. *Labyrinthos*. Coordinates seemed to point near the center of the island, not Knossos on the coast. That has to be our target."

"Getting there won't be simple," Boris stated grimly, staring into the dancing flames, swirling the potent brandy in his tin cup. "Not with Orlov's people. Assuming some survived that rockfall. Likely turning this whole country upside down looking for you two now. They know you have the sphere. Flying out is impossible; your names will be flagged. Border crossings will be heavily watched, especially heading south towards Greece."

"We'll go overland," Sera decided, her voice firm despite her obvious fatigue and the pain lines around her eyes. "Through Greece is the only viable option. It's slower, riskier in some ways crossing borders on foot or local transport, but potentially easier to blend in than trying to use major airports or ports. From mainland Greece, maybe Thessaloniki or Athens, we can find a ferry to Crete. Disappear into the tourist crowds heading for the islands."

Boris nodded slowly, considering it. "It might work. Risky, but maybe the best chance." Taking a long swallow of *rakia*. "And Crete..." He paused, a thoughtful expression crossing his rugged face. "I have family there. Distant cousin, Nikoss. Good man. Runs a small taverna in Heraklion. He's... resourceful. Knows the island, knows the people. The real people, not just the officials. Knows how to keep quiet, how things work below the surface." He found a scrap of paper and a pencil stub in his worn jacket pocket, carefully writing down a name and an address by the flickering firelight. "Find him. Tell him Boris sent you, tell him... trouble follows you. He'll understand what it means. He can help you find your feet, maybe get supplies, information."

As Boris explained the best, least-watched routes towards the Greek border, pointing out landmarks on Leo's map,

Sera quietly cleaned and re-dressed her leg injury using the supplies Boris provided, her movements economical and efficient despite her obvious discomfort. Leo watched them both, a strange sense of dislocation settling over him again. Just days ago, his biggest worry was a misplaced footnote or a looming lecture. Now, he was hiding out in a remote Bulgarian mountain cabin with a highly trained, lethal spy and a gruff mountain guide who seemed part moonshiner, part resistance fighter, planning a clandestine infiltration of Crete based on a map revealed by an ancient obsidian sphere that pulsed with unknown energy. It was utterly, terrifyingly insane. And yet... a part of him, the part that had always yearned for adventure beyond the library stacks, felt undeniably, frighteningly alive.

Later that evening, after Boris had checked the perimeter one last time before retiring to the other cot, pulling a heavy blanket over his head with a decisive grunt, Leo found himself sitting by the crackling fire, staring into the hypnotic flames. Sera sat opposite him on a low stool, meticulously field-stripping and cleaning her Makarov pistol with practiced, economical ease, the metallic clicks soft but precise in the quiet cabin. The earlier tension between them, the awkwardness born of their vastly different worlds, seemed to have burned away in the crucible of the past few days, replaced by a weary, hard-won familiarity.

"You were... amazing back there, Sera," Leo said quietly, breaking the comfortable silence, the words feeling inadequate. "In the caves... with Orlov's men... And that rocks lide... I honestly don't know how you do it. How you stay so calm."

Sera glanced up from her work, pausing for a moment, her hands still. A faint, tired smile touched her lips, softening her usually guarded expression in the warm firelight. "Part of the job description, Professor," she replied, her voice softer than usual, losing some of its professional edge. "React, adapt, survive. And," she added, the teasing glint returning briefly to her eyes, "somebody has to make sure you don't get yourself killed stumbling over ancient clues or falling off cliffs." There was humor, but underlying it was a grudging, perhaps deepening, respect.

Leo managed a weak smile back, feeling warmth spread through him that had nothing to do with the fire or the *rakia*. "Well, for a historian who'd rather be facing a dusty archive than a KalashNikosv, I suppose I didn't do *too* badly today."

"You did good, Leo," Sera stated, meeting his eyes directly, and this time, the compliment sounded entirely genuine, stripped of any irony. "You figured out the rock eye, you understood the significance of the sphere, you didn't freeze up during the chase. You've got good instincts, Professor, even if you're clumsy as hell sometimes and think too much." She returned her focus to reassembling her weapon, the metallic clicks precise and final.

The atmosphere between them felt different now. Easier, warmer, a silent acknowledgment of their shared ordeal and reliance. A bond forged in adrenaline and shared danger, a mutual dependence that transcended their initial, assigned roles. He was still the brains, she was still the muscle, but maybe, just maybe, they were becoming a real team. He found himself thinking, not for the first time, of Thorne's comment about teamwork, about her being his field partner. It felt less like an assignment now, more like a reality. Like she was the exasperated but fiercely protective older sister he'd never had, and he was the smart, sometimes utterly clueless, little brother she felt compelled to keep out of mortal danger. It was a strange thought, but not an unwelcome one.

They rested at the cabin for two precious days, allowing Sera's leg to begin the initial stages of healing and finalizing their complex travel plans. Leo pored over maps of Greece and Crete, trying to learn everything he could about the island, its history, the geography near Kastelli, and the bewildering mythology surrounding the Labyrinth. Sera seemed to recharge in the enforced quiet, her usual sharp focus returning, her movements becoming less pained, though she still favored the injured leg. Finally, armed with plausible fake Greek identity documents Boris procured from sources unknown ("Old favors," was all he'd say), Nikoss's contact information scribbled on the scrap of paper, and a shared, unspoken determination hardening their features, they prepared to leave the temporary sanctuary of the cabin.

They thanked Boris profusely, trying to express the depth of their gratitude. The gruff mountain man simply waved them off, nodding and wishing them luck with a simple grunt before pressing a small, heavy package of extra sausage and bread into Leo's hands. Watching Boris disappear back into the dense, misty forest, melting into the trees like a spirit of the mountain himself, Leo's chest tightened with genuine regret at leaving their unlikely, dangerous, but undeniably loyal ally behind.

Then, under the cloak of a moonless, starless night, the rain finally stopped, Leo and Sera slipped away from the darkened cabin, heading south on foot through the cold, wet forest, towards the treacherous Green border, towards Greece, towards the ferry, towards Crete, and towards the final, most dangerous stage of their mission to unravel the secrets of the Labyrinth and the Delphi Protocol.

CHAPTER SEVENTEEN

Cretan Sanctuary

The ferry from Piraeus chugged slowly into the bustling, ancient harbour of Heraklion, Crete's largest city, under a sky that seemed impossibly, brilliantly blue after the muted greys they'd left behind in Bulgaria and the misty peaks of Romania. The warm Mediterranean air hit them like a physical embrace as they stood on the crowded deck amongst other passengers gathering their belongings, thick with the complex smells of the sea. Sharp salt spray, diesel fumes from the dozens of colorful fishing boats and larger ferries jockeying for position, the savory aroma of grilled meats and seafood drifting from waterfront tavernas. All mixed with the sweet, heady scent of jasmine hanging heavy from unseen trellises and something else, something green and resinous that Leo guessed was the island's ubiquitous olive trees carried on the breeze. The noise was a vibrant, almost overwhelming cacophony after the strained quiet of their overland journey. Ferry horns blasted deep and resonant, echoing off the massive Venetian fortress walls guarding the harbor entrance. Dockworkers shouted in Greek as they secured thick mooring lines. Vendors called out desperately from the quay, hawking sponges, cheap jewelry, and pistachio nuts. Scooters and battered pickup trucks rattled over nearby cobblestones while snippets of lively Cretan *lyra* music drifted from open cafe doorways. It felt intensely alive, chaotic, colorful, pulsing with a different energy. Freer, perhaps, but no less complex than the places they'd left behind. A world away from the tense quiet of the Bulgarian mountains.

Leo and Sera, clad in the deliberately unremarkable tourist attire they'd acquired during their brief, tense transit through mainland Greece. Faded jeans for Leo, simple cotton trousers for Sera, plain shirts, practical walking shoes, sunglasses firmly in place. Blended easily into the stream of passengers shuffling towards the lowered gangway. Leo squinted in the bright Cretan sunlight, feeling conspicuously pale and out of place next to the sun-browned locals and seasoned European tourists disembarking alongside them, already pulling out cameras. He clutched his worn leather briefcase, now containing not just his notes but the heavy, carefully wrapped weight of the obsidian sphere, feeling a fresh wave of anxiety mixed with a strange, almost electric anticipation. They had made it. Crete. The island of the Labyrinth, the final destination indicated by the sphere's impossible map. Now the real search began.

Sera, dark sunglasses hiding her eyes, moved with her usual quiet alertness, seemingly relaxed but taking in the surroundings with quick, practiced scans. Noting the layout of the port, the position of the casually uniformed Hellenic Police officers observing the disembarking passengers, potential points of surveillance overlooking the busy boardwalk, the flow of traffic leading away from the harbour, the mix of taxis and private cars waiting. Had Orlov's network anticipated their arrival by sea? Were watchers already waiting amongst the taxi drivers, the vendors, the loiterers? Impossible to know for sure, but essential to assume. Her hand never strayed far from the slightly larger, nondescript messenger bag slung across her shoulder, its weight a familiar, necessary burden.

Following the surprisingly accurate, hand-drawn map and directions Boris had painstakingly provided back in the mountain cabin ("Turn left at the fountain with the lions, then third right after the church with the crooked bell to wer..."), they navigated the maze-like streets of Heraklion's old town on foot, deliberately avoiding the wider main thoroughfares. They plunged into a charming, bewildering tangle of narrow alleyways paved with ancient stones. Venetian-era buildings lined the paths, their peeling pastel paint in shades of ochre, faded blue, and dusty rose. Ornate wrought-iron balconies overflowed with bright red geraniums and cascading bougainvillea. The alleyways opened suddenly into small squares shaded by ancient plane trees, where old men argued passionately over politics and games of *tavli* outside bustling *kafenia*. They eventually found the address Boris had given them. A small, traditional taverna tucked away on a quiet side street, blessedly away from the main tourist hustle near the archaeological museum and the Morosini Fountain. Colorful flower boxes, bursting with red and pink blooms, hung from the windowsills above blue-painted shutters, and the inviting aroma of grilled meat, oregano, lemon, roasting garlic, and strong coffee drifted out onto the cobblestones. A simple, hand-painted wooden sign above the bright blue door read "Nikos's Place" in both Greek and slightly faded English letters. It looked welcoming, unassuming, authentic. Exactly the kind of place Boris would have a connection to, rooted deep in the local community, off the official radar.

Inside, the taverna was cool and refreshingly dim after the glare outside, offering immediate respite. Blue-and-white checkered tablecloths covered sturdy wooden tables. Fishing nets, colorful woven rugs depicting Minoan motifs, faded black-and-white photos of stern-looking Cretan men in traditional dress with impressive mustaches (Nikos's ancestors?), and other assorted nautical paraphernalia decorated the whitewashed walls. Copper pots gleamed above the small bar area. The air smelled wonderful. Garlic, olive oil, grilled fish, roasting lamb simmering with herbs, sharp feta cheese, oregano. A handful of local patrons sat nursing small glasses of cloudy ouzo or tiny cups of thick, sludgy Greek coffee, chatting quietly but intensely in rapid-fire Cretan dialect. Fishermen perhaps, judging by their weathered faces, calloused hands, and sturdy builds. Behind the simple wooden bar, meticulously polishing glasses with a clean white cloth, stood a man of medium height, perhaps in his late forties or early fifties. His face was deeply tanned and weathered by years of sun and sea, framed by dark, receding hair liberally streaked with grey, and a thick, well-trimmed mustache that dominated his lower face. He looked up as they entered, setting down his glass and wiping his hands on a clean white apron. His dark eyes were sharp and intelligent, immediately assessing the unfamiliar newcomers who clearly weren't regulars.

"*Kalimera sas,*" he greeted them, his voice warm and resonant, carrying easily across the quiet room, but holding an unmistakable undertone of polite caution reserved for strangers. "Welcome. Can I help you find a table? Or perhaps something to drink?"

"*Kalimera,*" Leo replied, using one of the few Greek phrases he knew, feeling suddenly awkward under the man's direct, intelligent gaze. "We're... uh... looking for Nikos?". The man's gaze didn't waver, holding Leo's for a moment before flicking briefly, assessingly, to Sera. "You found him," he stated simply, his expression giving nothing away. "I am Nikoss. What can I do for you?" His eyes held a question, patient but expectant.

Sera stepped forward slightly, removing her sunglasses, allowing him to see her face clearly, meeting his gaze directly. "Boris sent us," she stated quietly, her voice low but clear, using the simple phrase Boris had instructed them to use back in the mountain cabin, a phrase that clearly carried weight between the cousins.

Nikos's professional caution vanished instantly, replaced by a look of startled recognition, followed immediately by genuine warmth that transformed his face. A broad, welcoming smile spread across his features, crinkling the corners of his sharp eyes. "Ah, Boris! *O trelos mou exadelfos!*

My crazy cousin in the mountains! How is that old bear? Still wrestling smugglers and charming the tourists?" He wiped his hands vigorously on his apron and came quickly around the bar, extending a strong, calloused hand first to Sera, then to Leo, his grip firm and welcoming. "Welcome, welcome! *Kalos Orisate!* Any friends of Boris are friends of mine, especially if he trusted you with my name. You must be tired from your journey. Come, sit, sit! At my best table, here in the corner. Let me get you something cold to drink. Retsina? Beer? Ouzo? And some *mezes* to start. You look like you need it."

He led them to a quiet, secluded table in the corner, slightly shielded from the view of the other patrons. Over plates of delicious, freshly prepared grilled octopus drizzled with lemon and olive oil, sharp local olives, creamy feta cheese sprinkled with oregano, crusty bread, and glasses of chilled, resinous retsina that tasted surprisingly refreshing, they carefully explained their situation to Nikos. They omitted the highly classified details. Section M, the KGB connection (though implied by the mention of "officials"), the true nature of the Delphi Protocol mission, the existence of the sphere itself which remained hidden in Leo's bag. They framed their story around Leo's academic research into Minoan history and the specific legends surrounding the Labyrinth, mentioning the discovery of the tablet and the map fragment pointing to Crete. They alluded carefully to their troubles in Bulgaria, vaguely referring to "overzealous officials" from the Ministry of Culture who seemed unusually, aggressively interested in their research into Thracian sites, necessitating their discreet travel and seeking local, trustworthy assistance.

Nikos listened intently, leaning forward slightly, occasionally asking sharp, insightful questions that cut through Leo's academic rambling, nodding thoughtfully as he absorbed their carefully edited story. He clearly had a quick, practical mind beneath his easygoing taverna-owner exterior; he'd likely heard many strange stories over the years in this port city. "The Labyrinth..." he mused finally, swirling the pale golden wine in his glass, his expression thoughtful. "*O Lavyrinthos*. Ah, yes. A story every Cretan child grows up with, whispered by our grandmothers. King Minos, the palace, the terrible Minotaur hidden in the maze... A place of great mystery, great power." He leaned forward slightly, his voice dropping. "Many people, the tourists, even some historians, they think the Palace of Knossos *is* the Labyrinth, with all its confusing rooms and levels. A reasonable guess, perhaps. But there are other stories, much older ones, the ones the shepherds tell in the high mountains, the ones the fishermen mutter after too much *tsikoudia*. Whispers that the *real* Labyrinth wasn't a palace built by man at all, but something else... something ancient, something found... something hidden in the depths of the island, in the secret places."

Leo's academic instincts took over completely. He peppered Nikos with questions about myth variations, local folklore, potential locations whispered about in village tales. Was there any archaeological evidence of a real maze, something physical hidden away from the famous Knossos site? While Leo dove deeper into research mode, Sera gently steered the conversation back to their immediate, practical concerns.

"Nikos," she began casually, topping up their glasses with water from a carafe, "these 'officials' we encountered in Bulgaria... they seemed very well-connected, very persistent. Boris was concerned they might have... associates, perhaps, people who operate internationally. Could they have interests even here in Crete?"

Nikos's friendly expression tightened almost imperceptibly. Sipping his retsina, his gaze drifting towards the sunlit street outside for a moment before returning to Sera, his eyes suddenly sharp, serious. "Crete is a crossroads, my friends," he answered finally, his voice lower now, more cautious. "Always has been. Many people pass through. Tourists, traders, sailors... and others." He paused significantly. "People who ask too many questions, people who don't fit in, people who work for powerful interests beyond our shores." He looked directly at Sera, a silent understanding passing between them. "The kind of people Boris sometimes has... strong disagreements with back in his mountains?"

Sera simply met his gaze steadily, letting the implication hang in the air. No confirmation needed.

Nikos sighed, running a hand over his mustache. "There are always whispers. Especially now, perhaps, with the American base at Souda Bay nearby, the tensions in the Med... Men who don't belong, watching, listening. Sometimes connected to powerful people in Athens, sometimes... further east." He shook his head slightly. "Nothing solid I could tell you right now. No specific names that spring to mind matching your description of the Bulgarian officials. But," he added, his tone becoming deeply serious, "if you believe you attracted *that* kind of dangerous attention, the kind Boris worries about, then you must be careful here on Crete. Very, very careful. This island is beautiful, welcoming, but even paradise has its shadows, its hidden dangers. And the old ways... they run deep here."

Later that afternoon, Nikos insisted they stay in the simple, clean rooms above the taverna. Lodgings usually reserved for visiting family or trusted friends. "Safer here than some anonymous hotel," he'd insisted. While Leo gratefully accepted Nikos's immediate, generous offer to explore his small but surprisingly extensive personal library of books on Cretan history, Minoan archaeology, and local folklore. A collection far more impressive than the taverna's humble appearance suggested. Sera put her own, very different skills to work. Using Nikos's quiet introductions and vouched reputation as a starting point ("Friends of Boris," was enough for most), she began discreetly tapping into the local information network. She spoke casually with trusted shopkeepers in the old market, shared coffee with weather beaten fishermen down at the harbour mending nets, listened quietly to the conversations of old men playing *tavli* in the shaded squares. She wasn't just looking for signs of Orlov's men or other Soviet assets; she was building an understanding of the island's complex rhythms, its potential dangers, its information brokers, gathering the kind of nuanced local intelligence you couldn't find in any official Section M report. Who was new in town? Who was asking unusual questions? Who seemed out of place?

Leo, meanwhile, lost himself completely in the Labyrinth, metaphorically speaking. Surrounded by Nikos's books in a quiet back room, the sounds of the taverna muted, he read voraciously about King Minos and his cursed wife Pasiphae, about Daedalus the master craftsman who designed the maze and the wings, about the terrifying Minotaur. Asterion. Sacrificed in its depths, and about the Athenian hero Theseus who navigated the maze with Ariadne's thread only to betray her later. He studied detailed maps of the excavations at Knossos, poured over competing theories about its construction and purpose, delved into fierce archaeological debates about whether the Labyrinth was myth, metaphor for the complexities of the palace, or a real, physical place whose location had been lost to time. The deeper he dug, cross-referencing academic theories with the fragmented folklore Nikos shared, the more convinced he became that the myth held a kernel of profound historical truth, twisted and embellished over millennia, but pointing towards something real.

Nikos, sensing Leo's genuine passion and perhaps recognizing a kindred spirit fascinated by the island's deep past, shared stories his own grandfather, a shepherd from the Lasithi plateau, had told him. Tales considered fanciful by outsiders but held as truth in the mountain villages. Stories of hidden cave systems riddling the island's central mountains. Entrances guarded by superstition, tunnels said to stretch for miles beneath the earth, connecting ancient sites, remnants, perhaps, of the vast, mysterious Minoan civilization destroyed by the eruption of Thera.

"Some say the Labyrinth wasn't *built* by Daedalus at all," Nikos explained one evening, as they sat on the taverna's small, vine-covered rear terrace overlooking the darkening harbour, the lights of fishing boats twinkling on the calm water. "They say it was *found*. Something ancient, already hidden deep in the earth when Minos came to power. Something powerful, maybe dangerous, that the king simply... took over, repurposed, built his palace near, to control it, or perhaps contain it."

As the days slipped by. Perhaps three or four. Leo's historical research and Sera's quiet intelligence gathering started painting a clearer, if still frustratingly incomplete, picture. The obsidian sphere, the 'stone that sees the stars', was almost certainly hidden somewhere connected to this Labyrinth legend, the true, hidden Labyrinth. But where? Was it beneath Knossos after all, in some undiscovered section? Was it within one of the vast, unexplored cave systems Nikos spoke of in the mountains? And the most pressing question: was Orlov's network, or someone connected to the Soviets, already here, searching too, perhaps guided by their own sources, their own interpretation of the prophecy? Sera's contacts had reported whispers of quiet inquiries being made by 'foreign businessmen' asking about land access near remote archaeological sites, but nothing concrete yet.

They knew, with growing certainty, they were in the right place. Crete held the key. But finding the entrance to the true Labyrinth, navigating its potential dangers, and understanding the spheres importance before their enemies did, would be their most perilous challenge yet. They needed a breakthrough, a specific location to focus their search.

Chapter Eighteen

Map of Stars

Sera continued her discreet probing of Heraklion's undercurrents. Spending hours seemingly chatting casually with fishermen mending nets at the Venetian harbour, browsing stalls in the central market while listening intently to conversations, sharing coffee with old men in quiet *kafenia* known to be hubs of local gossip, all the while building a network of eyes and ears across the city. Leo spent equivalent hours immersed in the surprisingly comprehensive library tucked away in a back room of Nikos's taverna. Surrounded by the comforting, dusty smell of old paper and sustained by Nikos's excellent, strong Greek coffee, he felt more in his element, though the stakes of this research were terrifyingly higher than any academic paper.

He devoured texts on Minoan civilization, pouring over Sir Arthur Evans' original excavation reports from Knossos, comparing them with more recent archaeological surveys and obscure academic journals Nikos had somehow acquired over the years. He searched desperately for any mention of Labyrinth legends tied to specific locations *beyond* the well-trodden ground of Knossos itself. Nikos's intriguing tales of hidden cave systems riddling the island's mountainous interior kept echoing in his mind. Could the Labyrinth be a natural formation, adapted and obscured by the Minoans? He traced geological maps, looking for extensive karst systems or unexplored entrances near known Minoan sites.

Days blurred into a cycle of intense research, shared meals with Nikos and Sera where they exchanged frustratingly scant updates, and restless nights filled with fragmented dreams of twisting passages and shadowy pursuers. Leo felt the pressure mounting; Sera's inquiries hadn't turned up any concrete sign of Orlov's network yet, but the feeling that they were being hunted, that time was running out, was a constant weight. They needed a solid lead, a specific location.

He was cross-referencing excavation reports of lesser-known Minoan villas with local folklore maps detailing supposed entrances to the underworld when a small, recent article buried deep within an international archaeological journal snagged his attention. He'd almost dismissed it, the title dry and academic: "Preliminary Survey of Newly Discovered Minoan Villa Complex near Kastelli Pediados." But something made him pause and read further. The article detailed the preliminary findings of a newly unearthed Minoan site further inland, south-east of Heraklion. The text was dense, cautious, filled with academic jargon, but one phrase jumped out from the page, making Leo's breath catch: "...site characterized by an unusually complex, multi-level subterranean architectural layout, featuring numerous narrow corridors forming a potentially disorienting maze-like structure beneath the main villa." Attached were a few grainy, black-and-white photographs showing complex, interconnected foundation walls disappearing into shadowed openings in the earth.

"Maze-like... subterranean..." Leo murmured aloud, his pulse quickening dramatically. He pulled out his own notes on the Delphi prophecy, the obsidian sphere, the map revealed in Belintash pointing specifically to Crete, the resonant word *Labyrinthos*. Could *this* be it? Not the famous palace at Knossos, deliberately misidentified in myth perhaps, but a different, lesser-known site hidden inland? A structure *beneath* the ground?

He showed the article to Nikos later that evening, spreading the journal pages on the small table between them and pointing out the key phrases and grainy photographs. Nikos leaned closer, adjusting his reading glasses, studying the pages intently, stroking his thick mustache thoughtfully.

"Ah, yes, the Kastelli dig," Nikos nodded after a moment, recognition dawning in his eyes. "I heard some whispers about this find a few months back from a cousin who farms near there. Caused a bit of excitement locally, something about unusual lower levels, but the official archaeological service from Athens has kept it very quiet since the initial survey. It's in a remote area, up in the foothills, difficult to get to. Definitely not on any tourist maps yet, not properly excavated."

"Remote... quiet... maze-like... subterranean..." Leo's excitement grew, pushing aside his fatigue. "Nikos, this feels right. The location, the description... it fits better than Knossos, which is too famous, too public, too obvious. Maybe the Labyrinth wasn't the palace itself, but something the palace was built *near*, or *over*, to hide or contain it?"

"Perfect," Sera added, joining them at the table after returning from her own lengthy, seemingly fruitless day of reconnaissance, shedding the weary persona she adopted outside the taverna. Her sharp eyes scanned the journal pages laid out on the table. "Remote and quiet is good. Fewer eyes watching, less chance of running into Orlov's welcoming committee. *If* they are here and looking in the right places. It buys us time." She looked directly at Nikos. "Can you get us there? Discreetly? Tomorrow?"

Nikos grinned, his usual easygoing confidence returning now that they had a potential target. "My friends, getting places discreetly on this island is a Cretan specialty, especially when avoiding Athenian officials or nosy outsiders. Leave it entirely to me."

The journey the next day took them out of Heraklion's urban sprawl, leaving the bustling city and the blue expanse of the sea behind them, heading deep into the island's rugged interior. Nikos drove his sturdy, unmarked pickup truck along winding asphalt roads that climbed steadily through stunningly beautiful countryside. The kind used by farmers and builders all over Crete. They passed sun-drenched olive groves clinging precariously to steep hillsides, the ancient, gnarled trees silver-green against the reddish earth. Sprawling vineyards heavy with ripening grapes carpeted the lower slopes, and small, sleepy villages, clusters of whitewashed houses with bright blue doors huddled around tiny Orthodox churches, seemed untouched by time. The air grew hotter, drier, scented strongly now with wild flowers, oregano, and the dusty scent of the parched summer earth. As they got closer to the Kastelli region, the paved roads gave way to rough gravel tracks, then finally to bumpy dirt paths barely wide enough for the truck, bouncing them along as they climbed higher into the arid, rocky foothills, leaving plumes of dust in their wake.

Nikos eventually pulled the truck off the barely discernible track, maneuvering it skillfully behind a dense thicket of thorny oleander bushes and covering it partially with a dusty canvas tarpaulin. "We walk from here," he announced, cutting the engine. The sudden silence was intense, broken only by the incessant buzz of cicadas. "The site is just over that ridge. Less chance of attracting unwelcome attention this way. The Athens team hasn't been back in weeks, according to my cousin, but still... better safe."

They hiked the last mile under the blazing afternoon sun, the heat pressing down on them relentlessly. The terrain was rough, rocky, covered in thorny scrub. Cresting the ridge, they paused, catching their breath, and looked down upon the ruins spread across the slope below. Even from this distance, the site was impressive, and clearly ancient.

Crumbling stone walls, bleached bone-white by centuries of relentless Cretan sun, snaked across the hillside, outlining a vast complex of rooms, corridors, and courtyards. It wasn't built on the grand scale of Knossos, lacking the reconstructed frescoes and towering columns, but its layout was undeniably intricate, almost bewilderingly complex, hinting at multiple levels and phases of construction. It was easy to imagine getting lost in such a place, easy to see how it could have inspired legends of an inescapable maze.

They descended carefully into the ruins, the silence profound now, broken only by the crunch of their boots on loose gravel and the ever-present, hypnotic buzzing of unseen insects in the dry scrub. The air felt heavy, still alive with unspoken history. Leo's archaeologist instincts kicked into high gear immediately. His gaze darted everywhere, taking in the Minoan construction techniques. The massive ashlar blocks, the characteristic tapered columns lying broken on the ground. The confusing layout, searching eagerly for any symbol, any carving, any architectural detail that resonated with the Delphi clues or the Labyrinth myth. Sera moved with her usual fluid vigilance, not looking at the stones but at the surrounding landscape, scanning the nearby ridges, checking angles, listening intently, ensuring they weren't walking into a trap or being observed. Nikos pointed out features based on the little he knew from local gossip about the initial dig. A large storage area with broken *pithoi* jars, what might have been a central shrine, the deeper, partially excavated subterranean levels mentioned in the article.

They worked their way slowly towards what seemed to be a large central courtyard, partially excavated, the sun beating down mercilessly, reflecting off the pale stones. And then Leo stopped dead in his tracks, his breath catching sharply in his throat, his hand flying to his chest as if struck.

"Sera... Nikos... *Look*." His voice was barely an audible whisper, filled with utter astonishment.

There, partially uncovered in the precise geometrical center of the courtyard, almost glowing with vibrant color in the harsh sunlight against the pale surrounding stone, was a mosaic floor of breathtaking complexity and exquisite beauty. Dust and windblown debris covered parts of it, and many small stone *tesserae* were missing or damaged by time and exposure, but the overall design was stunningly clear, remarkably preserved. It depicted a classic, intricate Cretan labyrinth pattern, instantly recognizable. And set dramatically within the very heart of the maze, rendered in darker, more dynamic tiles, were two figures locked in eternal combat: a heroic, muscular figure wielding a double axe. Theseus, surely. Standing triumphantly over a fallen, powerfully built bull-headed man. The Minotaur.

"*Panagia mou!* Mother of God," Nikos breathed, instinctively crossing himself, awe and a touch of superstitious fear mingling on his face.

Leo dropped to his knees beside the mosaic, reverence warring with intense academic excitement. His fingers gently, almost tenderly, brushed dust away from the intricate tilework, revealing more detail. "It's incredible... a literal depiction of the myth, right here at this site, not Knossos..." He traced the winding paths of the depicted maze with a fingertip. But as he studied it, his analytical mind kicked in, noticing subtle details beyond the dramatic central figures. The way the paths twisted and turned seemed... deliberate, too complex for a simple decorative pattern, almost like a schematic, a code. And then he saw it clearly. Woven skillfully into the decorative geometric border surrounding the maze, and placed strategically within the background areas of the main scene. Tiny patterns made of different colored tiles (dark blue, deep red, bright white), almost lost in the overall design unless one looked very closely. Especially noticeable were stellar patterns set against the patches of dark blue tiles clearly representing the night sky above the combat scene.

"Nikos," Leo asked urgently, his voice hushed with dawning realization, "has this specific mosaic been fully documented by the excavation team? Photographed in detail? Have these patterns been published anywhere?"

Nikos shook his head, still staring at the mosaic with fascination. "Like I said, Professor, this dig is recent, and the Athens team kept things very quiet after the initial survey. Politics, probably, funding disputes. I doubt they have released anything this significant yet. Why? What do you see?"

"Because this isn't just a picture!" Leo exclaimed, his voice rising with excitement, the pieces clicking rapidly into place in his mind. He pointed a trembling finger at the patterns of colored tiles Sera and Nikos now knelt beside him to examine more closely. "Look! Look closely here! These aren't random decorative elements! They're constellations! That's Orion, there's Taurus, and look, Lyra! See how they're positioned relative to each other, and relative to the Labyrinth pattern itself? It's a star chart, a celestial map, embedded right here in the mosaic!"

Sera's sharp eyes followed Leo's finger, her brow furrowed in concentration. Even without his astronomical knowledge, she could clearly see the deliberate, repeating patterns he indicated, patterns that bore no relation to the central myth depiction. "Okay, Professor," she stated quietly, her mind already racing ahead to the implications. "A star chart hidden in a mosaic picture of a maze. What does it mean? What's the code telling us?"

Leo's gaze shifted rapidly between the constellations depicted in the border and the twisting paths of the labyrinth mosaic itself. His mind raced, connecting the dots to the prophecy. The 'stone that sees the stars', the celestial alignments hinted at in Tatul and Belintash, Father Nicolae's talk of cycles... "It's the code!" he realized aloud, hitting his palm against his dusty thigh in triumph. "The path through the *real* Labyrinth isn't random! It's guided by the stars! Each turn, each junction corresponds to a specific star or constellation in this sequence!"

His finger, trembling with excitement, traced a path through the mosaic maze, carefully following the celestial sequence dictated by the star patterns he was rapidly deciphering in the border and background. Left at Orion, then right at Taurus, straight past the Pleiades cluster, avoid the path under Draco, turn towards Lyra... His finger stopped decisively, pointing at a specific point on the outer edge of the mosaic labyrinth, a point that corresponded geographically to a section of the actual palace ruins nearby. A section that looked less excavated than the rest, almost deliberately ignored or overlooked, partially overgrown with thick, thorny bushes.

"There," Leo declared, his voice filled with utter conviction, pushing himself to his feet. "If I'm reading this star map correctly... the entrance to the true Labyrinth isn't an obvious doorway in the palace structure itself. It's *over there*. Hidden along that outer foundation wall."

They scrambled eagerly over crumbling walls and piles of rubble to the section of the ruins Leo indicated. At first glance, it looked exactly like the surrounding area. Just a crumbling stone foundation wall covered in thick, prickly, sun-scorched bushes. But Sera, running her hand along the stonework, examining it closely, noticed subtle differences. Some of the massive stones here seemed slightly different in color and texture from the surrounding Minoan blocks, perhaps reset, as if part of the wall had been carefully dismantled and then rebuilt long ago to conceal something behind it. Pushing aside the heavy, overgrown, thorny vegetation with difficulty, ignoring the scratches, they found it.

A narrow opening in the rock face behind the foundation stones, almost perfectly hidden behind the thick curtain of green. It wasn't an architectural feature of the palace; it looked like the entrance to a natural cave or perhaps a crudely dug tunnel, deliberately obscured by the later palace wall construction. A draft of cool, damp, subterranean air flowed out, carrying the same faint scent they remembered from Belintash.

Nikos peered into the dark opening, his eyes wide with amazement and a touch of fear. "By the Gods... *Lavyrinthos*..." he breathed. "All my years on this island, all the stories my grandfather told... I've never heard of this entrance. Never seen it."

Leo looked at Sera, his face flushed with the triumph of discovery, but his eyes also held a shadow of deep apprehension. The celestial code, hidden for millennia in a beautiful mosaic, had led them to a secret entrance within the ruins of a maze-like palace. This had to be it. The beginning of the true Labyrinth. The path to the sphere.

"Ready to see what secrets this old island has *really* been hiding beneath the myths, Professor?" Sera asked, her voice low and steady, her hand resting almost unconsciously on the grip of her pistol beneath her loose shirt.

Leo took a deep breath, the hot, dry air doing little to calm the frantic beating of his heart. He met Sera's steady gaze, finding reassurance there. He nodded, his voice surprisingly firm. "Ready."

Nikos gave a determined nod, his initial shock replaced by a rugged, almost fatalistic Cretan enthusiasm for confronting the unknown. "Lead the way," he stated, pulling a sturdy flashlight from his own pack. "Let's wake the Minotaur."

Together, the historian, the spy, and the Cretan patriot prepared to step across the threshold, leaving the sunlit world of familiar ruins and decipherable codes behind for the waiting, ancient darkness of the true Labyrinth.

CHAPTER NINETEEN

Into the Labyrinth

Sera went first, her powerful flashlight beam cutting a determined swathe through the absolute, waiting blackness of the cave entrance behind the foundation wall. The air hit them immediately. Cool, significantly damper than the ruins above, and heavy, carrying the thick, cloying smell of wet earth, ancient mineral deposits, and something else... that instantly reminded Leo, with a shiver of unease, of the subterranean passages hidden Belintash. It was the scent of places long sealed off from the world, holding secrets best left undisturbed.

He pushed the troubling memory aside, forcing himself to focus, taking a deep breath of the stale air and concentrating on following the bobbing circle of light illuminating Sera's boots as she stepped cautiously over the threshold into the unknown. Nikos brought up the rear, pausing for a second to pull the overgrown, thorny vines back into place across the narrow opening, obscuring their entrance as best he could before squeezing his sturdy frame through himself into the darkness. The transition from the bright, hot Cretan day to the cold, subterranean blackness was abrupt and disorienting.

The passage immediately sloped downwards at a steep angle, the rough-cut stone slick with moisture underfoot, making footing precarious. It was narrow, forcing them into single file again, the oppressive darkness pressing in, seeming to actively swallow the powerful beams of their flashlights just yards ahead. The silence here was profound, different from the open quiet of the ruins; this was a deep, subterranean silence that felt heavy, ancient, broken only by the soft echo of their own careful footsteps, the rasp of their breathing, and the rhythmic *drip... drip... drip* of water seeping from unseen cracks in the low ceiling somewhere ahead, a sound that seemed to count off the seconds in the suffocating quiet, amplifying the sense of isolation and descent into the earth's depths.

"This place feels old," Nikos murmured from behind Leo, his voice hushed, yet sounding unnaturally loud in the enclosed space, making Leo startle slightly. "Much older than the Minoan palace ruins they built above it. Like it was here long before Minos, waiting."

"Stay alert," Sera cautioned quietly from the front, her voice tight, absorbing the environment, her senses clearly heightened. "These places can be unstable. Watch your footing, watch the ceiling for loose rock. And listen." She moved with a fluid, economical grace born of long experience in dangerous, confined spaces, her light constantly sweeping ahead, methodically checking the floor, walls, and ceiling for hazards or markings.

The passage quickly lived up to the Labyrinth's mythical name. It twisted sharply left, then right following what seemed like a natural fault line in the rock, then seemed to abruptly split into two equally uninviting, black tunnels. Sera paused, sweeping her light into both. "Leo? Your star code from the mosaic?"

Leo consulted the slightly smudged sketch in his notebook, his flashlight beam shaky. "Okay... according to the sequence... the turn after Lyra should correspond to... Cepheus... which was positioned... left, I think?" Following his uncertain direction, they took the left fork, only for it to end abruptly, disappointingly, in a solid, damp wall of rock twenty yards later. No way through.

"Dead end," Sera reported flatly, playing her light meticulously over the rock face, searching for any hint of a mechanism, a disguised seam, or a hidden catch. Nothing. Just solid, unforgiving stone.

"Damn," Leo muttered in frustration, checking his notes again under the dim light. "Maybe the alignment was relative, not absolute... Okay, let's backtrack. The sequence must have meant the *other* path at that junction."

They backtracked carefully, the minor setback adding to the growing tension and the sense of being deliberately confounded by the ancient builders. Taking the right fork this time, they soon found themselves squeezing through a section so narrow they had to turn sideways, their shoulders scraping against the cold, damp rock, Leo's briefcase bumping awkwardly against his hip. The air grew heavier here, almost sharp in their nostrils. Leo stumbled on a loose stone in the near-total darkness outside his flashlight beam, his hand brushing against the wall for balance, the rock feeling strangely pitted and rough here, almost like slag.

A faint scraping sound echoed from somewhere far ahead in the passage, distinct from the dripping water. Dust motes, previously undisturbed in the still air, danced suddenly in Sera's flashlight beam, disturbed by unseen vibrations from deeper within the earth.

"Careful," she warned again, her voice low, pausing instantly, holding up a hand, listening intently. "Could be unstable rock settling from the tremors outside. Or could be something else moving down here. Move quietly."

They continued deeper into the mountain's bowels, the passages branching and rejoining in a confusing, seemingly illogical pattern that seemed designed to confound and disorient. More than once, they had to pause at junctions while Leo, sweating now despite the subterranean coolness, tried desperately to recall the complex celestial sequence from the mosaic, attempting to match primitive carvings they occasionally spotted etched crudely on the walls. Rough spirals, faded starbursts, serpentine lines sometimes marked with traces of ochre paint. To the precise star map he held imperfectly in his memory. It was like navigating by rumor in pitch darkness, relying on fragmented clues millennia old.

"These symbols," Leo murmured, tracing a cluster of seven small depressions that vaguely resembled Ursa Major, carved near a low side passage. "They *are* consistent with the mosaic's star chart, but much rougher, significantly older. Like preliminary sketches, or maybe mnemonic devices for initiates using the Labyrinth. Someone was definitely using the stars to map this place long before the mosaic floor was even laid."

Following what Leo hoped was the correct stellar path indicated by a carving resembling the constellation Draco, the Dragon, seeming to guard a specific downward turn, they chose a less obvious side tunnel that seemed to descend more steeply than the others. The footing immediately became more treacherous, loose stones shifting and sliding under their boots, threatening to send them tumbling into the darkness below. Sera, in the lead, moving with slow, deliberate care, testing each step before committing her weight, suddenly threw out an arm, stopping Leo just inches from disaster, her body tense.

"Hold up! Edge! Look out!" Her powerful flashlight beam cut sharply downwards, illuminating a gaping black hole directly in their path, spanning nearly the entire width of the passage floor. It looked terrifyingly deep, the beam swallowed instantly by absolute darkness, revealing no bottom, only echoing silence. A faint, foul, sulfurous smell wafted up from its depths, stinging their nostrils.

Leo's heart leaped into his throat, pounding against his ribs like a trapped bird. He instinctively grabbed onto the tunnel wall, feeling dizzy. "A trap? A deliberately set pitfall to guard the way?"

"Could be," Sera replied grimly, kneeling cautiously near the edge, probing the darkness with her light, listening intently for any sound from below. Silence. "Or just a natural sinkhole, maybe a volcanic vent tube, waiting patiently for the unwary. The Minoans were clever builders, yes, incorporating natural features, but nature's traps are often more final." She carefully tested the narrow, crumbling ledge remaining along the right-hand passage wall with her boot. Loose rock skittered silently into the abyss. "Looks barely wide enough for one person at a time. Very unstable. The slightest tremor could send it down." She looked back at them, her face serious in the stark beam of her flashlight. "Stay tight against the wall. Move slow. One at a time. No sudden movements. And whatever you do, don't look down."

Sera went first, flattening herself against the cold, damp stone, moving sideways inch by painstaking inch, her flashlight aimed downwards to illuminate the treacherous footing. Leo followed, pressing himself against the clammy rock, the foul smell from the hole gagging him, his eyes fixed firmly on the rough texture of the wall directly in front of him, trying desperately not to imagine the dizzying, silent fall into the echoing blackness below. Nikos came last, his bulk making the passage even more perilous, breathing heavily but moving with surprising steadiness and care.

Safely past the terrifying hole, the relief was immense but short-lived. They continued their cautious descent, the air growing noticeably warmer now, the sulfurous smell becoming stronger, mingling with the persistent metallic tang. And then they heard it. Not dripping water this time. Not shifting rock.

Faint at first, seeming to echo strangely off the unseen cavern walls far ahead, distorted by the underground acoustics, but growing louder, clearer with each step they took. The unmistakable sound of human voices echoing up from the passages *behind* and below them. Harsh shouts, muffled by distance and layers of rock, but undeniably human. And getting closer.

Sera froze instantly, holding up a hand for absolute silence, killing her flashlight beam. Leo and Nikos stopped dead behind her, hearts pounding, straining their ears in the sudden, oppressive darkness, broken only by the dim beams of their own lights pointed downwards. The sounds were clearer now. Boots scrambling hastily on rock, the metallic clatter of dropped equipment, curt commands barked in clipped, unmistakable Russian.

"Orlov," Sera stated, her voice a tight, cold whisper, all previous weariness gone, replaced instantly by sharp-edged focus. She flicked her flashlight back on, keeping the beam low. "He found the damn entrance. Or maybe another one, deeper in. He's inside the Labyrinth. And he's not far behind us."

A fresh wave of cold adrenaline surged through Leo, colder than the cave air. The inherent dangers of the Labyrinth itself were suddenly, terrifyingly compounded by the relentless pursuit of their ruthless human enemy. The darkness, the pitfalls, the crushing weight of the mountain, the confusing passages. They were trapped underground, in a maze, with Orlov and his soldiers hunting them.

"We have to move faster," Nikos urged, his voice a low growl, his hand tightening on the heavy flashlight he held like a club.

They broke into a stumbling, difficult run, their flashlights bouncing wildly off the uneven walls, casting frantic, dancing shadows that made the passage seem alive with menacing shapes. The tunnel ahead opened abruptly, without warning, into a much larger cavern, the ceiling completely lost in impenetrable blackness high above the reach of their beams. And spanning the center of the vast, echoing cavern, illuminated starkly by Sera's sweeping light, was their next, formidable obstacle: a narrow bridge of worn, ancient-looking stone, arching precariously over another deep, black, silent chasm that seemed to drop away into the very bowels of the earth. The bridge looked impossibly old, its surface eroded smooth by millennia of seepage or perhaps even foot traffic, its low, carved railings crumbled away entirely in many places, offering no security whatsoever.

"Doesn't look particularly safe," Nikos stated grimly, the understatement echoing slightly in the vast, silent space.

"We don't have a choice now," Sera replied curtly, already moving towards the bridge, cautiously testing the first few massive stones with her boot, checking for stability. "It's the only way across this chasm. Let's hope it holds our weight."

Cautiously, moving slowly now, keeping distance between them, they stepped onto the ancient bridge, single file again, the terrifying chasm yawning on either side, seeming to exhale cold, dead air. Just as they reached the midpoint, the worn stone beneath their feet trembled slightly, distinctly. A low groan echoed through the cavern, seeming to come from the rock itself, deep within the mountain. Loose pebbles, dislodged by the vibration, skittered off the bridge's edge, disappearing instantly into the blackness below without a sound.

The entire cavern seemed to shudder again, more strongly this time, a deeper, more ominous tremor that ran up their legs. Dust rained down from the invisible ceiling high above. The ancient stone bridge swayed sickeningly beneath them, groaning loudly in protest, the sound of stressed rock grating horribly, as if the Labyrinth itself, disturbed after millennia of slumber, was trying to shake them off into the abyss. Behind them, Orlov's men were closing fast. Angry shouts echoed from the tunnel, boots scrambling over stone. Getting closer.

CHAPTER TWENTY

Bridge of Sorrows

The ancient stone bridge groaned again beneath their feet, a deep, protesting sound like a dying beast that seemed to rise from the very bowels of the earth, vibrating up through their legs. The black chasm yawned on either side, a dizzying, terrifying drop into absolute darkness that swallowed the beams of their flashlights, offering no hint of a bottom. More tremors, stronger now, shook the vast cavern, sending showers of dust and small rocks raining down from the unseen ceiling high above, pattering onto the bridge and skittering into the void.

Just as Leo, Sera, and Nikos reached the relative safety of the rocky ledge on the far side, Orlov and two of his soldiers burst from the tunnel entrance they had just vacated only moments before. Their heavy military boots pounded heavily on the stone floor, the sound echoing ominously across the chasm. Their powerful flashlight beams stabbed aggressively through the gloom, instantly pinning the trio against the far cavern wall like cornered animals. Their AK-74s were leveled immediately, grim determination etched on the soldiers' faces, their training overriding any fear the unstable environment might inspire. Orlov stood slightly behind them, despite the crude bandage wrapped tightly around his head, radiating an aura of triumphant, almost manic fury. His gaze, sharp and filled with chilling certainty, fixed on them across the swaying bridge.

"End of the line, Americans!" Orlov's voice, distorted by pain and raw rage, echoed across the chasm, bouncing off the unseen walls. "And you, Cretan pig! Did you truly think you could escape me? Did you think this mountain would protect you?"

Sera instinctively shoved Leo and Nikos further back, towards a dark, narrow opening she spotted low down in the cavern wall behind them. Another potential passage, an escape route if they could reach it. She stood her ground resolutely at the edge of the bridge, her Makarov held steady in a two-handed grip, rapidly assessing their grim options. The bridge was impossibly narrow, crumbling visibly at the edges, offering absolutely no cover and no room to maneuver. Retreating back the way they came was certain death. Going forward meant facing Orlov's rifles across this treacherous span. Below them lay only darkness and the promise of a final impact.

"Don't move!" one of Orlov's soldiers shouted in heavily accented English, taking a hesitant, exploratory step onto the near end of the ancient bridge.

As he put his full weight down, the bridge lurched violently sideways with a horrifying, grating scrape of stone on stone. A large section of the already-damaged, eroded stone railing directly beside him broke away entirely, tumbling silently into the abyss without a sound. The soldier scrambled back hastily, his face suddenly pale beneath his grime, losing his footing slightly on the ledge.

"*Tha pesi!..*it's going to collapse!" Nikos yelled from behind Sera, his voice tight with rising panic, gesturing wildly towards the swaying structure.

Orlov and his men hesitated, their advance momentarily frozen by the bridge's obvious, terrifying instability. In that split second of indecision, Sera saw her only chance. It wasn't about winning a firefight; it was about buying precious seconds for Leo and Nikos.

"Leo! Nikos! Into that passage behind you!" she commanded urgently, nodding sharply towards the dark opening she'd spotted in the cavern wall. "Don't wait! Go! Now!"

Before they could protest or fully comprehend her intention, Sera spun back towards the bridge and, taking a deep breath, charged *onto* the swaying, groaning structure, firing her Makarov in a rapid, suppressing burst towards the figures on the far side. The sudden, unexpected aggression threw Orlov and his men completely off balance. Orlov cursed violently in Russian, ducking back behind the tunnel entrance, while his soldiers returned fire wildly, their automatic rifle shots echoing like thunder in the cavern, bullets ricocheting dangerously off the ancient stone all around Sera.

She dropped low, pressing herself flat against the worn, uneven surface of the bridge, using the slight curve of the ancient structure and the swirling dust dislodged by the impacts as meager cover. She fired again, methodically, aiming for legs, arms, anything to slow them down. The bridge groaned ominously beneath her, threatening to give way completely at any moment. Another tremor shook the cavern, stronger this time, and she felt the stone shift sickeningly under her body. She knew she couldn't hold them for long. She risked a glance back. Leo and Nikos were scrambling desperately towards the dark opening in the cavern wall. Good. Almost there.

Seeing her chance, needing to break contact before the bridge disintegrated or the remaining soldier found his aim, Sera fired one last shot. Hitting the closer soldier squarely in the thigh, eliciting a sharp cry of pain and sending him tumbling backward. Then turned and sprinted back with desperate speed across the swaying, vibrating bridge towards the passage where Leo and Nikos waited, urging her on.

Just as she reached the edge, muscles screaming, ready to leap the final few feet to the relative safety of the ledge, a deafening *CRACK* echoed through the cavern, louder than any thunder, louder even than the gunfire. The section of the bridge where Orlov and his wounded soldier stood, buckled downwards catastrophically, tilting at a precarious, impossible angle. They scrabbled desperately for purchase on the crumbling, disintegrating stone, their shouts turning to screams of terror.

"Go, go, go!" Sera screamed, seeing Leo hesitate at the passage entrance, his face a mask of fear for her. She launched herself forward, shoving Leo and Nikos forcefully together into the dark opening just as the entire cavern seemed to explode in a cataclysm of sound and motion.

With a thunderous, earth-shattering roar that dwarfed the earlier rockslide, a massive section of the cavern ceiling directly above the ancient bridge gave way completely. Tons upon tons of rock, ancient debris, and crystalline formations crashed down, engulfing the already collapsing bridge in a deadly avalanche of stone. The impact was immense, throwing Sera violently forward into the passage, the shockwave slamming the breath from her lungs and momentarily deafening them.

Dust billowed outwards instantly, thick, grey, and choking, instantly filling the cavern and the passage entrance, reducing visibility to zero. Leo and Nikos, already stumbling blindly into the darkness of the new passage, turned back coughing violently, their flashlights cutting utterly feeble beams through the impenetrable, swirling cloud.

The roaring and rumbling slowly subsided, replaced by the echoing crackle of settling rock. When the worst of the dust began to settle, revealing glimpses of the cavern beyond the passage mouth, the bridge was simply... gone. Vanished utterly. Replaced by a gaping black chasm dropping into unseen depths, partially filled now with a smoking, steaming pile of freshly shattered rubble far, far below. There was no sign of Orlov or his men amidst the devastation.

And, horrifyingly, no sign of Sera.

"SERA!" Leo cried out, the name torn from his throat in a raw sound of anguish and disbelief. He lunged back towards the passage opening, towards the swirling dust cloud, ready to plunge back into the devastation, but Nikos grabbed his arm with surprising strength, hauling him back forcefully.

"Leo, no! Stop! It's finished!" Nikos choked out, his own face a mask of raw grief and horror, tears cutting paths through the grime on his cheeks. "The bridge is gone! Completely gone! She's...she's gone! Buried! There's nothing we can possibly do!"

Tears streamed down Leo's face, hot and stinging, mixing with the dust and grime. He sagged against the rough passage wall, the strength draining completely out of him, leaving him weak and trembling. Sera... she had charged back onto that bridge to save them. She had pushed them to safety just as the roof came down. And now she was buried under tons of rock, lost in the abyss, sacrificed for them. The mission, the prophecy, the sphere... none of it mattered anymore. The cost, suddenly, impossibly, was too high.

With heavy hearts filled with crushing grief and the unbearable weight of Sera's apparent sacrifice pressing down on them, Nikos numbly pulled a devastated, almost unresponsive Leo deeper into the dark, narrow passage, away from the scene of destruction. Silence pressed in, broken only by their own ragged, choking breaths, the distant rumble of settling rock from the collapsed cavern, and somewhere further down the passage, the faint, lonely trickle of unseen water. They were alone now, deeper than ever within the Labyrinth, their guide, their protector, lost forever.

CHAPTER TWENTY-ONE

Taps in the Dark

The passage beyond the collapsed bridge chamber felt suffocatingly silent, the darkness pressing in, heavy and absolute, broken only by the shuffling, unsteady steps of the two survivors and the distant, mournful echo of seeping water. Grief settled over Leo like a physical weight, a crushing shroud heavier than the tons of rock that had buried Sera. He stumbled forward numbly, relying entirely on Nikos's steadying hand on his arm, seeing only the horrifying, repeating image of the bridge vanishing into swirling dust and Sera... gone. Just *gone*. She had charged back to save them. Pushed them out of the way with her last breath. And paid the ultimate price. The Labyrinth, the ancient prophecy, the mission, the lurking Soviet threat. It all felt utterly, sickeningly meaningless now, like ashes in his mouth, irrelevant in the face of such a devastating loss.

Nikos, too, was withdrawn, his usual rugged Cretan optimism completely extinguished, replaced by a heavy, grim silence that spoke volumes. He navigated the twisting tunnels purely by instinct, his flashlight beam tracing a path through the oppressive darkness, his face etched with deep sorrow for the brave, fierce woman who had fought alongside them, who had become, in their shared ordeal, like family. They moved automatically, putting one heavy foot in front of the other, driven only by the primal, animal need to escape the suffocating darkness, though neither knew where they were going or what purpose remained.

"She was brave, Leo," Nikos stated finally, his voice rough, thick with unshed tears, echoing slightly in a slightly wider section of the tunnel where they paused, gasping, to catch their breath against the damp rock wall. "The bravest damn woman I ever knew. Like the heroines in our old stories."

Leo could only manage a choked nod, unable to speak past the hard, painful lump lodged stubbornly in his throat. He sank onto a low, damp rock, burying his face in his dusty hands, the image of Sera charging back across the swaying bridge, her face determined, sacrificing herself for them, searing his memory like a brand. *Impossible*. It felt fundamentally impossible that someone so intensely alive, so fiercely capable, so vital, could just be... erased from the world in an instant of falling rock.

As they sat there huddled together in the heavy silence, enveloped by shared despair and the cold indifference of the ancient stone, Nikos suddenly stiffened beside him, his head cocked sharply to one side, listening intently. "Shh," he whispered urgently, his hand gripping Leo's shoulder. "Listen."

Leo lifted his head numbly, straining his ears against the profound silence, expecting nothing but the familiar sound of seeping water echoing through the darkness. At first, that was all he heard. But then... beneath the drip ping... faintly... another noise. A rhythmic *tap... tap-tap... tap...*

It was incredibly faint, seeming to vibrate through the rock itself somewhere back the way they had come, impossibly near the devastated cave-in zone. Barely audible.

Nikos frowned, listening hard. "Water dripping? Strange echo maybe?"

Leo held his breath, concentrating every fiber of his being on the faint sound. *Tap... tap-tap... tap...* Pause. *Tap... tap... tap-tap...* It wasn't random like dripping water. It was deliberate. Rhythmic. A *pattern*. His heart gave a sudden, painful lurch, hope flaring so unexpectedly it felt like physical pain. He scrambled closer to the cold tunnel wall, pressing his ear hard against the damp, ancient stone, ignoring the chill. *Tap-tap... tap... tap...*

The pattern shifted slightly, became more complex. Short taps, long taps. Morse? No, simpler... more basic... but undeniably intentional. *A code*. A primitive field code Sera had briefly, almost dismissively, explained once, sketching it on a napkin back when they were first planning the trip to Bulgaria. *"Just in case we get separated and comms are out, Professor. Basic tap code. Commit it to memory. You never know."* He *had* committed it to memory, thinking it a quaint piece of spycraft irrelevant to his historical research.

Hope, fierce, painful, and utterly unbelievable, surged through Leo, so powerful it almost made him dizzy, threatening to buckle his knees. He pushed himself clumsily off the rock. "Nikos! That's not water! It's *her*! It has to be! It's code!"

Nikos stared at him, his face a mask of disbelief warring with a desperate, fragile flicker of hope in his grief-stricken eyes. "Sera? *Alla mou*... My God... impossible! The collapse... tons of rock..."

"Listen! Just listen!" Leo urged, grabbing Nikos's arm, shaking it slightly. "It's a code! Simple, but it's deliberate! She's alive! She must be trapped somewhere near the collapse!" He scrabbled on the floor, finding a loose, fist-sized stone, and started tapping frantically back on the tunnel wall. Three short, sharp taps, the simple 'acknowledge' signal Sera had taught him.

They waited, frozen, straining their ears in the absolute, echoing silence, barely daring to breathe. For a heart-stopping, agonizing moment, there was nothing but the drip of water. Leo's fragile hope began to crumble again into despair. Then, faintly, seeming to come from slightly further down the passage they'd just traversed, came the reply: *Tap... tap-tap...* Closer this time! Responding!

"She heard us!" Leo cried, tears of raw relief now streaming down his face, mingling with the dust and grime. "She answered! Which way?"

They followed the sound, scrambling hastily back through the passages towards the area of the bridge collapse, their flashlight beams dancing wildly, illuminating treacherous footing and dark corners. The tapping grew stronger as they got closer, more insistent now, guiding them like a faint beacon in the oppressive darkness. It led them not to the main gaping chasm where the bridge had been, but slightly further back, to a section of the passage just *before* the main collapse, an area choked with fallen rock and debris from the violently shaken cavern ceiling.

The tapping seemed to be coming from behind a massive, precariously tilted boulder jammed hard against the passage wall, surrounded by a treacherous, unstable pile of smaller rubble.

"Sera!" Leo yelled again, his voice hoarse, cracking with emotion. "Sera, can you hear us? We're here!"

A muffled reply, faint and strained, came from behind the massive boulder. "...Leo?... Nikos...?... Get... out... Unstable..." Her voice was weak, laced with pain, but it was unmistakably, gloriously hers.

"She's behind here!" Nikos exclaimed, hope flaring bright in his eyes. Working with frantic, desperate energy, ignoring the obvious risk of dislodging the massive boulder or triggering a further collapse, they started clawing bare-handed at the smaller rocks, pulling them away, tossing them aside, clearing a path towards the base of the huge stone that miraculously still stood. It felt like moving mountains, their hands quickly becoming scraped and raw, but fueled by adrenaline and desperate hope.

Finally, after minutes that felt like hours, they cleared enough rubble to reveal a small, dark gap near the floor, between the tilted boulder and the tunnel wall. Shining his flashlight beam carefully inside, Leo saw her.

Sera was wedged tightly into a small natural alcove in the rock face, partially shielded by the massive bulk of the boulder that had, by sheer impossible luck, jammed itself in a way that protected her from the main force of the devastating cave-in. She was covered head-to-toe in fine grey rock dust, making her look like a ghostly statue. Her face was pale and etched with pain beneath the grime, bruises already darkening on her visible skin, but her eyes met his in the flashlight beam. Fierce, intelligent, undeniably alive. A crude splint, fashioned from splintered bits of debris and strips torn from her own shirt, was bound tightly around her injured lower leg. She managed a weak, dust-caked grin that looked utterly incongruous on her battered face.

"Took you guys long enough," she rasped, her voice weak but laced with her usual dry wit.

Leo felt unexpected laughter bubble up, sharp and hysterical, mingling with the tears of relief still tracking down his face. Sheer, unadulterated relief washing over him, so potent it made his knees weak. "Sera! How... how in God's name did you survive that?" He reached into the gap, his hand trembling, gripping her outstretched, dust-covered hand tightly. Her grip, though weak, was firm. Real.

"Saw the alcove... last second... roof started coming down... dove in," Sera explained between shallow, painful breaths, wincing as Nikos carefully, expertly started using a smaller rock as a lever to shift some of the remaining rubble away from the opening. "Big one came down right in front... shielded me... mostly. Leg got pinned for a bit. Been tapping ever since... hoping you weren't... gone..."

"We heard you," Leo assured her, his grip tightening reassuringly on her hand. "We heard you. We thought..." He couldn't finish the sentence.

"Orlov?" Sera asked then, her eyes suddenly sharp despite the pain, her focus instantly shifting back to the mission.

"Gone," Nikos stated grimly, finally clearing enough space around the opening for Sera to potentially be helped out. "The bridge collapsed completely before the main cave-in. We didn't see exactly what happened to him or his men in the dust, but... no one could have survived that fall, or the rock burying them."

Sera nodded slowly, absorbing the news, her expression grim but relieved. "Good. That simplifies things. One less thing to worry about." She leaned heavily on Leo and Nikos as they carefully, gently eased her out of the cramped, dusty alcove and helped her to sit on a stable section of the passage floor. Her leg was clearly causing her significant pain, despite the makeshift splint, but the fierce fire in her eyes hadn't dimmed in the slightest. If anything, her brush with death seemed to have focused her resolve, burned away any remaining doubts.

"Thought I told you to keep the professor out of trouble, big sister," Nikos teased gently, relief making him grin broadly despite the grim situation, reverting to their childhood dynamic.

Sera shot him a look that was only partly feigned annoyance, then glanced at Leo, who was still looking at her as if he'd seen a ghost return from the underworld. "Looks like we all keep each other out of trouble, Nikoss," she said softly, a new depth of shared understanding passing between them.

"The mission..." Sera continued immediately, pushing past the waves of pain with sheer willpower. "The sphere... the map... Crete..." Her gaze was fixed, distant, already planning. "We're not done yet. Orlov might be gone, but whoever he worked for back in Moscow... they won't give up easily. They know the potential now. We just need to find another way out of this damned maze and get to Crete before they figure out how to intervene there."

Hope, which had seemed utterly, irrevocably extinguished just minutes before, flared back to vibrant life within the damp, dark passage. Sera was alive. Battered, injured, but alive. They were together again. The relief was palpable, a tangible force pushing back the oppressive darkness and the crushing weight of despair. The mission, against all odds, was still on.

CHAPTER TWENTY-TWO

Light of Annihilation

With Sera alive and back with them, hope reignited in the oppressive darkness of the Labyrinth. Fragile but fierce. They pushed onward, deeper into the unknown passages beneath Crete. They followed the path Leo deduced from the celestial carvings he'd glimpsed, Sera moving with slow, grim determination, leaning heavily on a sturdy walking stick Nikos had fashioned from a stalagmite fragment, refusing to let the throbbing pain in her splinted leg slow them down more than absolutely necessary. Nikos, his relief at Sera's survival palpable but overshadowed by the grim reality of their situation, scouted cautiously ahead, his flashlight beam probing the darkness. Leo walked beside Sera, offering support when the footing grew treacherous, constantly scanning the ancient walls for more clues, the significant weight of the obsidian sphere heavy and somehow menacing in the specially padded pouch Sera had fashioned inside his satchel. It felt like carrying a sleeping bomb.

The tunnels here felt distinctly different from the natural caves and rough-hewn passages they'd navigated earlier. The walls were smoother, more deliberately constructed, hinting at advanced engineering far beyond simple excavation. The air grew dryer, warmer, and the faint smell they'd noticed earlier became stronger, now overlaid with the distinct scent of ozone, like the air after a lightning strike. It made the hairs on Leo's arms stand on end.

After navigating another series of tight passages that seemed designed to restrict movement and several small, empty antechambers, the tunnel suddenly opened dramatically, breathtakingly, into a space so vast it defied belief. They emerged onto a wide, high ledge overlooking an immense cavern, its distant walls lost in shadow, its ceiling vanishing into absolute blackness far, far above the reach of their most powerful flashlight beams. The air here thrummed, not just with a low, audible humming sound that seemed to emanate from the center of the space, but with a palpable, almost physical energy that vibrated through the soles of their boots and resonated deep within their bones. Strange, faint blueish light pulsed rhythmically from the cavern's center, casting eerie, elongated, shifting shadows on the distant, unseen walls.

And in that center, dominating the vast, echoing space, stood the source of the light and the energy: a colossal, impossibly intricate structure unlike anything Leo had ever imagined, let alone seen in any historical text. It wasn't stone; it appeared to be built entirely from some dark, non-reflective, perhaps basaltic or unknown metal that seemed to actively absorb their flashlight beams, making it difficult to gauge its true texture or composition. It rose from the smooth cavern floor like a complex, multi-tiered, alien tree forged in some Cyclopean foundry. A dizzying web of interlocking rings, strange conduits pulsing visibly with faint blue light, and arrays of large, multi-faceted crystalline lenses angled towards the cavern roof, all crafted with a precision and geometric complexity that seemed utterly impossible for the ancient world, or indeed, any known civilization. It hummed with immense, barely contained power, a sleeping giant breathing energy into the stale subterranean air. This wasn't just an artifact; it was unmistakably a *machine*, ancient beyond reckoning yet disturbingly functional.

At its heart, nestled within the complex framework of dark metal rings and conduits, was a central pedestal. Upon this pedestal sat a perfectly spherical indentation, clearly designed to hold something of significant size. Something that was currently missing. The indentation itself pulsed with the same faint blue light as the rest of the machine, almost like a vacant throne waiting for its occupant.

Leo instinctively clutched his satchel tighter, the heavy weight of the obsidian sphere suddenly feeling immense, charged with significance. *This* was where it belonged. The size, the shape, the energy... *This* was the key. The 'stone that sees the stars' was the heart of this impossible machine.

"*Theos mou*... God Almighty..." Nikos breathed beside him, stunned into silence, crossing himself repeatedly, his face pale with awe and superstitious fear. The scale and sheer alienness of the device overwhelmed him.

Leo's mind reeled with a dizzying mix of profound terror and overwhelming exhilaration. The historian faced with the ultimate, world-shattering discovery. "This... this is it," he stammered, taking an involuntary step closer to the edge of the ledge, his eyes fixed on the empty, pulsing socket below. "This is what the prophecy, the sphere, the Labyrinth... the maps, the warnings... it all led to *this* machine."

Sera gripped her Makarov tighter, her knuckles white. Years of training screamed at her that anything this powerful, this unknown, was inherently dangerous, especially with its core component currently residing in her partner's satchel. "What is it, Leo?" she asked urgently, her voice low and tight, pulling his attention away from the spectacle. "Some kind of ancient power generator? A communications device? Or... a weapon?"

As if in answer, their combined flashlight beams, sweeping downwards, illuminated large panels set into the metal near the base of the colossal structure. These panels were covered in deeply etched inscriptions. Rows upon rows of ancient Greek letters, stark and clear against the dark metal, similar in style to those on the Delphi tablet but even older, more formal, more arcane.

"Let me see..." Leo scrambled hastily down a short, crumbling section of rock leading from the ledge onto the main cavern floor, rushing towards the base of the humming device, momentarily heedless of the potential danger in his academic fervor. Sera and Nikos followed cautiously behind him, Sera scanning the cavern entrances, Nikos watching the strange machine with wary apprehension. Leo ran his fingers reverently over the cool, impossibly smooth metal, his eyes scanning the ancient text, his mind working furiously, deciphering the archaic language, the meaning slowly, chillingly resolving itself.

"It speaks of... harnessing the very essence of the stars," he translated, his voice hushed, trembling now not just with awe but with dawning horror. "Drawing power directly from the cosmos... channeling celestial energy through a core resonator... a focusing crystal of immense density..." He glanced back towards his satchel, his blood running cold, knowing with absolute certainty what the 'core resonator' had to be. He traced one specific line of text, his finger shaking slightly. "It describes a beam... a focused energy projection capable of... *reshaping the world*." His eyes scanned further, landing on another chilling phrase, etched larger than the others, almost like a title or a designation. "'*Phos Exolethreuontos*'..." He struggled with the archaic form for a moment. "The Light... that Destroys... The Light... of Annihilation. A beam to scour the earth clean."

His gaze darted upwards towards the complex array of huge crystalline lenses positioned high on the structure, aimed towards the cavern roof, presumably towards the surface world far above. "Sera, Nikos... this isn't just a power source," he declared, his voice barely a whisper, horrified by the implications. "It's a weapon. An ancient superweapon. A weapon of unimaginable destruction, just waiting for its key. The sphere."

As if to demonstrate its latent potential, the energy humming within the device intensified slightly, the blue light flickering brighter. A narrow, pencil-thin beam of *pale* white light lanced out silently from the main focusing lens array at the very top, striking a section of the cavern wall high above them. Unfocused, weak, almost like a pilot light for a furnace. It simply illuminated the rock, lacking the terrifying destructive power the text described, but the potential was clearly, undeniably there, dormant, waiting to be unleashed once the sphere was inserted into the empty socket. The machine hummed softly, patiently, waiting.

Leo swallowed hard, the metallic taste of fear sharp in his mouth, his mind racing, connecting the ancient text to the deadly realities of the modern Cold War world. "The Soviets... Orlov... if they could get the sphere, put it in here, figure out how to *control* this... It's not like a nuclear bomb, spraying radiation and fallout indiscriminately. This text describes it as... *surgical*. A beam they could potentially target anywhere on the planet, striking with devastating, focused force, instantly vaporizing cities, military bases, anything... leaving nothing behind but glass. No warning. No defense. Instant annihilation on demand." The precarious balance of mutually assured destruction that kept the Cold War frozen would shatter instantly.

Sera's face was grim stone, her eyes hard as flint. She understood immediately, the tactical implications chillingly clear. "Ultimate power," she stated flatly, her hand tightening on her weapon. "The perfect first-strike weapon. Orlov knew. He, or the people he works for, knew what this thing was capable of, if they could just get the sphere."

Nikos stared wide-eyed at the spot on the cavern wall where the pale beam had struck, then back at the silently humming, impossibly powerful machine. "This thing," he breathed, crossing himself again, his voice filled with dread. "It waits. It sleeps. It could truly end the world."

"Precisely! And *you* hold the key!"

The familiar voice, amplified unnaturally by the cavern's strange acoustics, dripping with manic triumph and exertion, echoed from the dark passage entrance they had emerged from only moments before.

They spun around, weapons coming up instinctively. Orlov stood there on the ledge above them, flanked by his two remaining soldiers, their weapons raised and ready. He looked terrible. The rough bandage around his head heavily stained with fresh blood, his uniform torn and filthy, his face pale and contorted with pain. But his remaining eye locked onto Leo's satchel with a burning, fanatical light as he took in the sight of the colossal device and the crucial *empty* pedestal at its heart.

"So," Orlov spat out the word, a chilling, triumphant smile twisting his lips despite his obvious agony. "The nest is found. The instrument awaits." His gaze fixed predatorily on Leo's satchel. "Hand it over, Doctor. Now. Hand over the obsidian sphere. Its power belongs to the Soviet Union!"

He leveled his pistol, its barrel unwavering despite his injuries, aiming it directly at Leo's chest. "Do not test my patience. The sphere, now! You have brought the key directly to the lock for me! How very convenient!"

Leo, Sera, and Nikos stood frozen for a heartbeat, trapped between the dormant world-ending weapon humming behind them and the desperate, wounded, but lethally determined man determined to finally turn the key. The final confrontation had arrived, beneath the earth, with the fate of the world hanging precariously in the balance.

CHAPTER TWENTY-THREE

Confrontation

The vast cavern crackled with palpable tension, the very air thick with the low, resonant hum of the ancient device and the sharp, metallic scent of ozone generated by its latent power. Orlov stood poised on the entrance ledge above them, pistol aimed squarely down at Leo, his remaining eye fixed and burning with an intense, almost religious fervor. His two surviving soldiers flanked him, their AK-74s trained unwaveringly on Sera and Nikos, fingers tight and white-knuckled on their triggers, their expressions grimly professional. The faint blue light pulsing from the dormant machine cast long, dancing shadows, making the cavern feel vast and menacing.

"The sphere, Doctor," Orlov repeated, his voice dangerously soft now, dropping the earlier rage, adopting the chillingly calm tone of a predator savoring the final moments before the kill. "Hand it over. Your interference, your meddling in matters far beyond your comprehension, ends now. This power will serve the glorious Soviet Union, forging a new world order. And you," his gaze flickered briefly towards Sera and Nikos, "will have the...

distinct privilege of witnessing the dawn of that new era before you die."

Sera shifted her weight almost imperceptibly onto the balls of her feet, her body coiled like a spring, ready to move despite the throbbing pain in her leg. "We won't let you have it, Orlov," she stated clearly, her voice cold and steady, projecting a confidence she didn't entirely feel, trying to draw his fire, buy Leo a second. They were outgunned, trapped deep underground in the heart of an enemy's potential superweapon. "This thing... it's too dangerous for anyone, especially fanatics like you."

Leo clutched the satchel containing the heavy obsidian sphere, his mind racing frantically. They couldn't fight their way out against rifles in this open space. Could he stall? Could he possibly reason with a wounded, cornered madman clearly obsessed with obtaining this power? He saw the absolute, unshakeable conviction burning in Orlov's eye and knew instantly negotiation was futile. Orlov was beyond reason.

"You understand *nothing*, Doctor," Orlov sneered, dismissing Leo's unspoken desperate plea, his lip curling. "Power isn't dangerous; weakness is dangerous. Power is meant to be wielded! Now! The sphere!" He gestured impatiently with his pistol towards one of his men. "Seize the historian and the sphere! Shoot the others if they interfere! The woman and the Cretan... eliminate them regardless once the sphere is secure."

CONFRONTATION 249

The soldier closest to Leo, the one Sera had wounded earlier on the bridge but who was still functional, lunged forward down the rocky slope from the ledge, his rifle held ready. In the same instant, Sera moved like lightning. She didn't fire at Orlov on the ledge; she aimed low, firing a single, precise shot from her Makarov that slammed into the advancing soldier's good knee. He screamed, a high-pitched sound of agony, collapsing in a heap on the cavern floor, his rifle clattering away.

The cavern erupted into chaos. Orlov's remaining soldier immediately opened fire from the ledge, spraying bullets wildly down towards Sera and Nikos, who simultaneously dove for cover behind the intricate metal framework of the ancient device near the pedestal. Sparks flew violently as rounds ricocheted off the strange, dark metal with loud *pings* and *whines*, the material proving surprisingly resistant. Sera returned fire from her new position, her silenced shots almost inaudible beneath the roar of the AK-74, but her accuracy forced the soldier to keep his head down, firing blindly from the ledge. Nikos, armed only with the heavy metal flashlight he'd kept from the escape, stayed low behind a thick metal conduit, desperately looking for any opportunity, any weapon, any way to help.

Leo scrambled back frantically, ducking behind the main pedestal supporting the sphere socket as bullets whined past his head, smacking into the rock wall behind him. Heart pounding, hands shaking, he fumbled with the satchel clasp, pulling out the obsidian sphere. It felt unnervingly cool and strangely heavy, almost dense, in his trembling hands, pulsing faintly with its own inner blue light, seemingly undisturbed by the violence erupting around it.

"Get the sphere!" Orlov roared from the ledge, firing his own pistol down towards Sera's position, the shots again pinging harmlessly off the device's bizarre, resilient metal framework. The soldier Sera had just wounded on the floor saw his chance while she was momentarily pinned down by Orlov's fire. Ignoring the searing pain in both his shattered knees, fueled by desperation or fear of Orlov's wrath, he lunged again, crawling agonizingly across the floor, this time straight for Leo, his hand grasping, trying to wrench the satchel and the sphere away.

"No! Get away!" Leo yelled, struggling desperately to hold onto the precious, terrifying artifact.

Sera saw the renewed attack on Leo from the corner of her eye. With a sudden burst of speed, ignoring the risk from the soldier still firing from the ledge, she launched herself away from her cover, tackling the crawling soldier hard around the legs just as his fingers brushed against the smooth surface of the sphere Leo held. They crashed heavily to the stone floor in a tangle of limbs. The impact jarred Leo's grip. The obsidian sphere flew from his grasp, hit the floor with a surprisingly dull thud, and then skittered away across the smooth stone like a giant black pearl, rolling towards the dark center of the cavern floor.

"Idiots!" Orlov bellowed in absolute frustration from the ledge. Blinded by rage, he fired again, wildly, ignoring Sera grappling with his wounded man. The shot missed them completely but struck a complex junction box mounted on the side of the ancient device near the base.

Sparks showered outwards violently with a loud electrical *crackle*. Lights flickered erratically across the entire machine's surface. The steady, resonant hum faltered, dropping in pitch, then suddenly rising into a discordant, angry whine that grated on their nerves. The pale pilot beam emanating from the main lens array high above wavered violently, spitting pulses of unstable white energy before sputtering out completely. The machine groaned, a deep, mechanical sound of distress.

Seizing the moment of chaos while Orlov and his remaining soldier were momentarily distracted by the device's malfunction, Leo scrambled desperately on hands and knees across the floor towards the rolling obsidian sphere. His fingers closed around its smooth, cool surface just as it was about to disappear into the deep shadows near the cavern wall. He felt that familiar, faint electric jolt again as he touched it, stronger this time, a strange sense of urgent connection, almost like the damaged device recognized its missing heart and was calling to it.

He looked back frantically at the empty socket on the pedestal. The celestial symbols carved around it were glowing faintly now, energized by the device's unstable state, shifting slightly. He recognized them instantly. The patterns from the mosaic, the crude star carvings in the tunnels. They represented specific constellations, specific alignments... *Lyra*, the text had mentioned *Lyra* for harmonious resonance... for stable operation... but what if...? What if harmony wasn't the answer now?

Orlov, recovering quickly from his fury, saw Leo retrieving the sphere. He turned his attention back towards Leo, who now knelt exposed on the open cavern floor, clutching the sphere protectively. "Foolish historian," Orlov snarled, starting to descend from the ledge, limping heavily but moving with purpose. "You cannot comprehend the power you hold! Give it to me! Now!"

Leo looked at the pulsing sphere in his hands, then at the glowing, empty socket on the pedestal, then at the advancing, determined Orlov. An idea, wild, desperate, born of fragmented knowledge gleaned from ancient texts and a sudden surge of defiant courage, sparked in his mind. It was insane. It might overload the entire cavern. It might kill them all instantly. But letting Orlov get the sphere was unthinkable; stabilizing the device for him was impossible. Disrupting it further, causing catastrophic failure... it was their only, desperate chance. He had to try to disrupt the harmony, not restore it.

Ignoring Orlov's raised pistol, ignoring Sera's shout ("Leo, no!"), Leo surged back towards the device pedestal, clutching the heavy sphere. His hands shook violently as he lifted the obsidian orb towards the waiting socket. He remembered the alignment sequence related to Lyra that the inscriptions hinted was for stable power... but what if he deliberately *reversed* it? Intentionally twisted the sphere as he inserted it, misaligning its internal matrix with the energy conduits represented by the glowing star symbols around the socket? If such a thing even existed.

With Orlov just yards away now, his pistol raised, his finger tightening on the trigger, Leo took a final, ragged breath and shoved the obsidian sphere back into its socket, twisting it hard counter-clockwise with all his strength, trying to force an alignment *opposite* to the sequence his research suggested was correct.

For a terrifying heartbeat, nothing happened. Absolute silence descended, except for Orlov's heavy, ragged breathing and the frantic pounding of Leo's own heart echoing in his ears.

Then, the device *screamed*.

The low hum exploded instantly into a deafening, high-pitched, metallic shriek that vibrated through the very stone beneath their feet, shaking the entire cavern violently. The lines of energy across the dark metal framework flared with blinding intensity, pulsing not blue, but a furious, chaotic, angry *red*. The pale pilot beam was gone, replaced by wildly uncontrolled arcs of raw, crimson energy lashing out from the main lens array like angry, destructive tentacles, striking the cavern walls with explosive force.

Orlov stopped in his tracks, his intended shot forgotten for a moment, his remaining eye wide with sudden shock and visceral alarm. The sheer, untamed, raw power now surging violently from the ancient device was far beyond anything his scientists back in Moscow had predicted or could possibly hope to control. This wasn't a weapon; it was Armageddon unleashed.

The furious red energy beams whipped randomly around the vast cavern, striking walls, ceiling, and floor, instantly vaporizing solid rock, carving new, unwanted passages, sending molten stone dripping down the walls. One thick beam lashed downwards with impossible speed, straight towards Orlov. He roared, a primal sound mixing defiant fury and sudden, abject terror, finally squeezing the trigger reflexively.

The bullet spat from his pistol towards Leo. But in the same microsecond, a shimmering, almost invisible field of distorted, heat-hazy energy erupted violently outwards from the overloaded device, surrounding the central structure like a protective, incandescent bubble. The bullet struck the shimmering field and simply... vanished. Deflected, disintegrated, erased from existence.

Leo, hands still pressed against the now searingly hot sphere locking it into its misaligned position, felt a massive surge of raw power course through him, a dizzying, overwhelming connection to the ancient, screaming machine. It felt like grabbing onto raw lightning. He had done *something*. He had overloaded it, turned its immense power against itself, but it felt utterly, terrifyingly unstable, on the verge of catastrophic, final meltdown.

Orlov and his remaining conscious soldier (the one Sera had tackled, now fighting to get away from her) scrambled desperately for cover behind rock pillars as the red energy beams danced manically, randomly around the chamber, tearing huge chunks from the walls, bringing sections of the ceiling crashing down. Sera, reacting instantly to the new danger, dragged Nikos bodily behind a large cluster of thick, crystalline stalagmites, shielding their eyes from the blinding, pulsating red light.

The obsidian sphere lodged in the heart of the device now glowed with an unbearable, pulsing red heat, cracks beginning to appear on its previously flawless surface. The shriek deepened, the vibrations intensified, shaking the entire cavern so violently it was hard to stand. The ancient machine was literally tearing itself apart from the inside out, awake, furious, and utterly beyond control. And no one knew what would happen when it finally, inevitably broke.

CHAPTER TWENTY-FOUR

Overload

The ancient machine continued screaming its death throes, unleashing a bone-deep wail that seemed to bore straight into their skulls. Crimson energy erupted in wild arcs from the lens assembly, carving molten scars across stone that had stood untouched for millennia. The cavern floor bucked and heaved like a living thing, threatening to throw them to their knees. Pulverized rock cascaded from above in choking clouds, turning the air thick and gritty. Through the swirling debris, the obsidian sphere blazed like a malignant star at the machine's heart, each pulse sending waves of scorching heat across their exposed skin.

Sera and Nikos remained pinned down behind their crumbling cluster of stalagmites, shielding their faces from falling debris and the intense light, the intense heat radiating from the device core washing over them. Leo stood frozen for a split second beside the device's pedestal, stunned into immobility by the sheer, untamed, catastrophic power he had unleashed. He hadn't destroyed it cleanly, but he'd definitely thrown a massive wrench into its ancient, alien works.

Through the maelstrom of noise, light, and vibration, Orlov proved his ruthless, almost inhuman tenacity. Shouting desperate orders in Russian over the deafening roar, somehow making himself heard, he rallied his remaining conscious soldier (the other lay groaning, clutching his shattered knees near the entrance passage). Using the flickering, unpredictable red light as strobing cover, they moved with brutal efficiency, circling wide around the dangerously unstable device towards Sera and Nikos's position. Before Sera, disoriented by the flashing light and noise, could react effectively from her pinned position, the soldier lunged forward, slamming the hard butt of his AK-74 viciously into Nikos's head just as the Cretan tried to rise. Nikos collapsed with a grunt, sprawling onto the vibrating rock floor. Simultaneously, Orlov, ignoring the agony in his knee and head, lunged at Sera, using his bulk and sheer desperate strength to knock her pistol aside, disarming her and shoving her roughly back against the cavern wall, pressing the muzzle of his own service pistol painfully into her ribs.

"Don't move!" the soldier yelled hoarsely, scrambling back towards Nikos and aiming his rifle unsteadily towards the groaning man on the floor.

Sera froze, breathing heavily, the rough rock scraping her back, acutely aware of Orlov's pistol pressing hard against her side, the smell of his sweat and blood suddenly sharp in the ozone-filled air. They were caught. Utterly exposed.

Leo watched helplessly from across the chaotic chamber near the pedestal, his heart sinking like a stone into icy water. His desperate gambit had created chaos, thrown the enemy off balance, but it hadn't secured their escape. Orlov, wounded, bleeding, likely half-blind, but dangerously focused and driven by fanaticism, limped heavily towards him, dragging a captured Sera along roughly as a shield, his visible eye burning with cold, triumphant fury.

"Now, Doctor Saint," Orlov snarled, his voice grating, strained, barely audible over the continuous shriek of the dying machine. "Enough games! It appears your friends find themselves in a rather... delicate position. One wrong move from you..." He nodded pointedly towards the soldier who now had his rifle aimed alternately between the subdued Sera and the groaning, barely conscious Nikos. "Your little sabotage attempt was... inconvenient. Destructive. But," he glanced towards the still-pulsing red sphere, "your little trick didn't completely disable it. The core still holds energy. I suggest you reverse whatever you did. Stabilize it. Now. Or your friends will pay the ultimate price for your academic cleverness."

Leo's mind raced, faster than ever before, sorting through impossible options. He looked at Sera's hard, defiant face. She gave a minuscule shake of her head, almost invisible. Then he looked at Nikos struggling to regain consciousness on the floor, vulnerable under the soldier's rifle. He couldn't let them die. Not after everything. He had to cooperate, or at least appear to, buy them one last chance. "Alright," he stated, forcing his voice to sound steady, trying to project a calm he was galaxies away from feeling, raising his hands slowly in a clear gesture of surrender. "Alright! Just... don't hurt them. Please."

"A wise decision, Doctor," Orlov replied, though his eye remained cold as ice, devoid of mercy. "Now, approach the controls. Slowly. Do not try anything foolish. And explain *exactly* what you did to cause this... instability."

Under Orlov's intense, unwavering scrutiny, and with the constant, implicit threat to Sera and Nikos hanging heavier than the mountain above them, Leo moved cautiously back towards the device's humming, vibrating control console near the pedestal. The angry red energy beams still lashed out intermittently from the main lens array, less frequently now as if the power fluctuated, but still dangerously unpredictable, carving molten scars into the rock walls. The deafening shriek had subsided slightly into a deep, guttural, unstable groan, like the machine was tearing itself apart from the inside.

Leo pretended to study the glowing symbols around the sphere's socket and the various levers and crystalline dials on the console, feigning confusion and deep concern, running trembling fingers over the strange, cool metal surface. "I... I think when I twisted the sphere, I overloaded the primary resonance matrix when I misaligned it with the Lyra constellation input," he improvised, trying to sound like an academic completely out of his depth, recalling technical terms from physics papers he'd barely understood. "The energy flow is highly unstable. It could... it could cascade into total core collapse at any moment."

"Then *stabilize* it, Doctor!" Orlov snapped impatiently, shoving Sera slightly forward for emphasis, making her stumble. "Before it destroys itself...and us with it!"

Leo nodded quickly, feigning panic. "Yes, yes, of course. Just... give me a moment to analyze the harmonic feedback loop..." He ran his hands over the controls again, his mind desperately searching for a real solution, a final, suicidal gambit. He remembered the inscriptions near the base, the specific warnings about chaotic energy release if certain shutdown protocols were activated *incorrectly*. He'd triggered *something* like that with his random twist, but not completely. Could he push it further? Intentionally trigger the catastrophic failure sequence? Could he cause a feedback loop that would destroy the core entirely, maybe cause a localized implosion, burying the weapon forever, rather than letting Orlov regain even partial control? It was an incredible risk; the energy release could vaporize them all instantly. But it was the only way to be sure.

He pointed with a shaky finger to a series of larger, complex symbols glowing on the main console. "This sequence here," he announced, trying to sound like he was having a sudden breakthrough, injecting false hope into his voice. "I believe it controls the primary focusing array and the energy regulation conduits. If I can just re-calibrate the harmonic frequency using these input regulators..." It sounded plausible, highly technical, hopefully enough to fool Orlov, whose scientific knowledge was likely less than his own, for just a few crucial seconds.

Orlov leaned closer, peering intently at the console, his suspicion momentarily overridden by his desperate desire to salvage and control the immense power within his grasp. "Do it then, Doctor. Carefully. And quickly."

Leo placed his hands on the controls, his fingers hovering over a large crystalline dial that seemed to pulse faintly and a series of smooth, touch-sensitive panels etched with the star symbols. Taking a deep ragged breath, he glancing quickly towards Sera. Hoping she understood, trying to convey his intention with his eyes, that she was ready to react instantly. Instead of inputting the stabilizing sequence he'd described, he recalled the specific fragment from the inscriptions. A complex emergency shutdown sequence, one the text warned could cause a catastrophic energy feedback, an implosion, if initiated while the core resonator was already in a state of critical instability. *This is it*, he thought. *No turning back*. He slammed his palm down hard on the touch-sensitive panels in the proscribed 'shutdown' sequence and simultaneously twisted the main crystalline dial hard to the left, deliberately forcing the unstable energy flow *away* from regulation, directly into overload.

For a split second, an eternity, nothing happened. The machine groaned. Silence, except for Orlov's heavy, ragged breathing and the frantic pounding of Leo's own heart echoing like thunder in his ears.

Then, with a sound not just like the universe tearing itself apart, but like metal screaming in agony, the device *exploded* inwards. The pulsating red light from the sphere flared instantaneously to an unbearable white-hot intensity, blinding them all. The groaning noise became a physical blow, a concussive wave that threw them back. The entire colossal structure shuddered violently, visibly buckling and twisting. Cracks spiderwebbed with impossible speed across the dark metal framework. The shimmering protective energy field flickered violently, then collapsed completely with a sound like shattering glass. The remaining erratic energy beams vanished, sucked back violently into the core, only for the entire machine to begin vibrating with terrifying, uncontrollable intensity, shaking the very foundations of the cavern.

"What have you done?!" Orlov bellowed, stumbling back in disbelief and sudden terror as the cavern floor beneath them began to heave violently, massive cracks appearing instantly in the walls, splitting the rock face, and huge chunks of stone and crystalline formations started breaking free from the ceiling directly above them. The air filled with the roar of collapsing rock. The entire chamber was coming down around them.

This was it. Leo locked eyes with Sera across the chaos for a fraction of second. *Now!*

While Orlov and his remaining soldier were momentarily stunned, paralyzed by the sudden, catastrophic escalation, Leo acted without conscious thought. He shoved the heavy, sparking control console with all his might towards Orlov, sending it crashing into the Colonel's legs, knocking him off balance just as a large slab of rock the size of a small car detached from the ceiling and crashed down exactly where Orlov had been standing. Orlov cried out, a thin shriek of pain and fury, as the edge of the rock grazed his shoulder, pinning his arm beneath its immense weight.

In that instant of distraction, Sera exploded into action. With vicious precision, she drove her elbow hard into the ribs of the soldier still holding her, breaking his grip with a sickening crack. As he doubled over, gasping, she simultaneously kicked Nikos's legs, shouting "*Tora!*" (Now!), urging him towards the relative cover of a massive fallen rock pillar near the passage mouth just as more of the ceiling gave way with a deafening roar. Nikos, groggy but reacting on pure survival instinct, scrambled desperately behind the pillar.

"This way! Quick!" Leo shouted above the cacophony, spotting a narrow, jagged fissure opening up in the far cavern wall as the chamber literally tore itself apart. A fissure that hadn't been there moments before, created by the device's self-destruction. He sprinted towards it, adrenaline lending impossible speed to his usually clumsy legs. Sera was right behind him, grabbing Nikos by the arm, helping him to his feet and half-dragging the disoriented Cretan along with her.

They plunged together into the narrow crack in the rock just as the main chamber behind them collapsed completely inward with a final, deafening roar and a blinding flash of white light, sending a massive shockwave of superheated dust and displaced air blasting after them down the new passage. They could hear Orlov's enraged, pain-filled shouts abruptly cut off, silenced forever by the falling mountain.

They didn't look back. They stumbled deeper into the newly formed, unstable passage, leaving the screaming, self-destructing ancient device and the wounded, likely buried, Colonel Orlov behind them in the utter chaos of the collapsing Labyrinth. They had survived the final confrontation, but the mountain itself, shaking in its death throes, seemed determined to bury them along with its deadly secrets.

CHAPTER TWENTY-FIVE

The Final Collapse

The narrow fissure Leo had spotted, torn open in the cavern wall by the device's self-destructive fury, was their only way out. They plunged into it desperately, leaving the roaring chaos, the blinding white light, and the certain death of the collapsing device chamber behind them. This passage wasn't ancient or deliberately carved; it felt raw, jagged, new-born from the mountain tearing itself apart. The air was thick with choking rock dust, hot and tasting of sulfur and vaporized stone, and the floor was a treacherous, uneven slope of shifting, freshly fractured rubble that slid under their boots. The terrifying sounds of the main chamber's utter self-destruction echoed behind them, a continuous, deafening rumble that vibrated through the very stone they crawled through, threatening to bring this fragile escape route down on top of them as well.

Sera, grimacing visibly against the intense pain radiating from her splinted leg, somehow took the lead again, her flashlight beam cutting weakly through the dense, swirling dust cloud. Nikos half-supported, half-dragged Leo, who was still shaken and disoriented from his confrontation with the device and the desperate escape, his ears ring-ing from the final explosion. They moved as quickly as they dared down the unstable slope, acutely aware that the passage itself felt terrifyingly unstable, groaning and shifting around them with each powerful aftershock from the collapsing chamber behind.

After what felt like an eternity scrambling blindly through the tight, suffocating crack, praying it wouldn't become a dead end or their tomb, the passage suddenly widened, opening out into another vast, echoing space. They cautiously stepped out onto a wide rock shelf, finding themselves in a cavern even larger, it seemed, than the one that had housed the destructive device. Its distant walls were lost in shadow, and its ceiling vanished completely into impenetrable darkness high above, far beyond the reach of their wavering flashlight beams. The air here was strangely still after the chaos behind them, cool, and heavy with the scent of deep, undisturbed dampness. The only sound was the faint, rhythmic, almost hypnotic lapping of unseen water somewhere nearby in the blackness.

Sera swept her flashlight beam slowly across the immense space. It revealed a huge subterranean lake stretching out before them, its surface black, glassy, and perfectly still, reflecting the narrow beams of their flashlights like a dark, distorted mirror stretching away into the infinite darkness. The water appeared to fill most of the cavern floor, extending into the blackness, its full size impossible to gauge. Strange, pale rock formations, like bleached bones or melting wax, dripped down from the unseen roof in places, hinting at millennia of slow geological processes.

"Where in God's name are we now?" Leo whispered, his voice hoarse with dust and awe, momentarily forgetting their desperate situation, captivated by the sheer scale and unexpected, eerie beauty of the hidden underground sea.

"Deeper," Nikos murmured, his voice hushed, his expression grim as his gaze swept the immense cavern walls, searching for any sign of another passage, another way out. "Much deeper. Deeper than any known caves on the island. This place... it shouldn't exist according to any map." He shivered slightly, despite the still air. "It feels... wrong. Like a place meant to stay hidden."

As they moved carefully along the edge of the dark lake, their flashlight beams probing the shoreline, searching for another tunnel, another possible escape route, Sera's light snagged on movement near the far wall. A flicker of motion in the deep shadows beyond a cluster of stalagmites. "Hold up," Sera warned instantly, her voice a low whisper, raising her Makarov again, the faint click of the safety echoing in the vast silence. "Company."

They approached cautiously, weapons ready, using the clusters of stalagmites and other rock formations along the lake's edge as intermittent cover, moving silently now, their footsteps muffled by the damp rock. As they drew closer, the figure resolved itself in the combined beams of their lights. Slumped against the cavern wall, near the mouth of a narrow, slime-slicked fissure that reeked of sulfur and freshly shattered rock – a passage clearly not meant for human transit – was Orlov. He was a nightmarish vision: his uniform was shredded, caked in mud and something darker that looked like congealed blood. The crude bandage around his head had slipped, revealing the horrific, empty socket beneath, and fresh gashes crisscrossed his exposed skin. He looked less like a soldier and more like something clawed back from the abyss, utterly broken, yet his one remaining eye burned with a disturbing, feverish intensity as he watched them approach. The heavy service pistol lay near his outstretched, trembling hand, as if he lacked the strength, or perhaps the will, to lift it. The bridge collapse must have thrown him or one of his men towards a lower gallery, some unmapped capillary of the Labyrinth, and his relentless will had driven him through that hellish, uncharted maze to arrive here, somehow, impossibly, ahead of them.

"You..." Orlov rasped, the sound dry and grating in the silence, like stones scraping together. He coughed, a terrible, wracking sound that shook his battered frame, spitting more blood onto the cavern floor. "You survived the collapse too. Impossible..."

"Looks like it," Sera replied coldly, her voice flat, devoid of sympathy or triumph, her pistol still aimed steadily at his chest. "It's over, Orlov. Finished. For you, at least."

A weak, rattling sound escaped Orlov's lips. A ghost of his former arrogant chuckle, now laced with pain and delirium. "Finished?" he wheezed, his good eye flickering wildly between them and the dark tunnel behind him. "You think this is finished just because the chamber fell? Because *I* am finished?" He coughed again, a deeper, wetter sound this time. "The power... the potential... *Oko*... it is still there. You merely... delayed the inevitable. My people... the backup teams... the scientists..." He gestured weakly with a trembling hand towards the dark tunnel opening behind him. "They are still down there somewhere... deeper perhaps... alerted by the energy release... trying to understand... trying to control... They will succeed..." His voice trailed off in another fit of violent coughing that left him gasping for air.

Leo stepped forward impulsively, ignoring Sera's cautionary glance. Pity warred with revulsion as he looked at the broken man. "Orlov, listen to me! That device... the energy... it's unstable! Wild! Dangerous beyond measure! It needs to be contained, sealed away forever, not controlled! It could destroy everything! The whole island! Maybe more!"

Orlov's feverish gaze flickered towards Leo, focusing with difficulty. For a fleeting, startling moment, something other than fanaticism seemed to cross his remaining features. A flicker of doubt? Abject fear? A glimpse of the terrified man beneath the iron mask of ideology? But it vanished as quickly as it appeared, replaced instantly by the familiar cold fire of absolute conviction, perhaps amplified by delirium.

"Silence, historian," he croaked, spittle flecking his lips. "You understand... nothing. The Party... the Union... the future... requires strength! Requires this power! We will harness it... We will... prevail..."

Before Leo could argue further, trying desperately to break through the man's conditioning, a deep, powerful tremor shook the entire cavern, much stronger and longer than any they had felt before during the device's overload. The dark water in the subterranean lake surged violently, black waves slapping hard against the stone shore, sending spray high into the air. Dust and small rocks rained down heavily from the distant, unseen ceiling. The low, resonant hum that had filled the device chamber seemed to return, deeper now, more powerful, vibrating through the very rock beneath their feet, as if the entire mountain was groaning in its death agony.

Orlov's head snapped up, his expression twisting into a bizarre combination of primal terror and crazed, ecstatic elation. "*Da!*" he gasped, his voice suddenly stronger, almost manic. "They are doing it! My scientists... they survived... they are trying again! Trying to access the core!"

The ground beneath them began to heave and crack. New fissures snaked rapidly across the cavern floor near the lake's edge, widening visibly. The distant cavern walls groaned ominously under immense pressure. The air grew noticeably hotter, thick and charged with static energy that made their skin prickle. Water began pouring from new cracks opening high above, turning the distant dripping into a torrential downpour, the sound echoing like thunder in the vast space. The Labyrinth, ancient and powerful, was tearing itself apart.

From the dark tunnel opening behind Orlov, a faint, intense light began to pulse, growing rapidly stronger, casting his battered, slumped figure into stark, dramatic relief against the pulsating glow. It wasn't the steady blue light of the device on standby, nor the angry red of its overload. This was a blinding, pure white light, pulsing with unimaginable, raw power leaking from somewhere deeper within the mountain.

"We have to get out of here! NOW!" Nikos yelled urgently, grabbing Leo's arm and pulling him physically back from the cracking ledge near the water's edge. "The whole mountain is coming down on our heads!"

Sera spared one last, quick look at Orlov. He seemed completely mesmerized by the pulsing white light emanating from the tunnel, a madman greeting the apocalypse, perhaps finally achieving some twisted form of union with the power he craved. There was nothing they could do for him, or against him now. Their only chance was immediate escape. They scanned the vibrating cavern walls, searching desperately for another fissure, another passage, any way out, as the ancient Labyrinth prepared to unleash its final, terrifying fury and reclaim its secrets forever.

Chapter Twenty-Six

Blood and Stone

The groan rumbling from the mountain's heart deepened, evolving into a continuous, grinding roar that resonated not just in their ears, but deep within their bones. The cavern, which had felt ancient and vast moments before, now seemed fragile, actively tearing itself apart around them. The rock underfoot trembled violently, threatening to buckle. New fissures, like jagged black lightning, raced across the stressed walls, showering them with dust and smaller fragments. Down below, the subterranean lake, once placid and dark, had become a boiling cauldron. Inky water churned and frothed, waves smashing against the ledges with surprising force, spray reaching impossibly high. Behind them, the unnatural tunnel where the wounded Orlov stood pulsed with an intensifying white light, radiating a heat that could be felt even from a distance, stinging their skin and making the air shimmer. It felt like the very heart of the collapsing mountain was about to detonate.

"There!" Nikos's shout barely cut through the cacophony. He pointed, his arm trembling not just from exertion but the violent shaking of the ground, towards the far wall. A section of rock, easily the size of a small house, had fractured and partially fallen away under the strain, revealing a sliver of absolute darkness. A narrow opening, previously completely concealed. "A way out! It *has* to be!"

There was no need for discussion, no time for hesitation. Survival instinct took over. They scrambled, adrenaline masking the scrapes and bruises, leaping over widening cracks that threatened to swallow them whole, ducking as chunks of rock rained down from the groaning ceiling. A quick, involuntary glance back showed Orlov still standing near the tunnel entrance, seemingly transfixed by the blinding, growing light, a silhouette against the impossible energy. A moth drawn to a world-ending flame. They left him to his incomprehensible fate. They flung themselves towards the narrow opening, hope warring with terror. Just as the last of them, Sera, dove through, an ear-splitting CRACK echoed behind them. A vast portion of the cavern roof gave way with a sound like the end of the world, collapsing inwards in a cascade of stone and dust. A hurricane blast of hot, pressurized air, thick with pulverized rock, slammed into their backs, nearly throwing them off their feet even within the passage.

The new tunnel was immediately different. It climbed steeply, forcing them onto hands and knees almost at once. Unlike the Labyrinth's hewn passages, this felt raw, natural. Perhaps an ancient lava tube or a fault line sheared open by the mountain's agony. The air changed rapidly; the damp, earthy smell replaced by something warmer, sharper, tinged with the bite of sulfur and, strangely, the distinct brine of sea salt. The deafening roar of the collapsing cavern began to fade, muffled by distance and tons of rock, replaced by a new, rhythmic thunder. The primal, distant sound of massive waves crashing against a shore.

The climb was brutal. The rock underhand was often slick with moisture, offering treacherous purchase. Their lungs burned, muscles screamed in protest, but the promise of open sky, however distant, spurred them on. They clawed their way upwards, dragging each other along, refusing to succumb to exhaustion. Finally, after what felt like an eternity, gasping ragged breaths, they saw it. Not sunlight, but a patch of churning, bruised-grey sky visible through an opening ahead.

They burst out of the tunnel's confines, staggering onto a narrow, windswept ledge, gasping not just for air but against the sudden onslaught of a fierce, biting wind that tore at their clothes and whipped their hair across their faces. The transition was jarring. From the crushing, subterranean darkness to this raw, exposed precipice. Below them, hundreds of feet down, a turbulent grey-green sea smashed itself against jagged black rocks that clawed upwards like skeletal fingers. Geysers of white spray erupted with each impact, carried aloft by the gale. The sky overhead was a uniform, oppressive grey, heavy with the threat of an impending storm. It felt utterly desolate, the absolute edge of the known world.

They had escaped. The Labyrinth, the collapsing mountain. They were behind them. Relief washed over them, potent but fleeting, immediately chilled by the wind and the grim reality of their situation. And then, the relief shattered completely, replaced by a cold, primal dread.

Not twenty yards away, etched against the bruised and turbulent sky like a vengeful spectre, stood Orlov. He was barely recognizable, a thing of blood, soot, and raw, exposed flesh where his uniform had been vaporized or torn away. One side of his body looked as if it had been seared by unimaginable heat, the other crushed. He swayed precariously, each breath a ragged testament to a will that had spat in the face of certain annihilation.

But it wasn't just his impossible presence that stole the air from their lungs.

Clutched in his one remaining functional hand, held forth almost like a dark offering to the storm, was the obsidian sphere. It pulsed with a faint, sickly internal light, no longer the calm blue of Belintash, but a disturbed, erratic glow. The cataclysmic overload Leo triggered must have ejected it from the heart of the dying machine. Orlov, consumed by his obsession even as the mountain came down, must have lunged for it, the sphere itself perhaps momentarily cocooning him in some chaotic energy backlash, blasting him through a newly ripped fissure in the rock – a raw, agonizing passage that had somehow, impossibly, vomited him out onto this same cliff edge.

The questions of *how* were drowned by the terrifying *what*. Orlov was here. And he had the sphere. The triumph blazing in his eye was no longer just manic; it was the incandescent glare of a soul utterly consumed by a power it could never truly comprehend, a terrifying parody of final manifestation.

"The power... it chose *me*!" Orlov's voice was a ravaged snarl, nearly lost in the howl of the wind and the crashing waves. "Destiny! It is mine now!"

"It was never yours! It doesn't belong to *anyone*!" Sera screamed back, raw fury momentarily eclipsing her exhaustion and the throbbing pain in her injured leg. Before Nikos or Leo could react, she launched herself forward, a primal cry tearing from her throat, heedless of the treacherous footing and the dizzying drop just inches away.

A desperate, brutal struggle erupted on the knife-edge of the world. Orlov, seemingly fueled by the sphere's energy and a madman's conviction, met her charge with surprising ferocity. He twisted, absorbing her momentum, and landed a heavy, backhanded blow across her face that sent her stumbling dangerously close to the edge. Leo instinctively lurched forward to help, heart pounding, while Nikos frantically scanned their surroundings, trying to see any way to intervene that wouldn't result in all of them plunging into the churning abyss below. The wind howled like a hungry beast, trying to tear them from their precarious perch.

Amidst the chaotic grappling, Sera, regaining her balance with sheer willpower, drove a desperate kick towards Orlov's hand. Her boot connected squarely with his wrist. The obsidian sphere flew from his grasp, arcing through the air. It hit the rocky ledge with a sickening clack, bounced once, twice, and rolled, spinning precariously close to the sheer drop.

Leo saw his chance...perhaps their *only* chance. While Sera and Orlov were momentarily locked, grappling fiercely, he scrambled towards the rolling artifact. The familiar cool, smooth surface met his outstretched fingers just as the sphere teetered on the very brink of the cliff.

"NO!" Orlov roared, the sound inhuman. With a final, desperate surge of adrenaline-fueled strength, he shoved Sera violently away from him. She staggered back, crying out. Orlov spun, his entire focus narrowing with terrifying intensity onto Leo and the sphere now clutched in his hand. His pistol, battered but functional, came up again, leveling unerringly. "MINE!"

Clutching the sphere as if it were a shield, Leo backed away instinctively, the rough rock scraping under his boots. He felt empty space behind him, the roar of the waves seeming to surge louder, hungrier, directly below.

"Leo, get back from the edge!" Sera yelled, regaining her footing, her eyes wide with raw terror.

Orlov ignored her completely, stalking forward, his movements jerky from his injuries but his aim unnervingly steady. "Give it to me, historian!" he commanded, his voice dripping with arrogant certainty and madness. "You are a fool! An insect! You cannot possibly comprehend its power, let alone *control* it!"

Leo stood his ground, feet planted near the precipice, defiance hardening his features. He held the sphere protectively against his chest. This artifact held the potential power to reshape, perhaps even end, the world; it couldn't fall back into the hands of this madman. The wind screamed around them, pulling at them, the tension stretching thin and brittle, ready to snap.

Then, Orlov fired.

Leo saw the blinding muzzle flash, a micro-second of detached surprise his only reaction. Then came the impact – not the searing tear of a bullet, but a solid, jarring shockwave that slammed into his chest, as if he'd been struck by an invisible battering ram.

The obsidian sphere, pressed tight against him, took the slug dead center. For an infinitesimal moment, the point of impact glowed with an intense, furious white light. The sphere didn't just absorb the projectile's kinetic force; it seemed to react to it, its own ancient, unstable energies ignited by the violation. Instead of merely shattering, it unleashed a violent, concussive pulse of its remaining power, a localized detonation of raw energy that vaporized the incoming bullet and blew the sphere itself apart from within.

Thousands of razor-sharp obsidian fragments, now inert and cold, sprayed outwards. Many embedded themselves harmlessly in Leo's heavy shirt and the reinforced vest beneath, but the sheer force of that final, energetic discharge lifted him bodily from the crumbling ledge, feet scrabbling for purchase that wasn't there. For one horrifying, weightless second, he hung suspended over the abyss. The world narrowed to Sera's horrified face, contorted in disbelief, and her raw, visceral scream of grief and rage echoing against the wind. Then gravity asserted its undeniable claim, and he tumbled backwards, over the edge, falling helplessly into the empty, wind-torn air towards the churning sea far below.

As Leo fell, witnessing his plunge seemed to break something in Sera. Pure, animalistic fury surged through her, overriding pain, fear, and exhaustion. With a guttural cry, she launched herself at Orlov again. Distracted by Leo's sudden disappearance over the edge, perhaps momentarily stunned by the unexpected destruction of the very artifact he craved, Orlov was caught completely off guard. He hadn't anticipated this ferocious, grief-fueled onslaught.

Sera slammed into him with the force of a battering ram. He staggered backwards under the impact, his remaining boot slipping on the wet, uneven rock near the very edge he had just forced Leo over. He flailed wildly, arms pinwheeling, trying desperately to regain his balance. The arrogant certainty vanished from his face, replaced by sudden, abject terror in his single, wide eye.

Sera pulled back from her attack, her chest heaving, watching him with a horrifying, detached mix of grim satisfaction and numb disbelief. Orlov teetered for a frozen moment on the brink, silhouetted against the vast, indifferent sky. Then, with a final, choked cry that was ripped away by the wind, his feet left the rock, and he plummeted downwards, tumbling end over end, vanishing from sight into the grey chaos below.

Seconds later, almost lost beneath the relentless roar of the waves, came the sickening, final sound of impact against the jagged rocks far below. The grey-green sea churned, indifferent, swallowing his broken body without leaving a trace.

Chapter Twenty-Seven

Rescue from the Edge

The wind screamed around the isolated cliff edge, a relentless, primal force that whipped Sera's loose strands of hair across her face, stinging her eyes and carrying the sharp, metallic taste of salt and ozone deep into her lungs. She stood frozen, feet rooted to the rough stone, her breath coming in ragged gasps that hitched in her throat. Below, the grey sea churned and boiled like a malevolent entity, relentlessly smashing against the black rocks, its depths having swallowed Orlov whole. He was gone. The sphere, the object of so much struggle and death, was nothing more than shattered fragments embedded in Leo's vest. And Leo... Leo was gone too, tumbled into that unforgiving void. The sudden, brutal finality crashed down on her, a physical weight that seemed to hollow her out, leaving an echoing emptiness where moments before there had been adrenaline and fury. She felt utterly adrift, lost on this desolate precipice at the world's end.

Slowly, unconsciously, her legs gave way, and she sank to her knees on the unforgiving rock. The sharp edges bit painfully into her skin through the tears in her trousers, but the physical sensation barely registered against the overwhelming, raw ache constricting her chest. Failure. Cold and absolute. She hadn't saved the sphere. She hadn't stopped Orlov in time. She hadn't protected Leo. Tears welled, hot and immediate, blurring the turbulent scene below.

Nikos moved cautiously to her side, the ground unsteady even for him. He placed a hand gently, tentatively, on her trembling shoulder. His own face was a mask of grim shock, his usual resilience momentarily fractured by the horror they had witnessed. "Sera..." he began, his voice thick, hoarse with unspoken sorrow, but the words died, inadequate. What could possibly be said?

The silence stretched, immense and profound, broken only by the ceaseless shriek of the wind and the thunderous, rhythmic crash of waves far below. It felt terminal. The end of the quest, the end of their hope, the end of Leo.

Then, cutting through the roar of nature and the fog of despair, a voice drifted upwards. It was faint, strained, nearly swallowed by the gale, yet impossibly, achingly familiar.

"Seriously?" the voice rasped, laced with pain but undeniably sardonic. "Are you two just going to kneel up there feeling sorry for yourselves, or are you planning on giving me a hand out of this?"

Sera's head snapped up so fast her neck muscles screamed in protest. Her heart felt like it stopped, lodged painfully in her throat, before restarting with a violent, hopeful jolt that sent blood rushing to her head. Could it be? Dare she hope? She scrambled frantically, recklessly, back to the cliff edge, Nikos instantly beside her, both peering down into the churning spray and the deep shadows clinging to the rock face below. Was it just grief? A cruel trick of the wind whistling past the rocks?

Then her eyes adjusted. She saw him. Perhaps ten, maybe fifteen feet below the main ledge, Leo was clinging desperately to a narrow, jagged shelf of rock that jutted from the cliff face. An outcrop she hadn't even registered in the chaos. He was alive. Shockingly pale, his clothes torn and darkened with what looked like blood near his chest, but undeniably, blessedly, miraculously *alive*. One hand was clamped onto the narrow ledge, knuckles white with the strain, while the other arm was pressed tightly against his chest. He looked up, squinting against the wind and spray, and managed a weak, pain-twisted grimace that was clearly intended as a reassuring smile.

"Leo!" The name tore from Sera's throat, thick with unshed tears and choked with overwhelming relief. The hollowness inside her vanished, replaced by a dizzying, overpowering wave of emotion that almost buckled her knees again. "Oh, thank God! Leo, hold on! Just hold on, we're coming!"

Her mind snapped back into focus, assessing the terrifying reality of the situation. The ledge Leo clung to was terrifyingly narrow, barely wide enough for his body, glistening wet with sea spray, and looked perilously unstable. Getting him back up to the relative safety of the clifftop was going to be incredibly difficult, especially with her own injured leg protesting every movement and Leo's condition still unknown.

Nikos was already scanning the cliff face with a practiced eye, his gaze moving methodically along the rock beside them. "The fall... this outcrop must have broken it," he muttered, processing aloud. His eyes narrowed. "Okay. Look." He pointed about thirty yards further along the main cliff edge. "See there? Looks like an old goat path. Starts near that twisted juniper." It was barely discernible, a faint scar winding down the cliff face. "It's steep, looks dangerous as hell, but it should lead down closer to his level. I don't see any other way. It's our only chance."

Nodding grimly, her throat too tight for words, Sera followed Nikos. The path was even more treacherous up close. A series of rough-hewn, crumbling steps and narrow ledges hacked into the rock, descending at a dizzying angle towards the churning sea far below. Every single step demanded absolute concentration. Loose scree shifted underfoot, threatening to send them skittering into the void. The wind gusted unpredictably, trying to tear them from their precarious handholds. Sera's injured leg throbbed with every downward pressure, but the image of Leo, pale and clinging precariously to that ledge, burned in her mind, fueling her determination.

The descent was agonizingly slow, painstaking work. They moved with excruciating care, testing each foothold, mapping out the next few precious inches before committing their weight. The sea roared below, a constant, menacing reminder of the penalty for a single misstep. Finally, after what felt like hours compressed into minutes, heartbeats echoing the crashing waves, they reached a point on the winding track almost level with the outcrop where Leo waited. A narrow, crumbling bridge of rock connected the path to his ledge. They traversed it carefully, inch by agonizing inch, hearts pounding against their ribs.

Leo looked significantly weaker now, his face clammy with sweat despite the cold wind, but his eyes remained open, tracking their approach with weary relief. Sera reached him first, dropping carefully to her knees beside him on the frighteningly small space. "Leo," she said, keeping her voice steady despite the tremor she felt inside. "Talk to me. How bad is it? Where are you hit?"

"Chest..." he gasped, the word clearly costing him effort. "Hurts... like hell. Think... the sphere... it took the hit."

Gently, carefully, Sera eased open the torn fabric of his heavy shirt and the reinforced vest beneath. Her breath caught in her throat. Embedded deeply into the thick, tough material of the vest, stopped mere fractions of an inch short of piercing his skin, were dozens, perhaps hundreds, of razor-sharp, glittering black fragments. The shattered remnants of the obsidian sphere. Beneath the embedded shards, a dark, ugly bruise was already blooming across his sternum and ribs, attesting to the massive kinetic force of the impact. Cracked ribs were almost certain, possibly worse internal trauma from the blow itself, but miraculously, impossibly, the bullet hadn't penetrated his flesh.

"It shattered..." Leo murmured, staring down at the glittering fragments embedded in his vest with wide, disbelieving eyes. "The bullet... must have hit it square on."

"It saved you," Sera stated, the simple fact hitting her with the force of another blow, but this time one of profound relief. The ancient, potentially world-ending artifact, in its final act of destruction, had become his shield. She quickly, expertly ran her hands over him, checking for other serious injuries. Broken limbs, spinal trauma, arterial bleeding. Besides the horrific bruising, the obvious impact trauma making each breath painful, and numerous cuts and scrapes likely sustained when he landed hard on the jagged ledge, he seemed miraculously, astonishingly intact. "Okay, Professor," she managed, her voice thick but regaining some of its usual edge. "Looks like you're just too damn stubborn to die easily. Think you can move?"

Getting him *off* that precarious ledge and back *up* the treacherous goat path was a monumental struggle, demanding every ounce of strength and willpower they possessed. Leo was incredibly weak, barely able to stand, let alone climb. He leaned heavily on both Sera and Nikos, sometimes sagging between them, his face etched with pain despite his attempts to hide it. Every upward step was a desperate battle against gravity, against crippling exhaustion, against the throbbing pain. His from the impact, hers from the injured leg. They moved inches at a time, pausing frequently to rest on slightly wider patches of path, the wind constantly threatening their balance. They worked as a team, Nikos's raw strength and intuitive knowledge of the terrain proving invaluable, Sera providing clipped, tactical guidance and sheer, unyielding determination, while Leo grit his teeth and forced his protesting body upward. Whispers of encouragement passed between them, a lifeline in the face of overwhelming difficulty. Giving up wasn't an option.

Finally, bruised, battered, scraped raw, utterly depleted but blessedly, miraculously alive, the three of them clawed their way over the lip of the main cliff top. They collapsed onto the windswept ground, lungs burning, muscles quivering uncontrollably, heedless of the rough rock beneath them. The sun, nearing the horizon, was beginning its final descent, casting immensely long, dramatic shadows across the land and sea, painting the turbulent, stormy sky in breathtaking, violent shades of bruised purple, fiery orange, and blood red.

They lay there for a long time, perhaps minutes, perhaps longer, simply breathing, the silence broken only by the wind and the eternal rhythm of the waves below. The vast, indifferent expanse of the sea stretched out before them, a stark reminder of the violence they had endured, the abyss they had faced, and the terrible price they had almost paid. The Labyrinth was conquered, its secrets likely buried forever in the mountain's collapse. Orlov, driven by madness and power, was gone, consumed by the sea he sought to command. The sphere, the catalyst for it all, was destroyed. In one sense, it truly felt over.

But as Sera looked at Leo's pale, pain-lined face, now slack with exhaustion, and felt the deep, throbbing ache radiating from her own leg, she knew with weary certainty that the journey back from the edge, both physically and emotionally, was only just beginning.

CHAPTER TWENTY-EIGHT

Calm After the Storm

A profound exhaustion, bone-deep and heavier than any physical weight, settled over them as they lay collapsed on the rough, exposed stone of the cliff top. The relentless wind, which had screamed and threatened only moments before, now seemed to sigh around them, a mournful lament rather than an assault. For the first time in what felt like an eternity, it felt strangely cleansing, washing away the immediate terror, even if the deeper aches remained. Leo was propped carefully against a lichen-covered boulder, his breathing shallow but blessedly steady. One hand gingerly probed the horrifyingly large, rapidly darkening bruise blooming across his chest beneath the shredded remnants of his vest, still peppered with sharp, glittering fragments of obsidian. Sera sat beside him, the adrenaline finally draining away, leaving behind a weariness etched deep into her features. Her eyes, though, were clear, focused, as she carefully inspected the crude but effective bandage Nikos had applied to her injured leg. Nearby, Nikos stood sentinel, slowly scanning the rugged, unforgiving coastline, his weathered face a complex mixture of profound relief and weary disbelief at their survival.

"You absolutely sure you're okay, Professor?" Sera asked, her voice quiet, roughened by dehydration and strain. "Nothing feels... loose? Or rattling? Nothing broken besides maybe a rib or three?"

Leo managed a weak, tight smile, the effort visible. "Pretty sure the sphere took the brunt of it. Absorbed the impact, I guess," he rasped. "Feels like I went ten rounds with a grizzly bear and lost decisively, but... I'm alive. Breathing. Which is more than I expected a few minutes ago. Thanks to you both." His gaze met Sera's, holding it for a moment, filled with a gratitude that went beyond words, underscored by the depth of understanding forged in the life-and-death crucible they had just barely escaped.

"We all saved each other," Sera deflected automatically, though a faint, unexpected warmth spread through her chest at his sincerity. She glanced down again at the glittering black shards embedded in his vest. "Still can't quite believe that actually worked." The sphere, the terrifying nexus of ancient power and modern ambition, was gone, literally shattered into harmless pieces. The horrifying potential it represented, the destructive force Orlov craved, neutralized in a hail of splintered rock.

Nikos turned back from his coastal survey, running a hand through his wind-tangled hair and shaking his head slowly. "Orlov... gone. Just... gone," he murmured, the finality still sinking in. "The sphere... gone." He looked back inland, towards the distant, hazy location of the palace ruins, invisible from this remote stretch of coast. "And the device down there?"

"Buried under half a damn mountain by now, I'd wager," Sera replied, grimacing as she pushed herself stiffly, painfully, to her feet. "The entrance chamber we used collapsed completely. Even if any of Orlov's people somehow survived that initial blast. Which I seriously doubt. That whole section of the Labyrinth is sealed tight. Whatever other secrets were hidden down there... they're likely buried for good, lost to time."

Leo nodded slowly, the movement careful. "The mission... the reason Section M sent you, the reason I got dragged into this... it's finished." The words hung strangely in the air, feeling almost anticlimactic after the relentless chaos, the desperate chases, the betrayals, and the sheer violence of the past weeks. The ancient whispers from Delphi, the shadowy Soviet threat, the pursuit across continents... it had all culminated and ended here, on a desolate Cretan cliff edge, amidst shattered obsidian fragments and with the churning grey sea swallowing their enemy whole.

"And good riddance to the lot of it," Nikos muttered with feeling. He looked critically at Leo, his practical nature reasserting itself. "But saying it's finished doesn't fix *you*. We need to get you somewhere safe. Somewhere with a real doctor, not just Agent Nightingale's... battlefield improvisation."

Sera shot Nikos a half-hearted glare at the familiar, unwanted nickname but nodded in immediate agreement. "He's right, Leo. Much as it pains me to admit it," she said, her tone softening slightly as she looked at his pale face. "We need to get off this cliff, get inland, and make our way back towards civilization. Back to Heraklion. Back to Nikos's taverna."

The journey back was an arduous, draining trek, arguably even more grueling than the desperate climb up the goat path had been. Getting the injured Leo safely along the rugged clifftop trails and then carefully navigating inland, deliberately avoiding any main roads or potentially watchful settlements until they were much closer to the relative anonymity of Heraklion, consumed the better part of the following day. They moved with painstaking slowness, resting frequently in sheltered hollows, supporting Leo between them when the terrain became too difficult. Their shared exhaustion hung over them like a heavy, damp blanket, punctuated only by the necessities of movement and survival. Once again, Nikos's intimate knowledge of Crete's hidden paths, ancient shepherd's tracks, and strategically located, dilapidated shelters proved utterly invaluable, allowing them to travel largely unseen.

By the time they finally staggered, dust-covered, limping, and utterly spent, back into the deep shadows and comforting, quiet familiarity of Nikos's small taverna nestled in the labyrinthine streets of Heraklion's old town, night had fallen thick and heavy once more. Nikos's wife, Eleni, took one look at their state and ushered them inside with quiet, urgent efficiency, her initial shock quickly replaced by practical concern. Warm water, clean clothes, strong, reviving coffee, and plates piled high with simple, hot food appeared as if by magic. While they recovered slightly, Eleni discreetly arranged for a trusted local doctor, known for his skill and his ability to keep confidences, to examine Leo and Sera's injuries without attracting undue attention.

The verdict was cautiously optimistic. Leo was severely bruised, suffering from massive impact trauma, and likely had at least two cracked ribs, but thankfully, there was no sign of internal bleeding or other life-threatening damage. Complete rest was ordered. Sera's leg wound, while deep and ragged, needed proper cleaning and stitches but was already showing signs of healing and would mend completely with time and care.

A couple of quiet, recuperative days passed. Leo rested upstairs in one of the taverna's simple guest rooms, feeling battered and sore but suffused with an immense, quiet gratitude for being alive. News began to filter back through Nikos's extensive network of local contacts. Shepherds, fishermen, shopkeepers. Petros, the shepherd from the hills near Kastelli who had initially guided them, sent word via a cousin. He reported that the entire area surrounding the palace ruins had experienced a massive, localized ground collapse shortly after they would have left the mountain. Where the central courtyard had been, there was now only a deep, unstable sinkhole. And the hidden entrance to the Labyrinth. The official story being cautiously circulated by baffled local authorities was a freak, unexplained 'seismic event'. Of the significant contingent of Soviet personnel Orlov had brought with him, there was absolutely no sign; they seemed to have vanished overnight, presumably caught in the collapse or withdrawn in utter secrecy.

Later, a discreet, heavily coded message arrived for Sera through secure, pre-arranged channels. It confirmed what they suspected: General Orlov was now officially listed by Moscow Centre records as "missing, presumed deceased" during unrelated operations in the Bulgarian sector. A neat, bureaucratic tidying-up of a disastrously failed, off-the-books operation. Section M's reply to Sera's brief, encrypted situation report was equally terse and devoid of sentiment: "Objective confirmed neutralized. Threat eliminated. Stand down. Await extraction." It was truly, finally, unequivocally over.

That evening, feeling significantly stronger, though still moving stiffly, Leo felt well enough to join Sera and Nikos on the taverna's quiet, vine-covered upper terrace. The warm night air was fragrant with the heavy scent of jasmine blooming nearby and the distant, clean fragrance of the sea. The low murmur of conversation and faint music from the city below felt peaceful, blessedly normal. They sat in comfortable silence for a long while, watching the lights twinkle across the harbor, sipping cool, retsina that Nikos had poured. The shared ordeal hung unspoken between them, a bond forged in fire and darkness.

"So," Nikos finally said, breaking the companionable silence, swirling the pale wine in his glass as he looked thoughtfully at Leo. "It is back to the dusty university library now, Professor? Back to your quiet books and ancient maps?"

Leo offered a genuine, tired smile. "Maybe eventually," he admitted, the thought surprisingly less appealing than it might have been a month ago. "Though I suspect after all this, deciphering dusty scrolls might seem a little... tame." He glanced over at Sera. She was leaning against the terrace railing, gazing out at the dark expanse of the sea, seeming more relaxed, less coiled and watchful, than he had ever seen her. "And you, Sera? Back to the shadows? Vanishing like smoke?"

She turned from the railing, meeting his gaze directly. A flicker of something complex, unreadable, crossed her usually guarded features before settling. Warmth? Vulnerability? Uncertainty? "The shadows are always part of the job, Leo," she stated softly, her voice low. "Some things don't change." She paused, a small, almost imperceptible smile touching the corner of her lips. "...But maybe," she added, her gaze holding his, "maybe not always alone."

Just as another comfortable silence settled, infused with new possibilities, a familiar, gravelly voice boomed cheerfully from the doorway leading onto the terrace.

"Did you miss me?"

They all turned, startled. Leaning casually against the wooden doorframe, a dusty, overloaded travel bag slumped at his feet and a wide, infectious grin splitting his rugged face, was Boris.

"Boris!" Nikos exclaimed, genuine pleasure lighting his face as he jumped up to greet his unlikely friend with a hearty clap on the shoulder. "Manos mou! What in the world are you doing here?"

Boris shrugged expansively, hefting his bag and walking onto the terrace as if he owned the place. "Heard through the grapevine you might be having a small celebration," he said, his eyes twinkling with amusement as he looked from Leo to Sera and back again. "Couldn't possibly have my favourite friends finishing the big adventure without me, could I? Besides," he added, giving Nikos another friendly thump on the back that made the Cretan rock on his feet, "your cousin Dimitri down at the port makes the best damn grilled octopus on the entire Mediterranean, and I've been dreaming about it all the way from Sofia."

Leo found himself laughing, a genuine, unrestrained, relieved laugh that eased some of the lingering tension in his chest. Sera simply shook her head, but the small smile lingered, softening her features. Nikos beamed and immediately fetched another glass, pouring a generous measure of retsina.

Leo reflected, looking around the small group gathered on the terrace under the Cretan stars, they were the most improbable collection of individuals imaginable: the academic historian pulled violently from his books, the lethal spy learning to navigate something other than darkness, the fiercely patriotic Cretan resistance fighter turned taverna owner, and the gruff, pragmatic Bulgarian mountain guide with a surprising loyalty. Bound together by a crazy, perilous journey that none of them had sought but all had somehow survived. The wider world would never know the truth...how close it had potentially come to disaster triggered by an ancient artifact, or the dark secrets and shattered ambitions now buried forever under the Cretan soil.

Leo raised his glass, feeling a sense of closure, and perhaps, a new beginning. "To unlikely partnerships," he proposed again, his voice stronger now, clearer. "And to good friends, old and new."

Nikos, Sera, and Boris raised their glasses, touching his gently in the warm night air. The ancient, ominous whispers from Delphi were finally silent. The mission was well and truly done.

For now.

Epilogue

Echoes and Beginnings

Section M, Quantico, Virginia—Four Weeks Later

The debriefing room felt even colder and more sterile than Leo remembered. Maybe it was the contrast after the warmth and vibrant life of Crete, or maybe it was just the harsh fluorescent lighting reflecting off the polished steel table. He sat opposite Agent Marcus Thorne, feeling oddly out of place again, despite everything he'd been through. Sera sat beside him, composed and alert, her leg fully healed, leaving no trace of the ordeal except perhaps a new hardness in her eyes.

Thorne finished reviewing the final page of the thick file labeled "DELPHI EYES ONLY," closed it decisively, and steepled his fingers, regarding them both with his usual unreadable expression.

"Operationally speaking," Thorne began, his voice flat and professional, "the primary objective was achieved. The artifact known as the obsidian sphere was neutralized, Colonel Orlov is confirmed deceased, and known Soviet assets related to Project... Labyrinthos... have withdrawn. While Orlov is eliminated, intelligence regarding the 'Comrade Supreme' who initiated his directive remains inconclusive. The ultimate architect of Project Oko is still in the shadows. However, the immediate threat posed by the energy device discovered in Crete appears to have been contained, largely thanks to its own self-destruction and subsequent geological containment."

He paused. "Your methods, however, were... unorthodox. The collateral damage to the archaeological site was significant, requiring considerable inter-agency cleanup and narrative control."

Leo shifted uncomfortably, but Sera met Thorne's gaze without flinching. "Orlov forced our hand, sir. Neutralizing the device and preventing its capture was the priority."

"Indeed," Thorne conceded, a flicker of something in his eyes as he looked at Sera, then Leo. Maybe grudging respect. "Your combined skillset, while unconventional, proved unexpectedly effective in achieving the primary goal, despite... considerable improvisation."

He allowed himself the barest hint of a smirk. "Frankly, some analysts in Ops have already started referring to your rather unique pairing... half-jokingly, perhaps... as the *Saint and Sinner*' team. A historian who quotes ancient texts under fire and an agent who seems uniquely adept at navigating chaos." He tapped the closed file, the smirk vanishing. "Regardless of unofficial labels, the final report notes your unique synergy, Doctor Saint's historical analysis proving crucial alongside Agent Volkov's tactical expertise." He almost seemed to be testing the waters, seeing how they reacted to being evaluated as a unit.

Leo glanced at Sera, a slight flush rising on his neck at the 'Saint and Sinner' comment. She simply raised a single, cool eyebrow in Thorne's direction. They hadn't really discussed their future, their 'partnership', beyond surviving the mission. But sitting here, back in the cold reality of Section M, he knew he couldn't simply return to his quiet library life, not completely. The world felt different now, history felt more alive, more dangerous.

Thorne picked up a different, much thinner file from the table. Its cover was blank except for a single, stamped word: "PENDING."

"While the Delphi incident is closed," Thorne continued, opening the new file, "other... anomalies inevitably arise." He slid a single reconnaissance photo across the table. It showed what looked like an ancient, submerged ruin taken from the air, water unnaturally clear around strangely geometric shapes on the seabed. Coordinates were stamped in the corner, indicating a remote location deep in the South Pacific.

"Anomalous energy readings detected near these coordinates three days ago," Thorne stated simply. "Coinciding with unusual tectonic activity in a region supposedly stable. Preliminary analysis suggests the underwater structure is pre-Polynesian, possibly connected to myths local islanders have about a 'sunken city' and 'stones that weep'."

Leo found himself leaning forward instinctively, peering at the photo, his historian's mind already clicking, connecting dots. Sunken city... singing stones... energy readings...

Sera looked at the photo, then at Leo, then back at Thorne, her expression carefully neutral, but Leo could see the spark of professional interest ignite in her eyes.

Thorne watched them both. "Requires further investigation, naturally. A situation that might benefit from... historical context combined with certain field skills." He closed the new file. "Just background for now. Your extraction transport is arranged for 0800 tomorrow. Get some rest. Both of you."

It wasn't quite an order, but it wasn't just a suggestion either. It was an open door, a hint of the next puzzle, the next potential crisis waiting in the shadows of the past.

Leo and Sera stood up. As they turned to leave the cold briefing room, their eyes met for a brief moment. No words were needed. The world was full of ancient secrets and modern dangers. Their work, it seemed, was far from over.

Acknowledgements

This book would not be in your hands without the help of several important people.

To the friends and family members who acted as my first readers and critics: thank you. Your honest feedback, insightful questions, and unwavering enthusiasm were essential in shaping *The Delphi Protocol* into its final form. You spotted plot holes, questioned motives, and cheered successes, making the solitary act of writing feel like a shared adventure.

My sincere gratitude also goes to Arpad Horvath, a true friend and author, whose crucial encouragement provided the spark that ignited this entire writing journey.

Thank you all for being part of this story.

www.ingramcontent.com/pod-product-compliance
Lightning Source LLC
Jackson TN
JSHW021452130725
87441JS00002B/7